THE AMBASSADOR CHRONICLES

James Voorhees

Bonfire Books

ISBN: 978-1-964126-15-9 Hardback
ISBN: 978-1-964126-14-2 Paperback
ISBN: 978-1-964126-13-5 Ebook

Printed by Bonfire Books LLC, in the United States of America

First printing edition 2025.

www.jamesvoorhees.com

To my family and friends who have inspired so much of the enduring charm in each of these characters.

INTRODUCTION

Welcome to THE AMBASSADOR CHRONICLES. This is a compilation of 10 short stories previously published as single Ebooks. Each story is meant to give the reader an introduction into a particular character who plays a crucial role in THE AMBASSADOR CHRONICLES series. In these stories, just like in our lives, no one knows the effects that we have on others or the roles we play in their futures.

Follow the journeys of Seer, Sorcerer, Monk, the Queen of Witches, Princess, AZ, Tinker, The Twins, Ghost, and Vampire over a forty-five-year period that ends where THE DRAGON CONSTELLATION begins. Read the stories in chronological order as the prophecy unveils itself to you and learn about the fated and unexpected interactions that the characters have played in each other's lives from the beginning of this exciting saga.

Seer

All will come to light

Chapter 1

"Kindron?" his mother called out. "Kindron, dear! Please come back inside. I promise that no one will ask for you to do that again." Mrs. Smug continued to urge him back into the villa as she scanned the gardens for her son. "He... Mr. Scanlon... has been escorted out of the party and off the estate grounds." She looked back and forth for any sign of the boy. "Your father will no longer be doing business with him," she added as a final, yet failed, attempt for her son to come out of hiding.

Kindron had run out of the party when his father's drunk business associate had pulled him aside and tried to force Kindron to enlighten him with his gift. Roger Scanlon, the clever business associate of Mr. Smug, had recognized in Kindron the gift of seeing someone's future. He had first realized it when he had seen Kindron in the office a year ago. Kindron was a child, only five years old at the time. He had noticed Kindron's fear of shaking hands, the tension on his face, the struggle in his eyes. Scanlon knew a "seer" when he saw one, for he was one himself. Since that first meeting, he had attempted to gain Kindron's good faith with kindness and presents. However, Kindron never took to him.

At the party, Scanlon had spent most of the time maneuvering to approach Kindron with determination. He wanted to ensure that continuing to do business with his father was for his own financial gain. His own limited gift did not allow him to see far enough for his personal satisfaction. Scanlon finally cornered Kindron and grabbed him by his bare hands. Scanlon expected that with this touch he would see a future of riches. Instead, he was forced back to the present by Kindron scratching his face, pulling away, and running out of the party.

It was not Scanlon's aggressive behavior that scared Kindron, it was what he saw. Kindron saw fire and pain. He saw his parents consumed by blackness. He saw a funeral that was poorly attended. Kindron did not understand.

"Kindron!" his mother continued to yell out. She sighed in frustration and went back to the party. She knew that her son would come back in when he was ready.

His mother's pregnancy had not been easy. She had been overly emotional throughout the partial term pregnancy. Kindron was delivered two months early and so quickly, almost like he had thrown himself from his mother's womb. As an infant, Kindron cried with every touch. His mother's emotional instability had quickly resolved at the time of his delivery. She was kind and learned quickly to hold him with a blanket. He refused feeding from her breast so she was quick to change and feed him from a bottle.

However, Kindron's father felt differently about his son. He began to feel rejected with each resisted touch. Kindron's father was a man of power. He was strong, respected, and controlled. He wanted to express love to his son but was unable to due to his son's constant crying whenever he picked him up. Kindron's father had no power in the relationship.

When Kindron was three months old, his parents had finally found a nanny who was able to keep him from crying when he was touched. The nanny, a Witch, had been recommended by a friend of his mother. She was able to educate Kindron's parents on the nature of their son and the reason behind why physical contact was difficult for him. She told them that Kindron was a "seer". Kindron had the ability to see into a person's future.

She taught the Smugs how to handle their baby. Kindron's parents made some changes that allowed them to hold their son and to express love the only way they could. They wore gloves to hold him; they kissed him on his clothes. They simply needed to keep a barrier between them: no skin-to- skin contact. He became a happy baby.

They were grateful for what they had been taught. They offered the Witch a position in their home, but she refused. She had done what she had come to do and it was time to move on. She urged his parents to not draw attention to his power. "Others would look to take advantage of him," she told them "Many seers become outcasts." Kindron's power appeared to be quite strong, as per the Witch. She had not experienced one as powerful as he before.

As a child, Kindron did not understand why but he knew he was different. At school, children did not want to play with him, and he gladly became an outcast. Children like to play physically; they touch and push. They hold hands as they walk and tap each other on the shoulder. They hug. All these aspects of childhood caused Kindron both emotional and physical pain.

He did his best to avoid physical contact. The slightest touch would open a floodgate as an instant flash of every life event and every emotion that the other person would ever experience would come to him at once. They would not see the visions but would experience that floodgate of emotions that rushed their awareness. The magnitude of the emotions could not be described by a mortal mind. The closest interpretation of the overwhelming sensation would be pain. Anyone Kindron touched would react by blaming him for causing them pain. And then, Kindron was left with the pain…Always the pain. Only the pain.

His visions tortured him. The longer he held skin to skin contact, the deeper and stronger his visions became. Kindron's vision was so strong that one time, a woman who had been holding his hand ended up suffering a heart attack from the surge of emotions and died as a result. It was too overwhelming for a child to understand. Even though his parents explained that it was an accident, Kindron stopped having any contact with anyone but them.

His father understood that Kindron needed to grow and learn about his gift in order to lead a fulfilling life outside of the villa. In the meantime, he would ensure that the estate was a safe space for his son. The Smugs led a prosperous and charmed life. His father's businesses continued to expand, and his influence grew alongside them.

His prosperity invited new business arrangements and new partners. It was a year ago when Rogert Scanlon came to his office with a good proposal. It was then that Scanlon first met Kindron. Scanlon had since pried about Smug's family life to confirm his suspicion. Kindron's father resisted in telling him about the boy and his gift.

Scanlon eventually confessed that he recognized Kindron's gift. He praised Smug for his acceptance of his son. Scanlon expressed to Mr. Smug support and acknowledged how hard that must be, as well as joy in them being able to find some sort of solution. Mr. Smug appreciated his candidness. He told Mr. Smug the story of another boy. The boy's parents had taken the opposite approach. They ignored their son and left him to learn about the world on his own. And he did, through harsh lessons. He did not explain that the boy was himself. He learned to use his gift for his own benefit.

Rogert Scanlon made it a habit to shake hands with his business interactions. "Just good business," he would say. However, the contact allowed him to "see" each of their futures. Although strong enough to get an idea of someone's near future, he was not able to elicit the reactions and have the same powerful effects as Kindron. He figured a more powerful seer would help him see better into the future.

A few years back, he had encountered another child who he recognized as a seer. That child was eight years old at the time and with much better control of his power than Kindron. His father loved to brag about how the boy's visions helped him to navigate through business to improve his financial holdings. Scanlon had attempted to get the child to aid him in the same way. The child refused and took off running out the door. He was struck down by a passing coach and died on the spot. Rogert Scanlon was seen attempting to revive him and had been praised by the boy's parents for trying to save their son. He never revealed that the boy was running from him when the accident had occurred.

Back at the party, Kindron's mother had gone back inside. Kindron continued to hide amidst the evergreens. He let out his breath and panted hard. He had been holding it to not give away his position. Kindron held his breath on a regular basis. It helped him to calm himself after he had a vision. He did not want to go back to the party nor did he want to be found. But he began to feel cold and the uncomfortable sensation of the pine needles sticking into him. He decided to find a more comfortable hiding spot. He stood up off the ground and looked at his disheveled appearance. Kindron did his best to wipe the dirt but knew that it would not come off. He felt that he should not go back in until the party was over. He did not want to disappoint his parents by presenting himself as less than perfect. He walked through the garden.

"Kindron?" his father said from behind him.

Kindron was quick to turn with concern in his eyes.

"No. No, Kindron. You are not in trouble," his father told him. "I'm just making sure that you are okay."

Kindron looked down at his soiled clothes.

"Your mother will forgive you," he told him and laughed. He wiped dirt on his own pants and smiled at his son.

Kindron said nothing. He attempted a smile but began to cry.

"Oh, Kindron." His father came quickly to him. He put his jacket over Kindron's head and pulled him in for a tight hug. He kissed him on his covered head making sure that he did not touch Kindron's skin. "It's not easy being you, Kindron. And I am sorry, but it is not going to be." Kindron's father held him at arm's length by the sleeves that covered Kindron's arms. "I do not know why you are so... special. But you are Kindron. You are special, you must be special. And you are strong, my boy. You have to be. Your mother and I will protect you from anyone who may look to hurt you. But Kindron, you will have to learn to be strong without us. You need to be able to learn who you can trust and rely on and who is looking to use you. Not all people are bad. Not all people are selfish and abusive. But some people are. And you need to know how to defend yourself against them."

Kindron's father pulled him in again for a tight hug. Kindron cried hard and his father did the same.

"I love you, my son. I love everything about you," he told him as the tears flowed.

They both dried their eyes and now it was Kindron who held his father at arm's length.

"I think we should go back in," Kindron said.

His father looked at the dirt and tears on their clothes and faces.

"Mother will understand. She won't be mad."

Kindron's father laughed and pulled him in again for a tight and loving hug.

"You're right," he said and with his gloved hand, he took Kindron's hand into his own and they walked back into the house.

Chapter 2

"Kindron!" his mother screamed as she pushed open the bedroom door and grabbed her son by the sleeves of his pajamas. "Kindron!" she repeated and shook him awake.

"Mother!" he yelled back in his confusion. "What is it?"

"Fire!" she looked back at the open door where he too looked and saw the reflection of the orange and yellow flames that were nearby.

Kindron did not start choking until he felt the smoke sneaking in along the ceiling. "Where is father?" Kindron begged through his coughing.

"Working with the staff to put out the fire," she told him with haste and pulled him from his bed. "We have to get out of the villa, Kindron. The fire is close to this part of the house."

Kindron's mother pulled him along towards the open bedroom door, accidentally grabbing his bare hand. Kindron immediately froze in place. In the vision, he heard his mother scream and saw her turn to light. Kindron snapped out of his vision as his hand lost contact with his mother's hand. Shaken by what he saw, he ran back towards the balcony.

She turned and opened her mouth to yell for him.

Kindron watched as his vision of his mother being engulfed in the flames came to be. She was swallowed by the heat and the light of the flames. Her burning body fell to the floor and attempted to crawl back to her son. She moved along the floor but then stopped moving. The fire that came off her corpse caught onto the tapestries, wood furniture, and drapes. Kindron was trapped by the flames that spread throughout his room. The smoke was becoming too much to bear. He dropped to the floor.

Kindron kicked open the balcony doors and ran to the rail of the third story balcony. Flames followed him. He closed the doors and felt a moment of safety. He looked over the edge of the balcony and saw his father.

"Father!" he yelled.

Kindron's father looked up at him.

"Stay there, Kindron! I will get a ladder," his father yelled back.

From the shadows, Kindron saw a figure emerge. He recognized Rogert Scanlon. Kindron turned and saw his father return with a ladder, alone.

Why? Kindron thought. Where are the servants?

Scanlon was quick to help Kindron's father who, without question as to why he was there, accepted his assistance with getting the ladder up to the balcony.

"Climb down, Kindron!" his father yelled over the roar of the flames. "Hurry!"

Kindron was trapped on the balcony and frozen in place. His father realized that he was not going to be able to move on his own. He turned to Scanlon, who nodded his head. Kindron watched and saw Scanlon hold the ladder steady as his father began to climb. Kindron attempted to move over the rail. He could not move. Kindron continued to watch Rogert Scanlon who was holding the ladder.

The heat and pressure of the flames shattered the glass of a window on the second floor and knocked Kindron's father off balance. Fiery debris fell from the broken window onto the dry ground at the base of the ladder. Kindron saw Scanlon take his flask from the inner pocket of his coat and douse it all over the wooden ladder. He was flicking it higher and even onto Kindron's father. Kindron saw this and wanted to scream for him to stop. But frozen in fear, he could only stare at his father whose sole focus was to reach him. Another explosion came from that same open window and more debris fell onto the ground, which was now aflame from the alcohol.

Mr. Smug reached the balcony. "I got you, my boy," Kindron's father said to him with a hero's grin. The expression was quickly stripped from his face as he now felt the burn of the flames that had made their way up the ladder and onto his clothes and engulfed him. He launched himself onto the balcony and rolled as the flames covered him.

Kindron watched in fear and reached out for his father. He watched helplessly as his father stood and fought the flames but fell over the rail of the balcony. Kindron's father had met the same tortured fate as his mother, consumed by flames and suffering in his death.

Kindron cried out and held himself as close to the rail as possible. He was stuck on the balcony, and no one was coming to save him. Through his tears, he saw that Rogert Scanlon was gone. His father's words rang in his ear. He would have to save himself.

Kindron heard the crash from behind him. He was pulled back to the present and realized that he had to be quick to save himself. He was three floors up and the ladder had burned and fallen to the ground.

Another explosion erupted from inside. The pressure from the blast pushed Kindron over the rail of the balcony. As he fell, he felt the terror of the fire, the sadness of his parents' death, and then anger at Scanlon who was behind all of it. He closed his eyes as blackness surrounded him. He no longer felt like he was falling. Instead, he felt himself being lowered to the ground.

As he opened his eyes, Kindron saw there were three of them. Three women. Their forms were so dark that they blended into the night. Only the outlines of their silhouettes were visible in front of the burning building.

Kindron felt as though he should be scared. But he had no room for fear. All he felt was anger, hate, and pain. These emotions were made stronger by the three figures in front of him.

He nodded.

The figures were gone.

Kindron passed out.

The fire went out.

Chapter 3

Kindron woke to the sun. He smelled the smoke from the destruction of his home. He heard the birds singing as if nothing had happened. Kindron had lost his parents to Rogert Scanlon. He knew that it was because of his gift. Kindron told himself that it was his fault that his parents had lost their lives in such a tortured and painful manner. Kindron brought his hands to cover his face and cried.

He sat up. He saw his father's charred body. The only thing that was identifiable was his father's ruby pinky ring. Kindron took the ring from his father's scorched finger, which broke off with a hard sound. Kindron was sure to not touch his father's blackened bones. He put the ring on his thumb. Mother, he thought to himself. He had to get to his mother's remains. Kindron made his way through the empty destruction. He was able to get upstairs. He looked into his burnt bedroom and made his way through the debris.

He saw what was left of his mother. He reached out to touch her, but her form disintegrated to his touch. He was unable to "see" anything. From the ashes, only her necklace was left remarkably intact. Kindron remembered that she always wore this necklace and displayed its red jewel over her clothes for all to see. Kindron took the necklace and placed it around his neck. He made his way back to the entry hall and out to the grounds. No one was there. Kindron turned and looked at the devastated remains of the villa. There was nothing left to salvage. This place was no longer his home.

He tucked the jewel into his shirt. He immediately felt the rush of rage. His eyes turned crimson. He felt his full unfiltered anger and had no desire to control it. "I will find you," he said to the air. "I will kill you." The rage built and caused Kindron to shake uncontrollably. He passed out and dropped to the ground. Steam rose from his closed eyes.

Chapter 4

The sun was high and warm on his face. Kindron felt something comforting for the first time since his parents had been brutally killed. He was unaware of the trees that lined the road. He was unaware of the birds flying overhead. Kindron wandered aimlessly on the country road. My parents are dead. My home is destroyed. The sun was bright in the cold winter air. Kindron felt that everything was in opposition to everything else. This is all your fault, he told himself. They died because of you. Kindron fell to his knees and sobbed.

He did not know where to go. He did not know who could or would help him. All he knew were the servants, and they had not come to the aid of his parents. Where were all the servants? he wondered again. They had all gone without a word. Tears turned to anger as thoughts of Rogert Scanlon reappeared. He continued walking.

Kindron was paying no attention to where he was going. The road led Kindron to the painted gates of the city of Tamsu. He looked at the soldiers who guarded this point of entry to the prosperous city. The guard to his right looked back at him with a scowl on his face.

"Where are your parents, boy?" he yelled to Kindron, displeased at the child not being in school and offended by his soiled presentation.

"What do you care?" he replied in anger. "They're dead!" Tears rolled as he said the words aloud.

The guard was taken aback and met eyes with his partner. They nodded to one another, and the second guard blew a whistle. The guard walked at a steady pace up to Kindron. He took him by the shoulder of his shirt. Kindron fought back and attempted to run. The guard held tight and pulled him from the crowd.

"Get off me," Kindron yelled.

The people on the street were quick to judge Kindron as an unruly child by his outburst and dirty appearance. The guard pulled him along by his collar and into a military headquarters as he nodded to the other guard at the door.

Kindron continued to fight the guard's grip. He was pulled into a room and thrown into the corner. Kindron fell to the floor and turned with anger in his eyes and breathing heavily through his nose, his hands balled into fists.

"It's okay, boy," the guard said. "Let it out."

Kindron felt the anger rush through him. He felt it build and pull his blood quickly to his head. His vision turned red. He rushed at the guard. The guard stopped him by holding him back at the sleeves of his forearms. Kindron kept pushing at him. He screamed out and then spit at the guard. The guard's grip slipped and Kindron's hands choked him at his neck.

Kindron's eyes glowed red. His grip was tight. His head shot upwards with his eyes burning and wide open. Kindron saw the guard in his vision. He saw the man on his knees in front of three black forms. He saw the guard crying and burning from the inside. He saw the guard attempting to peel his own skin to release the burning. Kindron saw one of the forms reach out.

He took the hand and immediately felt a shock.

Kindron released the guard.

The guard laid on the floor cramped in a fetal position. He was drenched in sweat and exhausted. He looked at Kindron with worry. He did not know how to move or what to do.

"What just happened?" he said to the boy after a pause. "That was pure evil." The guard found the strength to get up and went rushing about the office but with no sense of order or planning. "What happened to your parents? How did they die?"

"They were killed in a fire." He looked at the guard. "They were trying to protect me."

The guard saw the determination in Kindron's eyes. "From the fire?"

Kindron paused. "From Rogert Scanlon," he said.

The guard stopped in place as his eyes widened. "Cursed or not, you are a child." He turned and looked at Kindron. "We need to get you out of the city." He was quick to grab Kindron by the sleeve and pulled him up. "You are the boy he is looking for. He has even offered a reward for bringing you to him. You have to get out of Tamsu." He continued to rush about the office with no clear plan. "Do you have any other family?"

Kindron said nothing.

"Okay, I know where to take you." He grabbed a jacket and put it over the boy's head. "But keep quiet," he demanded. "We cannot trust anyone. He has eyes and ears everywhere."

Kindron still felt exhausted from coming out of his most recent vision. He allowed himself to go along with the guard. He did not resist.

"Why are you helping me?" he asked.

"Because Rogert Scanlon is pure evil," the guard told him.

Kindron allowed his eyes to close as the guard carried him.

The guard pushed his back into the door to the side of the headquarters. Kindron heard the street noise and knew that they were outside, and then the guard's footsteps. It went from a hard stone to gravel. We're leaving the city, he told himself. The footsteps stopped suddenly.

"Did you think I wouldn't know that you had him?" He heard Scanlon's voice ask as if joking.

The guard did nothing. He stood holding tight to the boy. Kindron pulled the jacket from his head and looked to see Rogert Scanlon standing with a line of guards blocking the path. "Put me down," he whispered to the guard. The guard resisted as Kindron began to squirm. "Put me down," he demanded. The guard obliged, expecting Kindron to run. He would block the men from coming for the boy as he escaped. To his surprise, Kindron walked towards Rogert Scanlon and the line of guards.

Scanlon smiled. "Good. You came to your senses, boy." Scanlon looked down at the boy with a look of success.

Kindron kept walking towards him, his anger building. He stopped right in front of Rogert Scanlon. Kindron reached out and grabbed him by his hand. Scanlon felt the electricity and dropped to the gravel road. The confused guards backed away slowly. Kindron's eyes turned red. He placed his other hand on Scanlon's face as the guards watched in terror as the man's body flinched and quivered as if in a fit.

Scanlon began to scream out in pain.

Kindron saw Scanlon's future. The three black shadows descended and encircled Scanlon as his blood boiled. They were not touching him, just pointing at him. Yet, he was experiencing a burning of his blood. Scanlon's eyes started to melt and run down his face. Kindron watched as Scanlon's skin followed and liquefied as his heart continued to beat.

Scanlon had caused his parents' deaths. Kindron believed this was the punishment he deserved. Now, Scanlon was paying the price. He was fully aware of the torture and felt the full intensity of it. This was all in the vision. It was Scanlon's future. Scanlon continued to scream out in pain.

One of the guards jabbed the blunt end of his sword into the back of Kindron's neck and knocked him unconscious. Kindron let go of Scanlon. They both laid on the ground. Scanlon was making attempts to catch his breath. His pain still felt real. He looked around at the circle of guards frozen in awe over the scene. He hurried to sit up and then to stand and compose himself.

He forced air from his nostrils like a bull about to charge. Scanlon pushed past the guards with an attempt at a strong gait. "Take him away," he told them. The guards looked at each other with concern as to who would chance touching the unconscious boy.

Chapter 5

Kindron awoke to a throbbing pain at the back of his neck. He saw nothing. Everything was black. The stone floor was cold. Kindron had become familiar with being uncomfortable. He began to perceive the presence of something. Kindron felt his skin get cold and the goosebumps rise. He held his fists tight.

A swoosh of hot air rushed by. Kindron ducked, barely avoiding it. Another rush came past him and knocked him off his feet. He hit the hard ground. Kindron screamed out. A third hot gust blew past him and whispered, "Kindron." He felt the essence of the three forms. By now, Kindron associated any pain with anger which was the trigger that brought them forward from the blackness.

These were the same forms that saved him from the balcony of the villa. They were the ones that appeared with the guard. They were the ones that came when he held onto Rogert Scanlon's hand. Kindron's fear calmed. He reached out and gripped what felt like an arm. The visions were immediate and strong. The pain increased as he felt a hand grab hold of his other arm.

"You must take revenge," a voice screamed in his head.

A second hand gripped Kindron's arm.

"We will help you," a second voice told him.

The two hands loosened their grip and turned Kindron to face the third form.

Kindron felt a new set of hands wrap around his head and pull him into what felt like a bosom. Kindron felt the hands soften and move down the sides of his head to embrace him. The pain was gone.

"You are stronger than other seers," the first Dark Sister told him. "Others can only see and absorb someone's future path."

"You have a rare ability to emotionally share what you see with the other person," said the second.

"You can open a mortal's psyche to everything at once. Concentrated it could destroy anyone you encounter," added the third. "It is not only a gift. It is a weapon."

Kindron held a single expression and longed for the destruction of Rogert Scanlon.

"Kindron Smug," said the raspy voice. "Kindron Smug," the second voice repeated. "Kindron Smug," three voices said in unison, with a clear feminine tone. "Kindron Smug," they repeated three times and then disappeared into a black mist that surrounded him.

Kindron felt their energies enter into his own and then leave. He felt angry and alone. The blackness was gone. He realized it was night and that he was in a jail cell.

A sliver of a window was high out of reach. The smallest amount of moonlight snuck through and gave shadows to the blackness. Kindron stared at the sliver of faint light, his sliver of hope, his hope to kill Rogert Scanlon.

Chapter 6

"Wake up, you bastard," screamed the angry voice of the jailer. He ran his baton against the metal bars making loud harsh clanks. He then threw a large bucket of icy water to torture Kindron further.

Kindron jumped to his feet as he looked for an escape. The jailer snickered.

"You're my burden now," the jailer told him and blew his cheap cigar smoke in his face. Kindron coughed and closed his eyes. He felt the pull of his shirt and the smash of his face against the metal bars. He smelled the onion and tobacco-tinged breath of the jailer close to his face. The jailer laughed and released spit onto Kindron's face.

The words of the three forms rang in his head. He knew his weapon, and he had the opportunity to use it. Kindron grabbed tight to the jailer's wrist. The jailer stopped breathing. Kindron took his other hand and put it on the jailer's face. Kindron dug his nails into the jailer's sickly yellow skin until blood was released. Involuntary contractions took over the jailer's body.

A rush of emotions came at Kindron. He started breathing heavily. He felt everything that the jailer would ever feel. He saw himself taking the man's life. He saw his death, and he did not let go. Kindron accepted what the blackness had told him in the night. He took his revenge and did not think to stop.

The man dropped and Kindron did the same. Upon his release, Kindron began to cry. He knew the jailer was a bad man, but did he deserve to die? His gift had killed before, but this was the first time he intended it to happen. He continued to cry until his thoughts drifted to Rogert Scanlon again. He rose and felt the power of what he had just done. He knew that he had the power to avenge his parents' murders, and he knew how he would.

Kindron saw the keys to the cell. He was quick to grab them off the dead man's belt and to unlock the door of the cell. Kindron stood for a minute. He had just killed a man. He had just killed him with his touch. He promised himself at that moment that he would do it again. And he knew that he would do it to Rogert Scanlon.

Kindron stepped over the jailer's body and walked out of the prison. No one else was there to challenge him. He simply walked into the city street and mixed with the morning crowd.

Chapter 7

Kindron did not know his way around the city but he knew where he would find a man like Rogert Scanlon. After a few blocks of searching, Kindron stopped and stared from across the street at the gates of the pompous guesthouse that served as the city's brothel.

"You're a mess," the smart-mouthed shopkeeper said to the boy. "And that's no place for a kid." Kindron looked up at the strikingly handsome man with flowing gray, white, and black hair. He looked above him and saw 'Parfumeur' on the sign. He inhaled in frustration, but the citrus and jasmine was calming, almost kind.

"Yes," the man said with a softer tone. "Our best seller." He extended his hand. Kindron immediately withdrew. The man cracked a smile and realized the boy's withdrawal was more than having been taught to 'not talk to strangers'. "No, no. Don't worry," he said. "You cannot hurt me," and ushered his touch. Kindron held back. However, the parfumier was fast. He had grabbed hold of Kindron's hand, skin to skin. Before Kindron could react, he was pulled into the store.

Kindron was shocked that he did not feel anything from the man. He could not "see" him; nothing about him. Not his present nor his future. Kindron found himself uneasy at the man's ability to "hide" from him. He looked up to a smiling face.

"My name is Thaddeus. I'm a vampire," he said very matter of fact, "an Immortal. Seers cannot 'see' Immortals."

Kindron attempted to pull back. He was more fearful at his lack of "seeing" than he was at the fact that he was touching a vampire. However, then that thought added to his fear.

"I'm not going to hurt you," the vampire told him. "And you are not going to hurt me. I can feel that your power is strong… stronger than any other that I have encountered."

Kindron could not look the vampire in the eyes. "My father had told me that my power made me special. But it turned me into a monster. My power killed a man. I watched as the jailer's heart exploded."

The vampire paused. He chose his words carefully. "Most seers are not able to do that. You do not know how to control your ability to 'see'."

Kindron shook his head, showing that he agreed. He did not offer that The Dark Sisters had taught him that.

"Where is your father now?"

"Dead," Kindron said flatly. "And my mother. The man who killed them is in there." He pointed at the brothel.

"You did what you had to do," the vampire said with comfort. "But know that if you go in there, you will kill again. And there will be no coming back from that."

Kindron looked at the vampire and squinted his eyes in determination and strength.

The vampire sighed. "I understand your... position." He let go of the boy's hand. "I know what you desire. I see it in your eyes."

Kindron looked at him with concern.

"You are not wrong to seek revenge," the vampire told him. "Whoever is in there deserves his fate, and you will avenge your parents' deaths." He kept his gaze on the boy as Kindron kept his on the brothel.

"You and I sit on opposite sides of the same coin," Thaddeus told him. "But it is up to us to flip that coin to expose our own truths. Our own paths." Kindron continued to look at the brothel without saying anything.

"I seek a love that I cannot have. And you... You lost a love that you can never regain." Kindron looked at him with a wrinkled brow that showed that he did not understand.

"As a vampire, I was sent to destroy humanity, but instead, I fell in love and could not. You were sent to be loved by your parents, but that love was stolen from you." Thaddeus looked to the sky and then back at the boy. "You seek justice, not revenge. A flip of the coin. I will help you."

Kindron softened his expression of confusion. His calming face showed that he understood and agreed. He nodded slightly.

"The one you seek can be found in there," Thaddeus told Kindron what he already knew and nodded towards the brothel. "Do what you must. Your truth is your destiny." Kindron looked back to the brothel and then back to Thaddeus. "I will help you get out of Tamsu... if you make it out of there."

"Thank you," he said with peace in his voice. Kindron walked towards the brothel.

Chapter 8

"How much you got, honey?" the drunken prostitute asked Kindron with an air of superiority. She joked at the boy's expense.

Kindron grabbed her wrist. She froze in place and began to cry. He released her. She did not know where Scanlon was. The man whose lap she was on threw her to the floor and came at the boy. Kindron grabbed his hand without a word. He dropped to his knees. Kindron let him go. He too did not know Scanlon's whereabouts within the brothel.

A member of the security team came at the boy. He reached out and grabbed Kindron by his exposed wrists. Kindron's eyes squinted, and his lips pursed. The burly man fell to the floor and loosened his grip. He did know where Scanlon was. Kindron removed his arms from the bouncer's light grip and placed his hands over the man's head.

The pain was so severe that the man's attempts to scream were in vain. He could only gasp as Kindron looked up to the top of the stairs. Kindron released his grasp and the man dropped to the floor. Kindron walked cautiously up the stairs, to the end of the catwalk that overlooked the salon. He stood at the glossy black door and reached out for the golden doorknob. Kindron was paying minimal attention to the stylish decor.

Kindron held the doorknob. His heart was racing and his hand began to sweat. He sensed his blood rushing through his body and heating up his core. Kindron felt his eyes turn hot. They were glowing red.

He attempted to open the door. It was locked. He kept trying to turn the knob and open the door. His eyes returned to their regular state, and he began to express concern. Scanlon is in there. I have to kill him. He slammed his body repeatedly into the door but it did not give. Then he ran down the catwalk, turned and ran back at the door. He threw himself hard into the door. Nothing.

Kindron dropped to the ground, crying at the foot of the door. He had failed. He had lost his opportunity to take revenge. This cannot be how it ends; Scanlon cannot win. Kindron slammed his open palm against the door. He did it again and again. He got to his knees and smashed his fists into the door. His knuckles were bleeding.

Kindron screamed out. His fists throbbed but the anger and hate burning inside pushed him to continue punching.

The door swung open as Kindron's bloodied hands came forward through the air. They met with the bare shins of the man inside the room. It was Rogert Scanlon.

"Who the fuck…?" Scanlon yelled out not seeing the boy on the floor.

Kindron grabbed and held tight to Scanlon's ankles. He looked up at his parents' killer. Scanlon's expression went from anger to sadness to pain to fear. Kindron's expression went from exhaustion to determination. He felt the surge again, stronger than before. Kindron felt his heart racing, This is it! He was going to take revenge. He allowed his energy to flow. He again felt his hands begin to sweat and his blood rush through his body and heat up his core. Kindron felt his eyes turn hot. They were glowing red once more. He looked up at Scanlon's face and squeezed harder.

Scanlon fell to the ground and could not move. Kindron's eyes were glowing hot crimson red. He heard laughter, but it was hollow, eerie and unnatural. The three black forms descended upon Scanlon and surrounded him, pointing. Kindron watched as the shadows grew closer and their laughter got louder. The laughter turned into Scanlon's screams and they grabbed him from his limbs and pulled on his melting form.

Kindron heard himself scream out. He squeezed his hands harder and felt Scanlon's fear. Kindron felt him burn, melt, and tear as the shadows dragged Scanlon to Hell and then… Nothing.

Kindron, still on the floor, was breathing heavily and sweating. The flashes had stopped and his eyes turned back to their regular state. He came back to the present. He saw his hands on Scanlon's ankles and quickly pulled his hands back to himself. He realized that Scanlon was dead. He cowered towards a corner and watched as Scanlon's eyes had melted out of their sockets.

Kindron heard the frightened breathing of a prostitute on the bed. Kindron was numb as he stood up but stayed in the corner for a moment. She held the bedsheets over herself and made every attempt to not be seen or heard. He could tell that she feared him. Kindron tried to control his breathing and began to feel strong.

Kindron moved towards her and heard her fear become more audible in her crying. Now drunk with power, he walked out of the room without any concern about the prostitute. She had no part in his revenge. He walked down the stairs, through the unaffected crowd, and out to the street. He looked ahead of himself, and in the distance, caught sight of the vampire, Thaddeus. In the light of day, he felt the rush of his own emotions. Kindron was in shock and everything that just happened replayed in his mind. Kindron reached his hand out before falling unconscious.

Thaddeus was quick to him with his Immortal speed before Kindron met the ground.

Chapter 9

The vampire had promised to help Kindron leave Tamsu if he made it out of the brothel. Thaddeus had secured him passage on a ship heading to Mortua. Kindron awoke to swaying that tousled his memories. Every rise and fall through the waves turned the pages of recent events in Kindron's mind. He felt no remorse about killing Scanlon, and none for taking the life of the jailer. He felt the loss of his parents and how much he missed them, their kindness, laughter, patience, and love. He squeezed his mother's necklace which was still under his collar and looked at his father's ruby ring that was turned to conceal the jewel.

"Watch it, kid," the sailor told him with a joking tone. "We're about to pull into port," he added and pointed to the active harbor of the city of Mortua. Kindron quieted his memories enough to reach up to the banister, pull himself up and be amazed by the city, its vibrancy.

The ship docked. Kindron felt lost, in the world and in his mind. He had been so consumed with destroying Rogert Scanlon. He had no plan now, no direction. He disembarked and wandered away from the vessel onto the busy cobblestone road.

"Hey!" yelled a strong voice from the carriage behind him. Kindron did not hear it. The driver stopped his horses. "Boy! Hey!"

"What is happening?" asked the passenger, who came down from the coach and walked to the boy.

"Boy!" the passenger yelled and attempted to shake him. Kindron gave no response, but instead fainted into the man's arms. The man looked up at the driver and motioned him to go on without him. He sighed. "My promise was to help to get you out of Tamsu, not take you all the way," Thaddeus said with a touch of regret about having to continue to assist Kindron.

Kindron awoke in the arms of the vampire as the Immortal walked along the snow-covered road. He could see the edge of the land in the distance and could hear the ocean beyond that as they traveled. Thaddeus had wiped himself from Kindron's memories. The boy looked up at him but said nothing. Kindron did not have the energy to fear the man carrying him. He had discovered the power of evil and he had avenged the deaths of his mother and father. He was empty. He could only surrender to his fate and accept the loneliness.

Kindron turned his head and saw the lights of the Monastery of the Brothers of the Order of Naa in the distance. Thaddeus stopped and gently lowered the boy.

"Go," he told him with no emotion.

Kindron paused. He kept his gaze on the building lights.

Thaddeus was momentarily distracted by the familiar scent of citrus and jasmine. "Wrong time," he said to his distraction as he sniffed the cold air for the direction of the source.

"This is your path." He spoke to Kindron before he seemingly disappeared. Kindron did not bother to question who or what the man was.

Kindron continued to look at the monastery. He turned his feet and stood for a second. He walked towards it with hesitation on the only road without looking back. The crunching sound of the snow covering the coastal road under his feet was hypnotic. He took in a deep breath and exhaled. It calmed him. He looked beyond his prolonged visible exhalation in the cold air. The monastery looked warm.

Kindron, for the first time since losing his parents, desired warmth. The smell of the burning fire seemed welcoming. He desired to feel welcomed.

Kindron started to sense emotions other than anger, other than hate. He felt a tear fall from his eye. Then, another and another. As he reached the monastery, the door was opened by a boy.

"Hello. I'm Phineas," the boy said and wrapped a warm blanket around Kindron as he escorted him into the warmth.

SORCERER

But the end is not clear

Chapter 1

"Oh!" the queen mother cringed her face as the offensive smell met her nose. She looked around the disheveled chambers with clothes and empty bottles left throughout. She snapped her fingers and a group of servants entered and began cleaning.

A maid pulled back the sheets on the bed and was met with the prince's naked body. She quickly looked away and threw the sheets back to cover him.

"Enough with wasting your life, Quentin," his mother ordered. "You are the Prince of Quorca. You have duties to the crown, and to the people."

Quentin rolled his eyes in his usual fashion, whenever anyone reminded him that he needed to "act appropriately for his station in life". Quentin did not care. He was the second-born prince and a prince is what he would always be. His older brother, Masquet, had been named king at the time of their father's death. Quentin missed his father, who had died a decade ago, and who had always encouraged Quentin to find his truth.

When he was a boy, Quentin's father had asked him what he wanted to be when he grew up.

"A sorcerer," he told him with such childlike excitement.

His father had immediately come up with a made-up spell and marveled at the brightness in Quentin's spirit, as he had played along.

"Do not encourage such foolery!" Quentin's mother had demanded. "How will you ever be a sorcerer, anyway?" she had asked the boy with a condescending tone. "You are not of a magical persuasion."

Quentin's smile had disappeared and he had lowered his head. His mother had walked away to address a pair of ladies but his father had whispered to him and gotten his attention. He had given Quentin a wink and casted a false spell from his imaginary wand. It made Quentin smile.

"Your antics will make him to be no more than a court jester at best," the queen had said to her husband and called for a nanny to collect the boy.

It was hours later that Quentin had learned of his father's passing. He had lost his only ally. He had lost the only one who had supported and encouraged him to be himself.

Chapter 2

"A wife?" Quentin laughed out. "I think not. What would all these other ladies do without me?" he further questioned. The royal dressers scurried to get Quentin's shirt buttoned up to the collar.

"Quentin, you will meet her and you will behave. It has been decided," his mother informed him as the royal dressers pushed down on his knee to force his heel into his shoe. "This is your chance to be something… to make something of your life. It's what your father would have wanted." She knew that guilt was a good weapon against Quentin.

"Mother! This is a definite 'no'!" he argued over the cravat being tightened around his neck.

"Too late, my son. Your stepfather has already sealed it," she said with her hand holding onto his chin and a gentle slap to his cheek. "Well, what I mean is that he has invited her and her parents to meet you. They are traveling and meeting potential suitors. I will make sure that you are her choice. You will make sure to accept my choice," she added and turned to admire the flowers on the stand in front of her.

Will I? he thought.

"I just hope that she will accept all of you," she said with sharpness in her insult and waited for a reaction that did not come. "After all," his mother added and sniffed the lavender, "you are a prince." Still nothing from him.

"I am more than just a prince, mother," he reminded her. The dressers spritzed a dash of cologne.

She hid her excitement at stirring a response from him. She was pouring her passive insults on thick to inspire Quentin's rebellious nature. She knew how to play the game with him, and she played it well.

Quentin's mother moved on leaving Quentin with a perplexed expression. All four dressers exited with her.

I know what you are doing, Mother. It will not work. Quentin paced the room. He pushed his hands forward and the windows blew open as he walked by.

Chapter 3

The following morning the queen mother forced her way into his sleeping chambers with servants moving quickly about the room. "Get up. You have plans today." The queen mother clapped and the well-dressed man in a plum-colored overcoat entered.

"Who are you?" Quentin asked the man.

"This is Thaddeus," his mother answered. "He is here to educate you on the proper etiquette of royal courtship. This is not going to be some brothel wench, Quentin. I want this union, Quentin. It will benefit the future of Quorca, as well as your future. Thaddeus is here to make sure that it happens."

"What?" he questioned and pulled the covers over his head.

She motioned with her eyes and head for the prince's royal dressers to get him ready. "You have twenty minutes," she announced to the room. "Quentin, we will meet you in the solarium." She looked at the four palace guards. "Twenty minutes." They clicked their heels in unison, acknowledging that they would get him there. Thaddeus offered his arm, which she took as they exited.

"Get off me, I told you," Quentin argued with the guards as they forced him into the solarium. The sun was shining bright.

"I will take it from here," Thaddeus told them. "Welcome, your highness," he said to Quentin as the guards walked off in a two-by-two formation.

"Fuck off."

"As expected," Thaddeus said, taking no offense to the prince's rudeness.

"Where is breakfast?"

"Finished and cleaned up," he replied.

"Go and get me something," he barked.

"No."

"What? Do you know who I am?"

"Yes," he replied. "You are no one. And that is why I am here. Your mother has concerns about the misguided direction of your life."

Quentin threw a decorative statue at Thaddeus. He moved quicker than humanly possible dodging the statue as it crashed against the wall.

Quentin's eyes opened in amazement.

"I am a vampire," Thaddeus confessed. "An Immortal."

Quentin looked up at the glass ceiling.

"That is a myth. Sunlight does not have any effect on me," he told him.

"Ah," Quentin said, unsure if he should be concerned or envious. "You have become everything that your father feared you would. Your mother feels you have lost your way."

Quentin made a sound that noted his disinterest in Thaddeus' comments. "Apparently, I never had a way."

"A future queen will not hold any interest in a useless prince. Let me be honest with you. You are the second son. You will not inherit this kingdom. You have no future as of now, other than drunk at the bottom of a barrel of wine… Domestic wine. You need to upgrade your skill and your perspective in life. Without that, she will have no use for you."

Quentin stewed in his anger. He knew that what the vampire said was true, but his ego was working overtime to not accept it.

"So, let us begin," Thaddeus told him, breaking the silence. He turned and began speaking as if at the beginning of a scholastic lecture. As he turned, he saw that Quentin had left the room.

Chapter 4

Thaddeus found Quentin on a large terrace that overlooked the royal gardens. He came to stand next to the young prince. The vampire turned and leaned onto the rail of the terrace. Quentin did not look at him; his distant gaze remained. Thaddeus unfolded his arms and assisted himself to sit on the rail.

"Everyone thinks that it is so easy being me," Quentin told him. He continued to not look at him. "I am the second son of a royal family." He now turned and looked at Thaddeus. "A prince. But as you have already said, I will always be just a prince. Do you know what it feels like to be born into your maximum potential?" Thaddeus maintained his silence. "Regardless of what I ever do, I will always be known as a prince." He turned away as he began to get emotional and continued to confess his silent concerns to Thaddeus. "And no one understands that I want more. I want to do something with my life. They all say that they want me to do something but want to control what that something is. I have no voice in my own life. Things were different when my father was here.”

“You were a child when your father was alive,” Thaddeus reminded him. “Yet now, you are an adult who acts like a child.”

“Who is treated like a child,” Quentin argued back.

“Who is very much acting like a child right now,” Thaddeus argued.

Quentin motioned to speak but knew that his continued arguing would only add to Thaddeus being right. He calmed himself and looked at Thaddeus. His expression showed defeat. “I’ve always only been seen as a backup. I’ve been forbidden to do more. So, why keep looking for more? You mentioned a ‘future queen’. Well, that would still make me only a prince.” He looked at Thaddeus who remained silent. “Forget it. Let’s get this over with.”

Thaddeus smiled and nodded. “You are wrong.”

“About?”

“You always had an ally. You always had someone who believed in you…and anything that you wanted.”

“My father. But he died a decade ago.”

“Yes, your father,” Thaddeus said. “Quentin. Your father’s final breath came with a wish…a prayer…to an angel before he died. He prayed for his children to reach their true potential.”

Quentin looked off and began to smile with thoughts of his father's humor and kindness.

"What is it that you want to do with your life?" Thaddeus asked, breaking the silence but allowing for the joyous memories of Quentin's father to linger in his mind.

"To become a sorcerer," Quentin answered to what Thaddeus had questioned. "I want to be a true and powerful sorcerer."

Thaddeus waited.

"I am already pretty good," Quentin told him, insecure with his lack of reaction. His ego was still attempting to hold itself high. "But I know there's more to learn to be a master."

Thaddeus spoke through his rustled brow. "Yet, you argue against being introduced as a potential husband to the Princess of Witches of all people."

Quentin thought about it. "The Princess of Witches?" He paused and remained silent in thought.

"Ah. She didn't tell you," Thaddeus said. "That is why you think that your mother is acting against you. I am telling you that she may still think that what you want is foolish, but it is what you want. And she supports you. She is holding to your father's dying wish," Thaddeus told him. "That is why I am here. And that is why she wants to introduce you as a potential husband to the Princess of Witches."

Quentin was quiet again, as he looked off in thought.

Thaddeus came to stand next to him. He leaned in and whispered, "I am going to help you, Quentin. You are going to be a great sorcerer."

Chapter 5

"First things first," Thaddeus said to Quentin as they were deep in the forest so as not to be disturbed. "You must know that your powers of sorcery did not come directly through your bloodline. As I told you, they are a divine gift to you as an answer to your father's dying prayer. You are the second son of King Kreviac and Queen Zerras of the Kingdom of Quorca. On your father's deathbed, he was able to gain the favor of an angel who answered his prayer for the true path of his children. Your brother was crowned king, which was expected, and you were given the gift of sorcery." Quentin was searching through his memories for signs of what Thaddeus said. "You want so strongly to be a sorcerer because you are a sorcerer. No one can ever take that away from you. It is divinely blessed."

"How do you know this?"

"I was there," Thaddeus told him. "My presence was requested to assist your father comfortably into the next dimension."

"And you saw the angel?"

"I am an Immortal," he reminded the prince. "I see all types of entities in all types of dimensions."

Quentin paced in thought. "It was just after my father died a decade ago that I began to be able to express my skill." He looked at the vampire. "I believe you."

"Good. Then, let us get started."

"The magic of a sorcerer holds a slightly different origin than that of a Witch. The magic of a Witch is a birthright. A Witch's power comes from within. The magic of a sorcerer comes from commanding the Elements and requires much more training and practice." Quentin was quiet, but his excitement took over his aura.

Silence followed.

"Good," Thaddeus said very matter-of-fact. "Seems you understand." The next few weeks were spent mainly with Thaddeus meeting Quentin deep in the woods in the early mornings. It was now Quentin who would be out of his bed earlier than the breakfast was prepared and without his mother barging in with guards to force him awake. This put a smile on the face of the queen mother.

"Remember, Quentin," Thaddeus yelled out from his distant position away from Quentin's focus, "up with your fourth digits." Quentin nodded.

"Why so far away?" Quentin yelled.

"I have no desire to have to recover, if anything goes wrong," Thaddeus told him.

"Thanks! A real confidence boost."

"Focus, Quentin. You know what you are doing."

Quentin did exactly that. He exhaled and moved his hands and arms in such a way to create a magical spell that manipulated the air and sent ripples towards the glass vase sitting on the tree stump. The vase lifted. It shook a bit at first but then steadied and held itself unsupported.

"Wrists and middle fingers down," Thaddeus called out. "Fire."

Quentin again exhaled and did as instructed. His forehead began to perspire and he felt a cramp in his right hand.

"Fourth digits up," Thaddeus reminded him.

He again did as instructed and the vase maintained its position. Quentin pushed hard through the cramp and the vase was engulfed in a flame. Quentin was immediately excited by what he was able to do but knew that he needed to stay focused.

"Thumbs," Thaddeus called out.

Quentin wiggled his thumbs in and out in alternating fashions and saw water fill the vase and pour over it putting out the fire.

"It's getting heavy," he yelled to Thaddeus.

"Earth," he said and nothing more.

Quentin turned his wrists slowly and a mound of dirt rose from the ground to stop where the vase was positioned in the air. It now sat full of water atop the dirt. Quentin screamed out in excitement. He ran over and hugged Thaddeus. "We did it!"

"You did it, Quentin. This is your truth. I am only here to train you to unleash it," Thaddeus told him.

Quentin could not stop smiling. He had achieved a union with the four physical Elements.

Chapter 6

Thaddeus entered the study. It had been set up like a chemistry lab. By whom, he was not sure. "What happened here?"

Quentin ignored him. He was concentrating on his studies.

"Quentin!" Thaddeus yelled. "What is happening here?"

Quentin was slow to look up at him. He was focused on his craft. "I am working on manipulating Ether. You are disturbing me," he told the vampire.

Thaddeus chuckled. "Look around," he told him. "You are disturbed. This is not the way." He looked around with concern. "Quentin. Ether is dangerous. It is without a ruler and therefore, corruptible."

"Then enlighten me on how to control it," the prince told him.

"You don't control it. Don't ever think that you can control magic." Thaddeus looked at him with a worried expression.

"How do I learn to command true magic?" Quentin asked the more appropriate question.

"By gaining favor of the Elements. All the Elements," Thaddeus told him. "I'm not sure what texts you have read, but it is that fifth Element, Ether or Space, that must be manipulated if you want to truly master magic and that can only come from understanding and practice." Thaddeus corrected him. "Ether is space. It is what lies in between."

"But different from air?" Quentin reached into his bag and pulled out a book. He searched through it and stopped on a page that mentioned Ether.

"Very different. Ether is space itself, not just the lack of something that can be touched." Thaddeus continued as Quentin was understanding. "It is corruptible if it is manipulated against the other elements. Ether has no ruler. It allows for passage from one dimension to the next, and having the skill to manipulate it without it turning dark is the test of a true master of magic... whether Witch, sorcerer, Fae, or any other magical being."

Quentin scratched his head as he was figuring out what Thaddeus said.

"You need to experience it," he told him. He turned and looked him in the eyes. "Experience, Quentin. Come with me."

"Where are we going?" Quentin begged.

"There is no better way to understand Ether than to open a portal to another dimension. We are going through the mirror, of course," Thaddeus told him.

"Oh yes. Of course. What?"

Thaddeus let out a breath, as if attempting to hold back his condescending laughter. "I see you have a lot to learn. Quentin. Getting through a mirror, into another realm of existence, requires the Element with no ruler, Ether. Having no ruler allows for that emptiness to exist, and that is what opens portals."

"Let's see." He stepped back and allowed Quentin space in front of the mirror.

Quentin inhaled and then slowly released his breath to be sure to control what he was about to attempt. He knew that it would require all his concentration. "Sorcerer," he told himself.

Thaddeus watched in silence. This was now Quentin's path. Quentin moved into a posture that showed a comfortable control of his energy. He opened his eyes and stared into the mirror. He began to move his hands in a way that looked as though they were becoming deformed. Each joint of each finger began to move without respect for the others. Quentin's face remained calm, and his breathing was relaxed and deep. He began to see what was on the other side of the mirror. He saw into a different dimension.

The shock of being able to see this caused him to gasp and lose his focus. He was again staring back at himself from the mirror. He looked for Thaddeus but was unable to find his reflection. He turned and saw him standing there.

"Vampires do not cast reflections," he told him. "A vampire can see through the mirror to what is on the other side. Seeing myself in the mirror would block what is on the other side."

"On the other side," Quentin tried to recall what was exposed on the other side of the mirror. "A greenish glow," he said as if in a vision.

"Ghosts," Thaddeus told him. "Let's try again."

Quentin walked up to and touched the mirror. He looked at his reflection quizzically. He was not fully sure what he did to be able to see through the mirror to the other dimension. "If I can do it again, will I see the same dimension, the same creatures?"

"Think of mirrors as doorways… A connection to a different location in this or another dimension. Now imagine a hallway that connects these doorways. That is the Mirror Realm. It exists outside of space and time. Mortals cannot enter without a spirit."

"And an Immortal?" Quentin asked.

"We are practically limitless," the vampire reminded him. "I have the ability to enter without being shrouded."

"Shrouded?"

Thaddeus searched for the right words. "Camouflaged by a spirit, most likely a ghost, to safely get through the Mirror Realm undetected."

"Okay," Quentin said with an eager nodding of his head. "Understandable enough."

"Good. Keep that thought in the back of your consciousness and conjure the spell again."

Quentin took a deep breath. He moved his hands in the same fashion as he had done prior, but this time, he added a pulling motion from his shoulder blades and lifted his arms. The response was quick. He was again successful with seeing into the dimension on the other side of the mirror. This time, the spirits did look out towards him. They looked at him, the vampire, and the room and surroundings. It was as if they had only now become aware of the world on this side of the mirror.

The ghosts became more curious and moved closer to the veil between the two dimensions. Quentin fought to keep his focus. He knew that he had to hold his spell to keep the opening between the dimensions. He watched as one of the ghosts began to come forward.

Quentin felt the air get thick and saw the world covered in a greenish hue as the ghost came over him and enveloped him completely. He began to feel the pull towards the mirror.

"Do not resist," he heard Thaddeus tell him.

This sense did not feel completely serene. There was a feeling of fear in the curiosity that the ghost brought forth. Quentin continued to allow what was happening. He trusted Thaddeus and more importantly, he trusted his abilities as a sorcerer. Quentin turned his head and watched as the world he knew disappeared and transitioned into the one on the other side of the mirror. I'm on the other side.

Quentin looked back and watched Thaddeus follow him, casually stepping into the mirror.

"Now what?" he asked Thaddeus.

"Now, we go back," he told him.

Quentin felt as though he needed to calm his breathing and just step backwards as he said the spell in reverse. It worked. Quentin was back in his dimension. He saw the natural colors of things and breathed with greater ease as the ghost's cover came off.

The green light began to sparkle and Quentin felt the ghost pull away from him just prior to entering the mirror.

"I'm not going back," he told them. The ghost immediately faded out of sight and his presence was no longer felt.

Quentin looked to Thaddeus.

"Hmmm. That will be a problem," Thaddeus was flippant with his response. "But one I am sure you will be able to manage… Quentin," Thaddeus told him. "You have now mastered Ether and conjured a portal. Not many can say that they have that ability. Congratulations!"

Yes! Quentin thought to himself, proud of what he had accomplished.

Quentin's attitude had changed. He was not only willing but truly excited to be introduced to the Princess of Witches. He was ready for his dinner engagement.

Chapter 7

"Mother," Quentin greeted and kissed her gloved hand. "Julian," he said to his stepfather with a snarl of his lip and no effort at any other form of protocol.

Julian nodded to his wife and walked away.

"Why you married him after Father's death, I will never know," Quentin told his mother.

"I promised your father that I would. He did not want me to be alone, and Julian is a good man. He looks out for me and for the crown."

Quentin ignored her.

"Where have you been?" his mother asked. "She is about to arrive."

"About to arrive? How rude! She should have been here waiting for me," Quentin joked.

"Oh, Quentin," his mother laughed. "You are in for a very rude awakening. This is not one of your common brothel mistresses. This is-"

The music from the horns cut Quentin's mother off. Everyone stood tall and motioned to get a look at who was coming in; everyone but Quentin, who looked away to collect his thoughts. He sniffed the air. An aroma of orange and vanilla floated in. It drew his desire; he was now interested. Quentin stood on a chair to get a better look. He became another of the onlookers hoping to catch sight of who was entering the ballroom.

The military escorts from the Kingdom of Witches made their way. They floated in and positioned themselves to push the crowd back. Once in position, they lowered themselves in unison to the floor.

Yaltheez and Elthian, the King and Queen of the Witches, entered the ballroom. They escorted their daughter, whose identity was hidden through a veil. She looked through squinted eyes and met Quentin's stare. He lost his balance on the chair but regained his composure quickly. The princess smiled. Quentin knew who the Princess of Witches was and the stories about her but had never actually laid eyes upon her. Very few had.

Her personal escorts, made up of four other witches, also accompanied her and her parents. A red fox walked along with her.

"I told you that you would approve," Quentin's mother told him and slapped his leg to have him come down from the chair. She offered her hand for him to escort her to greet the royals.

Quentin's brother, Masquet, who had been crowned the King of Quorca after their father's death, was greeting the royal family of Witches.

"Welcome," Quentin heard his mother announce with a surprisingly overjoyed tone. He always knew her to be direct and to the point, with no ceremonial grandeur. It drew his attention back immediately. He met eyes with the princess as she detached her veil. Her smirk was as cocky as his; his widened.

"Thank you for gracing us," Quentin interrupted and moved to kiss the princess' hand. The escorts were quick to draw their wands to hold him back. Quentin brushed his hand, and all four wands flew through the air and into a vase. His mother's lips were tight to keep her from screaming at him. Yaltheez and Elthian looked at one another in an attempt to hide their surprise.

"Impressive," the princess whispered to him as she offered her hand for his kiss. Quentin shrugged his shoulders playfully. The other four witches came closer. "Thank you," the princess said as if to say, "It's fine."

Quentin motioned to lead her outside for a private conversation. She, with her fox beside her, did not resist and walked with him.

"So, you are a sorcerer," she stated.

"Yes," he admitted. "It brings me joy. I used to think that it brought embarrassment to my family."

"Your magic brings embarrassment to your family?" The princess was taken aback.

"I thought that they didn't respect me," he told her.

"Well, your magic does come from an external source. It is more chaotic," she added jokingly, belittling him. "Maybe that is why they don't respect you. The magic of a sorcerer is without control."

"My skill comes from a balance with all five elements and exists outside of the laws that govern yours or any Witch." Suddenly, he was concerned that he just insulted the princess. "And besides that, I can whip up one hell of a potion," he joked to lighten the mood.

"Ah, an egomaniac," the princess added and laughed.

"Just a touch… It helps with the spells," he joked.

"Ileana," the princess said, introducing herself, "Princess of Witches." Her guard was down.

"Quentin Sinclair," he offered back. "Egomaniac and very talented sorcerer… and second to the throne of Quorca. But I'm not really in the mood to kill my brother off. I do not want to be king."

Ileana laughed. "That is a lot to say as an introduction. But you forgot funny. You are funny."

"Finally! A charming quality," Quentin joked.

"Yes," she agreed. "Finally." They stared at one another in silence for what seemed too long. "But I am guessing that there are more good qualities than you allow the rest of us to see."

Quentin felt the presence of the princess' escorts.

"So, if you don't want to be king, what do you want?" she asked.

Quentin paused and revealed an eager smile. He looked down at the fox who held his head cocked in interest. Quentin wanted to tell her everything. For some reason that he did not understand, he wanted her to know. He held his tongue and looked at the others. He squatted and petted the fox. "Will it ever be possible for us to be alone?"

"Yes," Ileana told him. "But not right now." Princess Ileana nodded towards his mother who was spying from behind the curtains. She walked past him and stood with her escorts. Her fox stayed with Quentin. The princess looked at the animal and nodded her head. The fox did the same. Then, she looked at Quentin with greater interest. "The time has come for me to take a husband. Don't worry. You are in the running," she joked. "We have just made the bond. And now, it is time for all the pomp and circumstance." She started walking, but the other ladies waited. Ileana stopped. "Are you coming?" she asked him.

Quentin shook his head. He was shocked by Ileana's confidence. "Yes. Yes."

They were announced as they reentered the celebration. A round of applause and the clinking of glasses was heard with the joyous yells of the excited crowd. Bottles of champagne, domestic from Quorca, flowed all night as the music, dancing, and laughter went through to sunrise.

Chapter 8

"There you are," Quentin's brother, King Masquet, yelled out as if scolding him. "You may have dazzled our visitors and fooled mother with your act last night, but the advisors do not have confidence that you can seal this deal. I need you in the planning room to argue your point and convince them and me that you are able to make this happen. Arguments for borders and political gains to be had in the meeting with the advisors. I need you to focus on your duties to Quorca. It is time for you to step up and take your place in this court."

"Masquet-"

"King Masquet," his brother demanded.

"King Masquet," Quentin said through a calming sigh. "I am completely taken by the princess and she by me. This marriage will happen, give Quorca an alliance with the Kingdom of Witches and everything that you want."

"Your duty is to be sure that this union occurs. You will meet me in the planning room where I have already gathered the royal advisors and understand that this is your path. This is your truth."

King Masquet stormed off. Quentin knew that he was expected to serve the Kingdom of Quorca before serving his own needs. His brother's demands were poorly delivered but were in line with what Quentin wanted for his life, so he decided that he would go to the planning room and hear what the advisors had to say.

Chapter 9

The ongoing discussions could be heard down the hall as Quentin joined his brother and the advisors in the planning room. His mother was also present at the gathering. The air was unusually chilled. The advisors argued for argument's sake. He immediately regretted coming to the meeting. His brother addressed the room:

"We will have joint control of the borders on and off the Kulkaati Penninsula. Our wines will finally be able to be exported for distribution to the finest shops and restaurants in the Kingdom of Witches and they will pay handsomely in tariffs. And the military strength will keep both us and them protected from any invasion."

The squabbling continued and sounded like a disturbingly harsh noise.

"I understand what you are saying." Quentin attempted to gather everyone's attention and quiet the room. "But I have found my path." He looked to his mother who had an unfamiliar twinkle in her eye.

"There's not enough magic to turn him into a responsible adult!" one advisor was overheard "whispering" to another.

"And how is he going to defend our borders? Building a wall out of all his empty wine bottles?" the advisor seated on the opposite side of the table replied.

These comments incited snorts, chuckles and murmurs. Quentin did not understand what exactly was happening. He was part of the royal family, after all, and that called for a measure of respect and decorum. The queen mother nodded in approval of what they said.

King Masquet sighed. He did actually give Quentin's argument a moment of light. But then he looked at the prince with an annoyed expression. "The time has come for you to grow up. You are not a Witch. Forget about forging magic and accept that you will be there as a political ally for Quorca. A marriage between you and the Princess of Witches needs to be sealed, but do not think that your parlor tricks will be enough."

"But my intentions are true!" Quentin countered.

"What is he going to do? Whoosh some air to sweep her off her feet?" someone across the room defiantly yelled.

"He has a better chance at being accepted by the circus than the royal family of Witches!" an advisor stood on the table and proclaimed. The room bursted out in laughter, maniacal and chaotic.

Quentin's brother and his mother repeatedly nodded in agreement with what was being said by the advisors.

"Mother," Quentin whispered as he leaned in. She refused to acknowledge him. "Mother," he repeated with a stronger tone to no response. "Mother!" he yelled and silenced the room as the echo of his scream remained in the air.

The queen mother turned to him and maintained the appearance of calm. Quentin noticed a swirling motion in her eyes. "Yes, Quentin?"

Quentin looked at her as if she were crazy. He looked around the room with the same puzzled expression. The conversation in the room had become louder and then bordered on hysteria. Quentin stood but was pulled back into his seat. He was surprised by the strength of the aged advisors who knocked him back and held him down.

Quentin's confusion turned to concern as Ileana, the Princess of Witches, entered the planning room with the red fox.

Quentin looked to his brother and his mother. They both sat, staring back with vapid expressions. They looked at one another and then began laughing with hysteria. He turned to Ileana, who was taking in the energy of the room. She cast a spell that knocked the advisor from Quentin.

"Quentin?" she asked.

"I don't know," he admitted.

Quentin took Ileana by the hand as she whistled for the fox. They made it to the middle of the room and jumped onto the oversized table. The others had all paired off and were still laughing uncontrollably at one another. The sunlight entered from the western windows, and Quentin saw a greenish hue on the beams of light that illuminated the room. "The ghost," he realized.

Quentin searched his mind for a spell to exorcize the spirit from the advisors. They had all turned their attention towards him and stopped laughing. The freakish smiles remained, but the expressions had turned sinister.

"We'll have to do this together," Ileana told him. "We can do this, Quentin. We can do this." He nodded in agreement with his lips pulled tight into a straight line. His thoughts stopped on the spell that he needed. Quentin dropped to his left knee and began chanting the spell. He twisted his trunk and moved his arms in circles as he stood and repeated the spell. He began yelling louder as he spun in a circle. Ileana cast a spell that kept a protective bubble of light around them. Everyone in the planning room stopped and several of them started to step back.

A strong wind began to blow off Quentin and from his fingertips came bolts of electricity. As the current flowed from him, it made contact with the light and intensified. The light extended in all directions and struck each of the advisors. They were all knocked onto their backs, unconscious. A greenish haze illuminated and surrounded them as a single circle on the floor. The ground began to shake, and a crack opened under the table on which Quentin and Ileana stood. It spread towards the outer wall, broke through it and onto the grass outside.

Ileana kept the protective spell around them as Quentin cast another spell. Rain began to fall inside the meeting room and covered the whole floor. They watched as the green-colored water flowed as a shrinking circle from each of the advisors and into the opening in the floor. He looked outside at the far end of the crack in the ground. There was a glow of green light. Quentin, Ileana, and the fox moved past the now sleeping bodies and walked over to see the light. There was a glowing swirl that held itself levitating in the open hole in the ground. It morphed into a glowing human form.

"It is you," Quentin said as he remembered the ghost as the one who did not go back into the mirror. "Why?"

The ghost said nothing.

"Not all spirits are good, Quentin," Ileana told him. Quentin looked disappointed.

Ileana moved her fingers and then arms in a way that cast a spell made of fuchsia light, which encapsulated the ghost.

Quentin looked back at the ghost, who was now weakened and contained by Ileana's spell. "You tried to harm the woman I love." Ileana was taken back by Quentin's announcement and the sincerity in his voice.

"We must send him back to his dimension," he heard Ileana say to him. She gave him a supportive smile and stepped back. He nodded in agreement.

"I have never opened a portal," she admitted.

"Well," Quentin said and looked at her. "You're about to. We need a mirror."

Ileana glamoured a window to have reflective properties. "That will do," she said with confidence.

Quentin thought of his lessons with Thaddeus. He focused his mind on Ether and on the spell that opened and closed the portal. Quentin was not sure where the other side of the mirror opened. However, he knew that getting the ghost into the Mirror Realm would get him out of his dimension. Quentin positioned himself in front of the mirror.

"Ileana," he said, failing to hide his adrenaline rush. "Keep the ghost contained. When I tell you, cast him through the portal." She nodded in agreement.

Quentin exhaled to gain control of his thoughts and emotions. He maneuvered his hands and said the spell to open the portal. Ileana held the ghost in a protective bubble. The ghost was now resisting.

"Quentin," she yelled. "He's becoming very aggressive in there," she told him as she maintained her spell and control.

"I will find you," the ghost threatened.

"Now!"

With her left hand, Ileana whirled the ball of fuchsia light and aimed it into the opening in the mirror. She then released her spell and ran to stand next to Quentin to protect him if anything came out. Quentin said the spell in reverse and moved his arms and hands in reverse to close the portal. Right before it closed, Ileana sent a bolt of light through. The sound of a distant mirror smashing was heard with an echo as the portal closed.

"In the Mirror Realm he stays," she said to Quentin, knowing that breaking the mirror on the other side of the portal would trap the ghost.

They grabbed one another in a tight embrace. The rain stopped. Quentin went over to feel the window that had been glamoured. Ileana reversed the spell and it returned to a clear window. Quentin smashed it to be sure that there was no reflective surface for the ghost to come back through. Ileana nodded to him with a sense of pride at what they had accomplished. "You are truly gifted," she told him. "You have control over all the elements."

Quentin walked back to her and dropped to his knee. He took her hand and she attempted to cover her excitement with the other hand.

"Princess Ileana," he began. "It would truly be my honor…"

She felt a rush of joy.

"If you would…"

The word yes was on her tongue.

"Tell me where your father is so that I can ask for your hand."

The princess' eyes widened.

"What can I say? I'm a traditionalist." Quentin shrugged his shoulders.

They smiled at one another.

"Quentin?" Ileana asked. "I need to know something before this develops any further."

"Anything," he said.

"In time, I will be crowned Queen of Witches…" She paused as to carefully select her words. "But you will be… still be… a prince. Are you sure that you will be okay with that?"

The fox came to stand between them. Ileana and the fox nodded to one another.

"No, my lady," he began. Ileana's eyes teared up. "I will be a sorcerer," he said with full confidence and bravado. "And you will be my queen."

Ileana's tears turned to joy as she held her hands to her mouth. Quentin grabbed her and kissed her deeply.

The fox pawed at their legs. "He's going to stay with you, Quentin. He has taken a liking to you… as have I." She kissed him on the cheek.

Quentin smiled and stood in quiet reflection. The fox rubbed his head on Quentin's leg.

MONK
Fire will rain down

Chapter 1

The day was perfect…A cloudless sky, cool air with a warm sun. The rustling of the grasses sounded refreshing. Phineas smelled the air for any unexpected aromas. Nothing. He allowed his hood to drop. He was on a beach that was near the monastery. The fresh sea air blew across his face and the waves sounded off rhythmically in the distance. He sensed for the first time in a very long time that if he ever stopped, it would be here. Phineas had been looking for his friend for more than twenty years.

Phineas and Kindron were orphans who had been taken in by the Monastery of the Order of the Brothers of Naa. Phineas was brought by a soldier as a newborn. His mother had died at the time of his birth, according to the soldier. When the soldier had found them, the boy was reaching for his mother's face with his tiny hand as she held him to her chest, still covered with blood. The soldier had lost his own son and always wanted the name to live on. The orphan had been given his name by the stranger, but no last name.

Kindron was not brought there as a baby. When he was six-years-old, he appeared at the monastery doors one winter evening, disheveled and shivering in the cold. He never spoke of his past. Kindron never took to any of the other boys and definitely not to the monks. He was a "seer" and had an ability that few understood and many viewed as entirely evil, including Kindron. He had the ability to visualize the future path of anyone who he touched and the intensity of every emotion that they would ever feel rushed to him and to them all at once. The experience was overwhelming for them and Kindron. It felt like excruciating pain. Kindron did his best to hide his power, especially from the monks.

When the boys first met, Phineas was ordered to become Kindron's guide and to show him around the grounds. He was told to orient him to the rules and the routine of the brothers.

Phineas was a bit of a rebel. He was smart enough to not get caught in any of his rogue behaviors which included sneaking into the library and reading through the texts that were off limits to the boys. He enjoyed learning about different powers that people possessed. He was interested in learning about Immortals and Witches and the things that the Order of Naa deemed against their teachings.

One night when Kindron could not sleep, he followed Phineas as he was sneaking out of the dormitory. He followed Phineas into the library. Phineas showed him the types of things that he had been learning in the night. He showed him books about fringe powers. Kindron allowed himself to share with Phineas about his own gift. Phineas did not judge him. Phineas assured him that he would keep his secret. He welcomed him into his nightly rule breaking. They became immediate friends.

Kindron had become an outcast among the boys. Phineas felt a need to protect him. On a particular day, Kindron was being hazed by a group of boys. He resisted fighting back for he did not want to expose his gift by touching anyone. One of the boys grabbed him by the face and attempted to push him into the wall. The touch immediately sent the boy and Kindron into a painful shock. Phineas saw this and kicked the boy away from Kindron. All the other boys took their friend and cried to the monks that Phineas had attacked him and something unnatural happened with Kindron.

One of the monks who recognized Kindron as a seer immediately brought it to the attention of Monsignor Quahin, the head of the Order of the Brothers of Naa. Quahin reinforced that Kindron was evil and must be cast out. Despite Kindron's pleas and cries, Quahin showed no mercy in throwing him out into the cold rainy night. He then turned to Phineas and administered punishment for disobeying the monastery rules. He would make an example out of Phineas. Monsignor Quahin beat Phineas with the torturous blades of his glove and did not stop until the boy was left with scars that ran across his face.

For a period of time, Kindron stayed in the forest near the monastery. Phineas would sneak out and bring him food and books. He spent nights teaching him what he learned during the days, and together, they discovered how to understand and control Kindron's special talents, or at least as much as two young boys could.

Phineas came almost every night. But one night, Kindron was not there. Phineas worried that he had been discovered by the monks. He spied around the monastery but heard no rumor of the boy being found in the woods. He returned every night for two weeks. Food that he left remained untouched and spoiled. Phineas searched for clues as to Kindron's whereabouts. Yet, there was not very much to look through.

By the end of the second week of Kindron's disappearance, Phineas found a sketchbook. He had given it to Kindron as a gift during a celebration of the Blood Moon. The sketches in it were all similar; three sinister shadows gathering around a child. The history of "The Hundred Years War" was taught to all children. He had read about Witches who were called "The Dark Sisters". He compared Kindron's sketches to what he found in restricted books of the library.

They were the same. He had no doubt this was a sign that The Dark Sisters had taken Kindron. Phineas knew that if they had him, he was not safe. He had to find him and save him.

Yet first, he had to learn more about The Dark Sisters. He spent his time at the monastery learning as much as he could from the number of texts in the library. He knew that the time would come that he would leave the monastery in the hope of finding his friend.

He had stayed in the monastery for years learning from the vast library. Phineas had been focused on finding Kindron since they were boys. He learned about the theories of what happened to The Dark Sisters after they disappeared during the Hundred Years War. And he followed leads that came regarding any seer who had been discussed in the gossip. However, none of it gave him enough reason to leave the Order until Monsignor Quahin abused his power in punishing another innocent boy.

Phineas had the unspoken respect of most of the brothers. They knew he would stand up for what was right whenever the monks overstepped. On this occasion, Quahin decided to make another example of a quiet boy who did not react immediately to his orders. He put on his bladed glove and took his abusive hand to the air. Phineas intervened by drawing his sword and slicing it through his wrist. He left the monastery with the boy who had no name. Phineas called him Tinker. He never looked back to see why the other monks did not attack him as he left. He only remembered the scent of a burning fireplace and noting that no fire was lit.

However, now, on this perfect day, the thought of a reunion with Kindron made Phineas smile. Despite his quick-witted demeanor, smiles were rare for Phineas. He felt his mouth contract into a half smile. The right side of his mouth pulled at the scars that crossed it. That feeling always brought him back to that moment in his childhood when the scar was created and stopped him from smiling.

Phineas shook his head to come back from his memories. This time, the lead seemed promising. "I will find you Kindron," he swore to the horizon with determination. "I will bring you home." Phineas laughed at the word. He had no home. He had been a nomad ever since leaving the Order of the Brothers of Naa.

A breeze blew, and Phineas heard the rustling in the grasses increase. He did not turn from his staring at the horizon and the sea. He whistled. A small red fox ran out of the high grass with a strong posture. Phineas looked at him and again attempted to grin.

"Not sure if you are smiling," he said to the fox as the animal circled and rubbed up against the form fitting pant legs of his Cerulean blue robes. He reached down and rubbed the playful animal's head. "We will find him." The fox ran off towards the beach.

A single bird flew in a circular pattern ahead of Phineas, in the direction to which the fox had run.

"That's progress," Phineas joked to himself. He followed the path of the fox and walked onto the beach with his silver and sapphire staff in his right hand and his sword gently clanking against his left hip.

Phineas shielded his eyes from the golden glow of the setting sun. The brightness and the reflection of the sunlight off the ocean were blinding. He took a pair of sunglasses that the boy, Tinker, had given him and placed them over his eyes.

Tinker was, without any argument, a genius. His mind worked in a way that he was able to figure out problems that were way beyond the understanding of others. Yet, he was still just a child. Tinker, as Phineas continued to call him, was constantly tinking about and creating new things. These sunglasses were the result of one of his discoveries.

With the sunglasses in place, Phineas saw the world to be more colorful with radiating auras coming off any living thing. He looked at the playful fox jumping in the sand and saw warm shades of orange vibrating around him. He looked to the sky and saw purples and blues emanating from the raven who continued to circle.

He lowered his vision and looked ahead to see the fox digging. The fox had exposed something shiny which reflected the rays of the setting sun. Phineas saw the raven come down and land on the glowing object. He rushed over and assisted the animals in digging out what was buried in the sand.

"A boat?" he asked. "A glass boat."

The raven cawed.

"Looks like we're heading across the sea." The fox looked at him with a quick turn of the head. Phineas laughed as he thought the fox's smile had disappeared. "This is a gift. From who? I don't know. But we're being guided," he said with a shrug of the shoulders. Phineas finished clearing the boat and got it into the water. He still needed to convince the fox that it was seaworthy.

"Come on," he said and encouraged the fox to jump into the boat. He was holding his sapphire and silver staff in the sand to keep the boat steady. The fox shook his head. "Now," Phineas demanded. The fox again shook his head. "We have to find Kindron," he said, pleading. The fox looked back and then ran and jumped into the boat. Phineas lifted his staff and allowed the boat to float out into the sea. He used it as an oar.

Chapter 2

What seemed like millions of stars illuminated the night sky as Phineas lay in the boat, looking up at their twinkling glow. His attention was drawn to an area that was void of stars, void of light. Yet, there seemed to be a pattern in the darkness. He paid it no attention but felt a tingle on the left side of his torso.

The fox was sleeping, nuzzled tightly at Phineas' neck. The raven twitched in all directions and watched the night. Phineas took the glasses and put them on. He saw lines of green light moving in the sky. He saw the waves of varied greens continue to move as if they were blowing overhead. He continued to watch until they lulled him to sleep.

The sun was rising and the fox awoke with a yawn. Phineas was seated and deep within his morning meditation. The fox elongated his red body and squinted at the rising sun. The raven was gone. The fox looked to the sky and over the edge of the boat. He felt the soft hand of Phineas stroking his fur.

"She's scouting ahead for us," he told his four-legged companion. "We need to be as best prepared as we can be for whatever we will encounter."

The fox turned his focus to the bottom of the clear boat and into the blue-green water underneath. He saw movement under the surface. Phineas realized his interest and turned his own attention to the bottom of the glass boat.

"Hmmm," he said as he watched the shimmering scales beneath the water. "Mermaids." He looked the fox in the eyes. "Sorry, buddy. You're probably hoping for fish." The fox followed the Mermaids' path past the edge of the boat. "Not gonna happen."

The raven returned with a strong "caw".

Phineas took to a high kneeling position and held his hand above his eyes to try and see land. Nothing.

The raven cawed again.

Phineas paused and then put the glasses on. He saw the lights in the sky but with less definition than at night. The colors had changed and, at the horizon, there appeared to be openings outlined by the wavy lines. He used his staff to steer the boat to the left and moved towards one of the openings. The raven landed on the bow and maintained her scanning. She was fearless. The fox appeared unsettled. His head kept turning from Phineas to the opening in the lights.

"We are here for Kindron," Phineas reminded the fox. They crossed the opening, and the waves of light seemed to close behind them.

Chapter 3

The opening brought them somewhere far from where they started. The changes were immediate. Morning had become evening. The color and temperature of the water went from light blue to emerald green, warm to cold. Phineas was trying to find clues as to whether they were in the same dimension. Hidden doorways allowed for movement throughout time and space. This portal could have brought them anywhere.

"So this is where they've been hiding the land," Phineas joked. The land in front of them seemed dark. It had an energy of secrecy. "Okay. Plan. Find Kindron and get him on the boat. Sail away and live happily ever after." The fox looked at him with his eyes squinted and attentive.

Phineas looked down at the fox who turned his attention forward. The raven took flight. "She'll bring us some information," Phineas told himself and the fox. He was unsure where and when they were at this point. He never enjoyed the experience of entering another dimension. Previous attempts to find Kindron had brought him into other dimensions and back. Phineas was already untrusting of anyone who they would encounter. His wits would have to be sharp.

As they got closer to the land, the sky was darker and the air was getting cold. A veil of icy precipitation was falling. Phineas surveyed the land and looked to the top of the mountains, but the clouds concealed their peaks. A thick fog quickly rolled in and surrounded the boat. Phineas could not see in front of himself.

He felt a hard stop as if an anchor had been dropped and caught with the floor of the sea. "Here we go," Phineas said to the fox. Even though he could not see it, he knew that the boat was at a distance from the shore.

Phineas smashed his staff hard into the surface in front of the boat. The surface held as the glass boat became covered in ice. The ice surrounding the boat seemed capable of bearing weight. He turned to the fox and nodded. The fox's eyes twinkled as he crouched into a low position, ready to stalk.

Phineas looked to the sky, but the thick fog obscured any visual landmarks or orientation. He dared not whistle for the raven for he did not know what lingered in the fog. The glasses, he thought and pulled them back to his eyes.

With the glasses on, Phineas began to see shapes in the distance. He saw the island and the mountain tops. Phineas looked up to the sky and was able to make out the shape of the raven circling overhead.

He waved. The raven cawed. Phineas took that as a good sign that it was safe to get out of the boat and to continue. He pulled his hood and buttoned his collar to mask his face up to his eyes. "We continue on foot."

The fox jumped from the boat without hesitation.

Chapter 4

Phineas and the fox walked across what he now knew to be a surface of ice. The falling snow limited traction but offered them a safe visual path. Phineas was guided by the distant shadows that he was able to make out with the use of the glasses. He watched as the fox stayed low and sniffed as if hunting prey. Phineas cracked a side smile to his left. He was confident that this time, they would find Kindron.

Beneath the icy surface, Phineas watched colorful lights move as if guiding them. The lights radiated from the tails of Mermaids, which began to move quicker in the direction of the beach. Phineas followed their lead and began to run. The fox too was running in time with the Mermaids and Phineas. Then the Mermaids stopped and formed a circle of light surrounding Phineas and the fox. He and the fox looked through the ice and saw the Mermaids grab hold of each other's shoulders. Steam rose from the ice, which melted enough to make room for them to rise above the surface. The Mermaids encircled

Phineas and the fox as they steadied the ice by propping themselves on their elbows and forearms, suspended on the edge of the ice.

"Yes," the first Mermaid said to him. "Who you seek is in this land."

"But no," said a second. "He is not who you remember him to be."

"They, the three, have taken him unto their path," added a third.

"A path for which there may not be a return," the fourth Mermaid continued.

"His mind is made up of lies," added the next. "You must regain his trust."

"But remember this, Phineas, the monk," spoke the sixth Mermaid. "Love him when he deserves it the least…"

"Because that is when he will need it the most," finished the seventh.

The Mermaids lowered themselves under the water and swam deep and far. Phineas watched as the lights of their tails faded.

One Mermaid stayed behind and stared quietly at Phineas. He walked over to her.

"Why do you linger?" he asked her.

She cocked her head and smiled but continued to stay quiet.

"I don't have time for Mermaid trickery," he yelled.

The glow off her tail illuminated Phineas from under the clear ice. She saw him raise an eyebrow.

"I was commanded," she admitted, breaking her silence. "By my queen."

"The Ruler of the Seas?"

"She rules all. Not just the seas," the Mermaid demanded. "She is part of everything."

"Is she going to help me?"

"She got you this far, but now, you are heading to a desert," the Mermaid said.

Phineas said nothing. The Mermaid took his silence as rudeness.

"The desert is not her domain," the Mermaid scolded him as the light in her tail changed to red. "Fire, Earth, and Air have greater authority. Why else would The Dark Sisters have brought your friend there?"

Phineas thought about it.

"Water, The Ruler of the Seas, has gotten you this far. The rest is up to you."

With that, the Mermaid dove under the water and Phineas watched as the light of her tail traveled quickly away from where he stood on the ice until it was no longer visible.

"Water," he said as he retraced the Mermaid's path from the ice to the sea beyond it.

"Well, fox," he said after a sigh. "Seems we have some work to do."

The ice floated up to the solid surface that was connected to the shore. Phineas stepped off in time with his confident gait and the fox jumping and running ahead. Phineas looked up to see the raven circling in the direction they walked. He was still able to make out her form with the glasses on, but she was invisible in the fog and clouds in the night sky.

Chapter 5

Phineas and the fox walked slower along the ice path. Phineas looked up and traced the raven's movements in the sky. The words of the Mermaids' song added to his worry about what he would encounter when he found Kindron, and he was sure that he would find him. The Mermaids had confirmed it. They were still on ice, but the ice had become grainy, as if the wind had blown sand upon it. "We have to stay on our path. Find Kindron and get him away from here."

Phineas looked up to the raven and then down to the beach that was growing ever closer. He watched as the raven dropped low and then rose high and fast. A line of fire shot up from the beach after the bird. The raven swerved and continued to fly in an evasive pattern.

"Down," Phineas whispered with force to the fox. The fox stopped. He looked back at Phineas but then ran towards where the fire was emanating. "No," Phineas attempted but knew that it would not make a difference. He heard the loud cracks coming from the ice and felt the surface under him start to shake. The ice began to explode and break. Phineas followed the fox and ran towards the beach. The surface became unstable and tilted with each footstep.

"Shit!"

What seemed like bombs in the ice exploded upwards with every point of contact that Phineas made as he ran towards the sand. He coordinated his stepping as he felt the poetry in the timing of the explosions and stepped in time with the music that was forming in his mind.

Unnatural, he thought to himself. The timing of the explosions was too perfect, not organic. But there was no time to stop and analyze the situation. Phineas simply had to avoid getting blown up in the explosions under the ice. He made it to the beach. The grainy sand gave him traction as he continued to run. Black magic, he reassessed and told himself.

The fox ran towards the source of the fiery blast that continued shooting up at the raven. The raven was continuing to fly erratically. Phineas ran towards where the blasts emanated. The raven and the fox were working together as a distraction. The raven dropped into a dive. The fox zigzagged. Phineas ran hard and pulled the tip from his staff to expose a sharp silver blade. He whistled for the others as he launched it upwards, aiming at the spot where the last blast of fire originated. The fox stopped and ran back towards him. The raven glided and circled back and up higher into the sky. The staff hit, causing a loud explosion. Phineas ducked with the fox close and the raven landed on his shoulder.

They watched as three figures were engulfed in flames from the explosion and ran towards the ice at the edge of the beach. "Followers of The Dark Sisters," Phineas said with a twitch of his nose. "They have Kindron."

Phineas paused. He and the others waited to see if there were any others who they would have to battle. Nothing. No one and nothing came. Phineas felt it in his gut that they were alone. He looked to the raven, and the bird took to the sky for surveillance. He looked to the fox who was quick to turn and ran to scout out the surrounding area from the ground. Phineas himself closed his eyes and focused his vision. He felt the energies around him. The fox. The raven. The three attackers were nothing more than burnt corpses. They no longer gave off energies. They were alone.

He turned to see the last remains of the body that had been consumed by the blasts. "Fire." Phineas walked to the closest body. The fox was sniffing and examining it. He took an abrupt offense to the scent that emanated from the burnt corpse.

Phineas walked over and used his hand to waft more of the aroma to his nose. He smelled the air and snarled his face in disgust.

He looked at the fox and nodded his head in agreement regarding the foul stench. "Evil," he said.

The fox shook his head and sneezed as if trying to get the smell out of his nose.

Phineas moved cautiously towards the other two bodies but held his breath. He had already gotten all the information he needed about their attackers. "They answer to…" he said to the fox. Phineas looked around. "The Dark Sisters," he yelled.

Chapter 6

The ice along the shoreline broke open as tentacles came through. The demon came quickly upon the beach as his mucous covered limbs climbed over the black sand. He grew in size and loomed over where Phineas stood as if to attack.

Phineas sighed.

"How dare you disrespect me!" exclaimed the demon, "I am Leviathan, Ruler of the Fifth Circle of Hell. The highest of demons."

"If that were true, you would not feel the need to explain it," Phineas remarked bluntly.

Leviathan pounded his tentacles. He hated how Phineas had the ability to get under his "skin". His gelatinous form engorged and exploded. Phineas was quick to cover himself under his robes. Leviathan's semi-solid pieces pulled themselves together to recreate the demon only to have him scream and again fall into pieces, but this time more liquid.

"This is exhausting," Phineas said to the fox. "We have to be on our way. The journey will take some time."

"More than you think," Leviathan said to him as he pulled himself into a more human-like form and stood behind Phineas. "But I can help."

"No, I don't trust you." Phineas told him and started to walk away.

"But you have not even heard what I have to offer," Leviathan argued.

"I'm good with that," Phineas replied. "Come on, fox."

The fox was sitting at a distance watching the interaction. He lifted his head and nodded at the demon. He quickly turned and was at Phineas' side and walked in stride.

Leviathan cracked a smile. Phineas continued walking and Leviathan became quickly angered at Phineas' rejection. "No!" Leviathan screamed. His beastly form engorged and again exploded. The explosion caught Phineas by surprise. He quickly dropped to a knee and shielded himself from the gelatinous ooze that spread through the air. "Gross," he said as the slimy residue dripped off his head.

Some of the residue got in his eyes. "Damn! That burns," he yelled and looked around for the demon ruler. Everything was hazy with the ooze in his eyes. Phineas started to blink his eyes and squint.

"Fucking demon," he added and shook his head. Is he working with them? The Dark Sisters? Phineas rubbed his eyes as he thought about who he was going to have to face to be able to rescue Kindron.

The raven returned to Phineas' shoulder.

"Where have you been?" Phineas asked her. Her head moved in a quick erratic twitch. She took off again, this time towards the mountains. "Come on, fox. We gotta go." Phineas and the fox followed her. Phineas realized that as he and the fox were dealing with Leviathan, the raven was scouting ahead. "We have enough to figure without his disruptions and tantrums."

His eyes continued to burn. He rubbed and then opened them wide. He realized that things were becoming visible. Phineas was able to see in the darkness. It was not the same as in daylight, but he was able to make out shapes, auras, and movement. It was similar to when he had the glasses on. He could see the raven flying high and was able to see the blue and purple colors that surrounded her as well as her path.

"A cave?" he questioned as they approached the opening in the rock. "And Leviathan," he added with a shake of the head. "I really don't feel like going through Hell." He looked at the fox who was looking back at him. "I mean that literally."

The fox took off and stopped at the entrance of the cave. He sniffed around and then entered. That's a good sign, Phineas thought.

Maybe it's not a portal to Hell. He squinted his eyes and made out the entrance to the dark cave and depth within it. "Leviathan. You watery, gelatinous piece of shit. Not sure if it was intended, but thanks for the gift." He entered the cave. "Raven!" he yelled and the bird too was quick to join them.

Chapter 7

Phineas had awoken from a dream with a quick sharp gasp. He saw Kindron tied and bound by black chains. The sky was black. The ground was black. A slight red light lined the distant horizon. Then, he heard Kindron scream. That was when he awoke.

Phineas knew that he was running out of time. The distant light in the horizon of the dream was fading. "Time to go, fox," he said to the sleeping animal who moved and gave himself a good stretch and a yawn. Phineas was momentarily lost in the orange and red aura that radiated off the fox. The raven flew ahead and scouted that it was safe. Phineas walked with the fox through the cave's tunnels.

The fox was by nature able to see through the darkness. Phineas moved to put the glasses on but realized that he did not need them. "Fucking Leviathan," he said with frustration and looked at the slight residue of the demon ruler on his robe. He chose not to question why he was gifted his vision by Leviathan. Yet, he was grateful for it. He had agreed to nothing. He owed the demon nothing.

As they continued, Phineas noticed something. He and the fox were turning their heads in the same direction at the same time. They were seeing the same thing.

"Hey!" he yelled to the fox. "These are your eyes. Aren't they?" He saw what appeared like a smile come across the fox's face and a nod in the darkness. "You agreed to this?"

The fox ignored the question.

Phineas began to purposely turn his head and look in directions that the fox did not. He was still able to see clearly through the darkness. The vision was his and was now independent of the fox.

Chapter 8

They reached an opening at the other end of the cave that had tunneled through the mountain.

Easier than I thought.

The raven had taken to the sky and scouted for trouble. She came back with a nervous energy. She flew around Phineas' head and cawed sharper, louder, and repeatedly. This behavior wasn't normal for the raven. Did she find Kindron? The bird was flying erratically. No. Not Kindron. It must be something grave, Phineas deduced. But not here or else she would've warned us from the sky. "The Queen?" he voiced softly as the raven increased the tempo of her caws. "Go to her. We'll take it from here." he commanded. The raven wasted no time in flying out of the cave on her path to the Queen of Witches.

The fox watched with angst as the raven flew hard in the other direction.

"She'll be fine," Phineas assured him.

The fox's low head showed that he did not lessen his worry.

"We need to stay focused on what lay before us," Phineas reminded him. "We have to find him, fox." He looked out into the open landscape. He saw nothing.

Just like in his dream, the landscape was black; the sand, the rocks and the sky. Phineas took in a deep breath and grounded himself. He felt no life here. They continued to walk along the open flat landscape.

The fox caught the scent of something. He turned to look at Phineas and ran on. Phineas ran to catch up. The ground at his feet was black and had a shiny and slimy quality to it. The fox was standing with a strong posture. He was looking straight ahead. Phineas looked in the same direction at the vast emptiness that lay before them. He noticed a single tree; there was no growth from it. He focused his vision to see what was next to the tree. His heart pounded in his chest. They had found him. Finally, they found Kindron.

Chapter 9

Just like the vision in Phineas' dream, Kindron was chained to a dead tree. It was slicked with oil. He was on his knees and whimpering. His shabby red robes were the only color visible through the blackness.

Phineas looked towards the horizon. He realized that, different from his dream, there was no light. Phineas felt his heart break. He felt that they were too late.

No! he demanded in his head. "Kindron!" he yelled out. "Kindron!" he yelled again but saw no reaction from his friend.

The fox looked at him with concern. He looked around with worry that Phineas' yelling had announced them to whatever evil lurked in this place.

Phineas began walking towards Kindron. He was stumbling a bit. As he moved closer to Kindron, he stumbled more. He thought it was the oil that was coming out of the tree and onto the ground but he also began to feel drunk. He initially attempted to pull himself together, but it took too much effort, unnecessary effort. He just allowed the sensation of being out of control build as he made his way to his friend.

"Kindron," he slurred as he reached out for his bound friend. "I found…" he attempted to speak and passed out.

Chapter 10

Phineas awoke to the sound of metal clanking. He found himself on his knees with his arms suspended above his head. He raised his face to look up and saw that he was bound to the dead tree. He attempted to get up, but he was unable to move. Phineas looked around in confusion.

"Kindron!" he screamed. "Kindron!"

"I am here," Kindron said with a sense of calm as he came around from the other side of the tree.

"Kindron," Phineas began with a gaspy breath and eyes teared with the thought that his twenty-year search finally led him to his friend. "Oh, Kindron…I found you."

"Yes. Yes, you did," Kindron answered with the same cold disposition as before. He walked slowly, dragging his feet in the oil slicked sand.

"I have been searching for you for over two decades. I have spent my life trying to find you and be a family again." Phineas realized that Kindron's mind had been polluted. Kindron's expression was so full of hate. The words of the Mermaids' song rang in Phineas' head.

His mind is made up of lies. You must regain his trust.

Phineas attempted to rationalize with him. "Kindron! We have to get out of here. Away from this place." Phineas looked around for the fox. He could not see him.

"What do you know about this place?" Kindron questioned. "I've been here longer than anywhere else. This has become my home," he announced and raised his arms as he spun in a circle. His smile was manic.

"Kindron!" Again, Phineas tried to get his friend to understand him. "This is not your home. This is your prison. You've been a prisoner here. The Dark Sisters-"

"The Dark Sisters?" Kindron was quick to yell back. "The Dark Sisters have unlocked my powers... I now know how to use them... I know how to control them!"

"We tried to do that for you when we were children-"

"Tried?" Kindron screamed as if he was crazy. "Tried," he said with a softened tone. "Yes. You tried." Kindron squatted and rubbed the back of his gloved hand across Phineas' facial scar. "And where did that get us?" He slapped Phineas in the same way the Monsignor

Quahin had done when Phineas was first scarred. The force of the slap drew blood which traveled down his face and pooled on his lips. "I was banished, tossed away! The Dark Sisters took me in. Nourished me. Empowered me!" Kindron screamed and went into an insane laughter.

Phineas tasted his own blood. He looked down and saw how the drops of blood scorched the sands. He saw the sands crystalize as his blood made contact. It all makes sense, he realized. The Desert of Xedu… Phineas remembered what he learned about this land in the library at the monastery, the sands were evil. He knew that he had come here with pure intentions. His intentions must have caused the reaction.

That will take too long, he joked to himself as he thought of bleeding himself to safety. And I might get a bit too lightheaded. Phineas mocked himself to find balance. He needed to ground himself. He had not expected Kindron to be this far gone. He had expected him to be a prisoner, a victim to the Dark Sisters, but the Kindron that he found had evolved into an evil presence.

"They told me that you would come," Kindron said, looking off into the distance. "They told me that you would challenge me and try to lead me from my purpose."

Phineas stayed quiet. He again replayed the words of the Mermaids' song.

Love him when he deserves it the least…Because that is when he will need it the most.

"You will not win, Phineas. You are my final test. Once I am through with you, The Dark Sisters will unleash me to take revenge on all those who ever harmed me. They have told me that my full power will be available to me after I dispose of the one thing that stands in my way of greatness…You."

"No, Kindron," Phineas begged as Kindron came closer to him with his bare hands reaching for the Phineas' bound arms.

"Don't worry! I will be sure to take you to the very end. To your very end."

Kindron felt a pull backwards into Phineas' life. He attempted to pull his vision forward but was met with resistance. As he was seeing Phineas' past, he felt his kindness and strength. He felt his protective energy and how Phineas had channeled his love into his quest to find Kindron. Kindron made another attempt to pull his vision forward. He felt Phineas' fear, his only fear. He was able to see that Phineas feared that he would not be able to save Kindron. He had never experienced this before. Instead of the expected clash of conflicting emotions, Kindron experienced a singular feeling. He was channeling love.

Kindron experienced peace. His gift went backwards when he touched Phineas. He did not see his future as was typical with the ability of a seer. He saw his past. He saw himself. He realized that he had a true presence and purpose in Phineas' life. Phineas had come to the Desert of Xedu to save him. Phineas had been searching for him and had worked tirelessly to make sure that he found him. Kindron saw that Phineas did all of this out of love. Kindron saw that Phineas' love for him was unconditional and that he would sacrifice himself to save Kindron. Phineas would never stop. Kindron was his family.

Kindron fell back in the sands. He was breathing heavily. Phineas was gasping for air. Kindron had taken him to the edge. He let go, but he could do no more. He could not touch him.

Phineas began to breathe softer. He stopped and looked off into the distance. A sliver of crimson light sat at the edge of the horizon. Phineas gasped.

What Kindron experienced when he touched Phineas broke him of his feeling of being alone. It broke him of the lies that The Dark Sisters had told him and educated him on. Kindron now understood that Phineas was his family. He was able to see that Phineas had sacrificed everything to find him and to save him. Kindron began to cry.

"Phineas," he spoke through his tears. "Phineas," he said with added strength. "Phineas, forgive me. I am so sorry," he pleaded. Kindron was facedown. "Phineas," he continued through his tears.

"You have no idea how lonely and painful and destructive this time has been."

"Kindron," Phineas whispered with all his strength.

"Oh, Phineas," Kindron answered with a stronger tone. "Phineas! I need to get you out of here." Kindron looked to the distance, to the horizon. "The time is now," he told him. "We must be quick. That sliver of light is our only way. It is a rare occurrence."

"Kindron," Phineas said with kindness. "Tonight is the third night of the Blood Moon." Phineas told him. "The Blood Moon is happening now. A time of love."

Kindron looked his old friend in the eyes and smiled. Phineas did the same.

"The Dark Sisters expected you to show up sooner or later." Kindron told him. "Apparently, destroying the Queen of Witches was a higher priority than destroying you."

Phineas held back from telling Kindron about the raven. He held back from telling him about the bird going to warn the Queen of Witches about the Dark Sisters. He could not yet trust Kindron. He thought about the fox. He worried for his safety. Did Kindron hurt him? Kill him? Phineas saw the fox tracks in the sand, but said nothing about that either. Where the fox had gone, he did not know. However, he knew that he was safe.

Kindron appeared to be lost in his thoughts. "Kindron," Phineas began. "We need to go. The Blood Moon will protect us. The Dark Sisters cannot battle the Queen of Witches and us at the same time, not during the Blood Moon."

"Kindron," Phineas continued with his kind tone. "We need to get out of here now, before they come back. Kindron you can be free to live the life of your choice. You need not follow anyone, not even me. You are loved and you are not alone."

They sat in silence on the slick sands.

"Come on, Phineas," Kindron sighed and said calmly. "We have to get out of here." He put his gloves on. Phineas continued to look at Kindron with worry as Kindron assisted him to his feet. Their skin did not touch. "They will be back soon," he continued. "The Dark Sisters. They have dethroned the Queen of Witches."

Phineas' concern grew.

"Everything will begin to change," Kindron told him. "Our futures will need vision."

Chapter 11

The day was perfect…A cloudless sky. Cool air with a warm sun. The air along the coast was salty and damp. Phineas walked back towards the glass boat as Kindron awoke.

"That might have been the first restful night I have had since I was a boy," Kindron confessed.

"For both of us," Phineas replied. Phineas smelled for any unexpected aromas. The scent of a fireplace burning seemed distant enough to be his imagination. Yet, somehow, he knew that it was real. Word had made its way that Ileana, the Queen of Witches, had fallen. Phineas felt his facial muscles tighten and contract with concern as they pulled at the scars that crossed his face and into his lips. He looked and saw Kindron sitting in peace with the glasses that he wore to see the waves of light in the darkness.

"They will conceal my eyes," Kindron said about the glasses. "You know, just in case I accidentally bump into someone. I don't want to freak people out when my eyes turn red."

Phineas smiled at Kindron's attempt at humor. He had found him. He had saved him. But this was only the beginning.

"Kindron!" he called to him. He paused, knowing that his next statement would not be taken well and that Kindron would need some time to understand Phineas' demand. "We need to go back to the Monastery of the Brothers of the Order of Naa."

QUEEN OF WITCHES

As the beast will appear

Chapter 1

Tension amongst the kingdoms rose as what would be known as the Hundred Years War loomed. Concerns regarding the rising power of certain kingdoms over others caused a sense of political paranoia and began to limit trade agreements. These limits started to have stifling effects on local, national, and global economies. That paranoia was directed at the Kingdom of Witches and was based on the notion that Witches, by nature, had an upper hand because of their magic, and therefore, power. Negotiations amongst the Council of Kingdoms had repeatedly come to a stalemate.

Queen Ileana, the Queen of Witches, had more than the Council of Kingdoms to worry about. Within the Kingdom of Witches, tensions were felt even more deeply as her Senate was not in full agreement with her campaign for political policies that would cater to ease the fears of those other kingdoms. She proposed limiting the use of magic to a level that would not grant witches or their businesses unfair advantages.

"The Dark Sisters", as they were referred to in the headlines, were a splintered faction of Witches who held seats in the Senate of Witches. They held to the doctrine that because of their powers, Witches should exist above all others.

The Dark Sisters used the impending Hundred Years War to secretly align with a few kingdoms ruled by royals who had been persuaded that with the use of magic their own interests would be secured. Through a magical blood oath called a "Bonding Ceremony", a ruler would be assured of their personal protection and continued power.

The Dark Sisters had conspired against Queen Ileana and gathered enough of a following to start a civil war just before she signed an agreement to prevent the Hundred Years War. Their timing was purposeful to undermine any progress she had made. However, they were disorganized and their attacks were scattered and uncoordinated.

This split within the Kingdom of Witches divided Queen Ileana's attention and resources. The uprising of dark magic fostered the catalyst that brought added distrust from the other kingdoms and led to their attacks on the Kingdom of Witches. The Hundred Years War had begun. The Kingdom of Witches was now under attack from most of the other kingdoms as well as from within.

As the wars continued, Queen Ileana was successful in gaining more support from her people who now saw the effects of unrestricted magic. The Dark Sisters' quest for power led to mixtures and misuses of spells that were offensive to the natural order of a Witch's essence. The effects of those spells were vile and caused physical deformities to the bodies of those who, whether reluctantly or willingly, became a part of The Dark Sisters' forces.

Queen Ileana's efforts procured the support of the other rulers and was able to suppress The Dark Sisters. Their followers who had survived had been rehabilitated and by the grace of the queen, welcomed back into the community of Witches. However, they each bore the mark, a physical deformity, of having been a follower of The Dark Sisters.

At the conclusion of the Hundred Years War, Queen Ileana signed the declaration to limit the power of magic. To ensure compliance with the ruling, the Witches were forced to burn their ancient texts; that the practice of magic would fall under control of a chosen council outside of the Kingdom of Witches and be limited to what was considered "…of no threat to nonWitches". Witches understood the need for control of the dangerous magic that had been conjured by The Dark Sisters and their forces.

The Hundred Years War ended over a century ago. In the time that followed, fewer and fewer Witches remembered how to practice advanced magic due to the lack of texts and hence, the lack of spells. Witches were only able to perform simple spells that could pass as parlor tricks. It was entertaining and turned the City of Witches into a vacation destination.

Ileana continued her rule over the Kingdom of Witches. She maintained a harmonious relationship with bordering kingdoms and with rulers who had come into power over time. She outlived many and welcomed their successors. The lifespan of a Witch, although not that of an Immortal, was considerably longer than a non-Witch. Some Witches were known to live thousands of years and not show the signs of aging that would be noted by a non-Witch. Her rule remained peaceful and magic remained controlled.

However, it was rumored that Ileana, the Queen of Witches, did secretly create an enchanted text that contained all spells. The rumors were never confirmed. She brushed off the comments as political heresy.

Chapter 2

Thaddeus stepped out of the magical coach that drove unattended. His long black coat rippled as it blew in the strengthening breeze. He allowed his hair to cover and uncover his eyes as it did the same. "Oh, yes," he said to the air. "Something is coming." Thaddeus walked up to the gates of the palace grounds as if he belonged there. The guards did not open them upon his arrival although his ego expected that they would. His face contoured with disappointment.

"Tell your queen that Thaddeus, the vampire, is here to see her," he commanded.

The group of inexperienced soldiers stood in place, each awaiting one of the others to do as he had instructed. Their collective refusal went unappreciated by the proud Immortal.

"Now!" he demanded with a frightening volume and quick disfigurement of his jaw.

The guards were quick to come together in opposition to the vampire.

He sighed with frustration. "Exhausting," he said. "Where's Quentin?" he asked. They responded with ruffled brows. "The prince," he enlightened them. "Where is Prince Quentin, the queen's husband?"

Prince Quentin appeared atop the wall surrounding the palace grounds and was laughing at the exchange happening below him. "This is unexpected," he yelled to the vampire as the guards held their place.

"But necessary," Thaddeus told him.

"She is not going to be happy to see you," he added.

"She never is," Thaddeus confirmed.

"Let him in," Prince Quentin told the guards.

Thaddeus walked through the gates and Quentin met him on the road leading to the palace. The prince gave him a full tight embrace. "It's the first night of the Blood Moon, Thaddeus. Nothing can be so urgent. Even the worst of us takes the time of the Blood Moon to stop and reflect if not celebrate."

The Blood Moon was a celebration of love that occurred when the cracked moon took on a red color and appeared like a heart in the sky. Its presence did not occur yearly but when it did occur, it would last for three nights.

Thaddeus stared at Quentin with worry, attempting to hide his joy at seeing his friend.

"It is good to see you, my friend," the prince told him and hugged him again.

"Hold that thought," Thaddeus told him. "I need to speak to her."

"Come on," Quentin said and guided him towards the glass palace.

Chapter 3

The queen sat regally on her golden throne as peacocks strolled without a care around the grand room which was illuminated by sunlight through the glass ceiling. However, Queen Ileana was unaware as she was lost in another vision. She saw the intensity of a fiery explosion and the glass ceiling of the palace shatter. Screaming and death. A raven. Water. She saw an emerald blade and flashes of light. And then, darkness. Nothing.

"My death," she said and dropped her confident posture as she exhaled with quivering breaths.

Prince Quentin led Thaddeus to the doors of the Art Nouveau-styled receiving chamber but waited outside. The queen was quick to regain her royal pose while still seated on her throne.

The vampire walked towards her and watched as the white peacock drew attention from the others.

"I don't want you here," Queen Ileana told him.

"I come in peace," he told her, "and with purpose. Your kingdom is in danger."

She did not react.

"And I need your help," he admitted to a raise of her eyebrow and a cocking of her head. The peacocks seemed to mimic her expression.

Thaddeus had selfish motives for looking to help Ileana. He was working off a prophecy that told of the end of time and what would be required to prevent that from happening.

"Ileana," he began. "They are back, and they come with such vengeance that if they win, they will join the fight to destroy all of time and space."

She again cocked her head as if not knowing to whom he was referring.

"The Dark Sisters. They have returned," he informed her.

Queen Ileana rolled her eyes. "Go away, vampire. And take your foolishness with you. The Dark Sisters have not been heard from since the end of the Hundred Years War. Now, do as they did and disappear."

"Ileana," Thaddeus pleaded. "I've seen it!" he urged.

"Where? I've heard nothing."

"A vision," he answered.

The queen laughed. "Oh, please," she said. "You're having visions? You're a vampire, not a seer, not a Witch."

"You must hear me out on this."

"I would call my guards, but why waste the time. If you do not leave immediately, I will dispose of you myself."

Thaddeus knew that the queen would hear no more of what he offered. He bowed with disappointment and exited the throne room, the palace, and the grounds. He said nothing more as the wind blew stronger.

As Thaddeus rode back to the City of Witches, he felt a rush force into his chest. The vampire fell off his seat with such force that he broke through the floorboards of the coach. The impact was painful as he made contact with the hard stones that paved the road. He laid there on the white surface, his face now bloodied.

Where did that come from?

The coach went on without him. He felt it again, the force in his chest.

"Your interference will be in vain," he heard the voices say in unison. Thaddeus looked around for the source. No one was there. The pain lessened. Thaddeus pulled himself up as his wounds healed and took deep breaths.

"Fucking Witches."

Chapter 4

Two days had passed since the vampire's visit. The queen was in her dressing chambers. She was momentarily alone as her dressers went to fetch the jewels that she would wear to the Blood Moon Ball. The vision came crisp and sharp. It was raw and full of fear. The screams were loud. The light turned to darkness and the darkness then turned to fire. Confusion. Destruction.

The Queen of Witches gasped hard as her consciousness returned to the present.

"Your majesty?" a dresser asked with concern as they had come back with the blue gemstones reflecting the light.

"Where did you find this?" Queen Ileana asked about the bracelet that was presented to her.

"A gift," her dresser remarked, "from Baltaan."

The queen stared in amazement at the robin's egg color of the bracelet. "It's beautiful. Yes.

The dresser placed it on the table as it would be added as a final touch.

"Call Aqielle and tell her to get me the stone," Queen Ileana demanded. "The reflective one." Her attendant ran to do what was instructed. My children must be safe.

"Ileana?" Prince Quentin came in with confusion at the rushed pace of the queen's dresser. "What is happening?"

"I am sending word to Queen Sharon of Mortua. It would be best for the children to not be in the palace during this…event."

"My queen, it is the last night of the Blood Moon. We need to celebrate our love, all love. And that includes our children," Quentin told her in his attempt to rationalize.

Ileana, the Queen of Witches, looked at her husband. She gently stroked his face with the back of her hand.

"Yes, Quentin," she began with a smile. "We must celebrate love." Ileana came close to him and sniffed at his neck. She exhaled with a sweetness on her breath. "Another reason to have the children out of the palace tonight," she said with a wink. "Our… love… is going to be epic on this final night of the Blood Moon."

Quentin smiled.

"Then, yes," he agreed. "Off to Mortua they go. It will be good for them to get some sea air, to visit with their godmother."

Queen Ileana kissed her husband and then backed away. "I must finish getting ready, my love. Please see to it that the children are ready to go. I want to see them as they leave."

"I will," he told her and bowed as he kissed her hand. With that, he took his leave and exited the queen's dressing chamber.

Ileana had just lied to her husband.

Aqielle, the queen's attendant, entered the room as the prince exited. She attempted to not appear rushed and bowed to him. She then ran over to the queen.

"The stone, my lady," she said and handed her a plum-colored silk that seemed weighted.

Queen Ileana rubbed the fabric over the slick surface of the stone.

"You remembered not to touch it," Queen Ileana said. "Good girl."

Aqielle bowed her head. Her father was a dignitary from Bacaa and had asked the queen to offer his daughter some form of apprenticeship. Aquille had grown in her time with Queen Ileana and had become one of her personal attendants. She, being not a Witch, had been educated to not touch the stone contained in the fabric for direct contact with it would turn her to dust.

"I have one last favor," the queen told her. She went on to explain that Aqielle would accompany the children to Mortua. They would be received by Queen Sharon and remain there until called for by herself or Prince Quentin.

"At which point, you will return to your father in Bacaa. Now, gather your things," she ordered. "I will pen a letter that you will present to the queen." She looked at the purple fabric that reflected the overhead light. "This," she said and then paused. "You will also present this to the queen in appreciation for her assistance and confidentiality regarding the children being there. No one else is to know that the children are there. Do you understand?"

Aqielle nodded.

"Do you understand?" the queen repeated with a stronger tone. "This is very important!"

"Yes. Yes, your majesty," she told her and began to cry. "I understand."

Queen Ileana realized that her attendant did understand. She understood too well. The Queen of Witches pulled her trusted girl in and squeezed tight. "There is no one else I can trust with this," she told her. "No one."

"I will protect them with my life," she responded.

The queen smiled and brushed the hair from her face. "You won't have to," she assured her. "Now go. I will see you soon," her second lie of the night.

The attendant bowed and rushed towards the door.

Chapter 5

The ball was in full grandeur. The invitations had read, For your love of love. And on this third night of the Blood Moon, the festivities continued. The evening's event hosted all of the highest-ranking members of the court and politicians from all over the Kingdom of Witches.

Ileana looked over towards Quentin. He was charming officials who appeared to be quite drunk. She cracked a smile. Quentin did make her laugh. He was a beautiful man and a trusted and loving partner.

She looked out into the crowd and found Baltaan in her striking green gown. Queen Ileana lifted her arm to show her the bracelet that she had gifted her and nodded a gracious Thank you. Baltaan returned her gesture with a smile and a just as gracious You're welcome.

"Queen Ileana," she heard and immediately became irritated at the familiar voice which spoke her name.

"Thaddeus," Ileana stated with an attempt to contain the distaste. The Queen of Witches extended her hand and the jewels on her wrist twinkled into his eyes. She was curious. "I thought that we had an understanding that you are not welcomed in the Kingdom of Witches."

However, at this moment, Thaddeus was quick to take Ileana's extended hand and kiss it. "May I?" Ileana raised an eyebrow in disapproval. The vampire escorted the queen onto the dancefloor.

"Why are you here?" she asked again.

"You know why I am here," he replied and spied the room from over her shoulder. "My understanding of things-"

"Is less than mine," she rushed and interrupted him. "My visions are clear."

"Then, the question should be, 'Why are you here?' The Dark Sisters are coming for you."

They stopped dancing.

"Ileana. They were able to enter my consciousness when I left the palace the other day."

The Queen of Witches gave the vampire an accidental but only slight glimpse into her concern. She contained it back before anyone but the vampire realized.

"Your family," he began. "You are placing yourself and your family at risk."

"Quentin can take care of himself. And the children are just fine. Sleeping," she said, lying for the third time this night.

Thaddeus looked over and saw Quentin engaged in conversation with several members of the military guard.

"He doesn't know?" he asked.

Ileana pulled her emotions back and held herself in a stoic posture. "Thank you for your concern, vampire. I am well aware of the forces that are looking to rise up against me."

Around them, the dancing and gaiety continued at the celebration. Ileana waved her hand to show the festivities in full colorful stride. "We can handle anything that comes our way," she told him. She was confident in her statement.

Four Witches came towards them, one from each direction. Thaddeus' attention spun from one to the other. He had seen each of them before, but was unaware of them as the Queen's Council. How did I miss that? he asked himself.

His swirling attention quickly focused on the first, Esmeralda, whose expression was seductive and longing. The second, Natasha, who had an androgynous appearance, showed strength. She was quick to look to the queen for approval and acknowledgement of her safety. He turned and found himself face to face with Ariel's caramel eyes which pulled him in and made him momentarily lose himself. And finally, he felt the chill from the gaze of the fourth Witch.

"Baltaan," he said with a flirtatious bow of his head to the bewitching woman.

"My council, as you must now know, is made up of the most powerful Witches in the kingdom." The four exquisite Witches encircled Ileana and the vampire.

"They are drawing you out. They mean to overthrow your rule and to destroy you at your core. They mean to torture you for as long as your magical energies can take and then to continue to do it in the afterlife."

"Well," she said as she took her hand from his. "Good luck to them." Ileana walked away with each of the four powerful beauties following her in a fanned-out formation. She showed no concern for his words nor his fears. Baltaan, the Witch walking closest to Ileana on her right, turned and looked at Thaddeus. She nodded.

Chapter 6

The dancing and the laughter continued at the Blood Moon Ball. The guests drank, ate, and danced without a care. Thaddeus kept his attention on the four beauties of the Queen's Council. His eyes were drawn to what looked like a tattoo on the right side of Baltaan's midsection as the cape of her gown blew and exposed her skin. He rustled his brow. The vampire looked around the ballroom. His attention was changing focus from the crowd to the shadows, from the elaborate decorations to the night sky outside.

"Sir?" an attendant asked as he presented a tray of champagne.

"Thank you," Thaddeus said through his frustration.

He reached for a glass and noted that the bubbles began to move fast and pop at the surface. The server held tight to the tray as it felt like it was shaking. Thaddeus looked at the man who looked back with a concerned expression.

"I'm not doing this," he told Thaddeus with confusion in his voice.

The glasses began to clink and to fall over as the shaking became stronger. Overhead, that same sound became louder and more intense as the chandeliers began to swing and hit each other. The guests who were not dancing were the first to feel the shaking under their feet. The crystal chandeliers started to hit with such force that pieces broke off and fell atop the guests. Everyone looked up as they heard loud banging and then saw the glass roof above them crack. It was only then that a sense of true fear set in and they all ran.

Thaddeus looked all around. He could not find Queen Ileana, nor could he find Quentin. Yet, he did find Baltaan. She was moving her hands in a spell casting pattern. He was blinded as the intense light and heat overtook the palace.

It came quickly. The smashing of the glass. The fierce heat that followed it. The falling star came crashing through the windows to the west. It came with such force that it felt like the world stopped turning. Chaos rang out. Thaddeus again looked back to where Baltaan stood. She was surrounded by a protective bubble that kept the heat from turning her to dust. Those around her were pulverized immediately as was everything in the path of the heat wave emanating from the impact.

Thaddeus had no choice. Even for an Immortal, the intensity of the heat was too much to bear. As he exited, he pulled two trapped Witches from the ruined palace, one of them being the server who had offered him the champagne. He realized that they were dead. Then, he too ran. He attempted to find a trace or a scent of where Ileana had gone. He searched for the members of her court. Nothing.

Baltaan, he said in his mind. After what he had seen during the attack, she was now his focus. He centered his vision. He had found her. Baltaan, the queen's greatest confidant and closest council was flying. Thaddeus took to the air. He could not catch her scent, but the lingering energies of her magic were scattered and left her exposed. He followed the trail of those energies which focused towards the night sky.

Thaddeus looked ahead as he flew without effort through the night. The lights of the City of Witches illuminated the point at the end of his path. Thaddeus was confused.

Why the city, Baltaan? Are you warning others? Why didn't you use that spell to protect the queen? That look you gave me, the markings on your side…A deformity, he deduced. You betrayed her.

Thaddeus felt the same pain that he had experienced in the coach. He fell from the sky and met the hard ground with full force. Thaddeus was quick to stand. His fangs protruded and he began running towards the City of Witches.

He took back to flight. However, he had lost her energy.
Baltaan, like Ileana, was gone.

Chapter 7

A flicker of light presented itself in the backroom of the empty shop. What began as a pin grew and became a fiery circle from which Ileana and Quentin stepped through.

"Ileana?" he rushed. "What just happened?"

"They are back," she told him with her stare directed straight ahead. She closed her eyes and took in a deep breath. She was focused on the space around them. It was empty. It was safe.

"The Dark Sisters," she confessed. "I used the party to draw them out. But they must have known. They must have been aware of my plan."

"And that is why you sent the children to Mortua," Quentin said with a sarcastic laugh. "You lied to me."

"I lied to everyone," she confessed. "I knew they had come back. I thought that I would be able to confront them, defeat them, but-"

"You must have been betrayed. You must have been. They had to have knowledge," he continued.

"What?" No."

"Ileana! They pulled a star from the Heavens," he yelled. "That takes planning and planning takes knowledge. You were betrayed."

They again sat quiet as Ileana's logical mind had to accept that he was right.

"So why did you bring us here? Why to the City of Witches when everything is probably in chaos and…" He stopped as he saw Ileana unravel into tears and moved to hug her. She accepted his touch and returned it as she released her frustration through her tears.

"We will fix this," he told her.

"We will," she agreed. "But first, we need to get what we came here for."

Chapter 8

Thaddeus entered the City of Witches. Walking with a quick pace, he looked around with an investigative stare. It did not seem as though news of the destruction had reached the city. He did not understand how the fallen star had not been seen. The palace, although miles away from the city, was visible and a fallen star would not have been missed.

How could that be? he thought. Unless...

Then he saw them. The Dark Sisters. Across the way, the three evil Witches stared him down. One by one, they turned and disappeared into the darkness behind them. As the first one stepped backwards into the darkness, he began to hear distant screams. A swirl of black smoke twisted around the second of The Dark Sisters and the screams became louder and closer. The third Dark Sister clapped her hands overhead and dissipated into the night.

Everyone on the streets was now in shock and looking towards the direction of the palace.

They shrouded the city. Thaddeus realized that his theory was correct.

The Dark Sisters had now removed that magical cloak and the news and messages had come rushing in. It was too late for anyone to do anything. The destruction had already taken place. Lives were lost and the palace was destroyed; the queen, her family, her council and court. They were instantly killed, massacred. The panic had begun. The highest-ranking officials in the Kingdom of Witches were all gone.

"But not you," Thaddeus said aloud. "Not you, Baltaan."

Ileana and Quentin walked through the city, their identities concealed. They watched as the fire of the fallen star continued to burn at the site of the destroyed palace.

"This is the work of The Dark Sisters," they heard whispered from a Witch on the street. "I always knew that the queen would fall."

"What?" begged the other Witch walking arm in arm with her.

"Once she gave into the other kingdoms and limited magic, she set us up for this. There will be no coming back. We will have to protect ourselves somehow, no one knows any real magic anymore."

"No one other than The Dark Sisters. We will have to keep a low profile to avoid being targets."

"The queen has destroyed us."

Quentin attempted to go and argue with them, but Ileana held him back. "They are right," she said. "Come on, we got what we needed."

She felt under her cape, the book was safe. The Book of Spells as she would refer to it (to no one other than herself) with its rose gold spine showed blank pages to anyone who opened it. Only a Witch would be able to bring forth the characters, symbols, and images onto the pages. However, a Witch would first have to figure out and master the spell to do so. Queen Ileana kept this a secret from everyone and kept it hidden in the City of Witches.

They turned a corner into a plaza and stumbled upon another conversation.

"I heard the entire palace was destroyed, there were no survivors," yelled a man in the crowd.

"Who will lead us now?"

"Will The Dark Sisters come for us next?"

The hysteria grew.

"We rallied behind Queen Ileana and now we can't even defend our families?"

They continued past the screaming crowd.

"All I thought of was our family, the children." Quentin said.

They looked around to see that they were not being followed. "The children are with Queen Sharon in Mortua. I told no one that they would be there."

"We need to go to them," Quentin was quick to start conjuring a portal.

"No!" she demanded. "Magic is a tracer." She held his hands and felt the energy of the spell that he was preparing dissipate. "We will need to travel without using magic."

Quentin nodded in agreement. "It will give us time to figure out our next move."

Chapter 9

It was five days later when Ileana and Quentin walked over one of the seven bridges that connected the city state of Mortua to the mainland. The sun was shining and the concerned whispers on the street mimicked what they had heard in the City of Witches. They made their way to the palace. Quentin was escorted to the children as Ileana was led into council with Queen Sharon.

"Now is the time to act, Ileana," Queen Sharon of Mortua told her. They sat across from each other in the reception room.

"Sharon," Ileana argued in a whisper even though they were the only ones present. "Do not let your pride destroy your kingdom like I let my pride destroy my own. We now know what they are capable of."

"They came for not only you but your entire political system." Sharon continued her argument. "The attack came when all the High Witches were gathered… at the palace. They were able to shroud the palace and the city. They pulled a star from the Heavens. That level of magic has not been seen in ages! That attack took too much energy. They must be in some form of recovery. Without you and the palace, war and chaos are not far. Now is your time to strike."

"Strike?" Ileana questioned. "With who? With what?"

"Mortua and Bacaa will both come to your aid. And Water, the Ruler of the Seas, has sent word with the Mermaids that she too will ally with us."

The city states of Mortua and Bacaa maintained a history of alliance and trust with Queen Ileana and the Kingdom of Witches. They were part of the larger and more powerful kingdoms. They believed that Queen Ileana had put into policy the enforcement of magic for the protection of the greater good. They always showed support for the Kingdom of Witches and fought beside her.

Queen Sharon continued. "The other Elements have not come forth, but I have not heard that they will join with The Dark Sisters. However, the King of Tebbs has already announced that he is looking to invade the Kingdom of Witches. He has dispensed ships which Water has kept from your kingdom. But she will not be able to do that for long as it will throw too much out of balance. We need to act now."

Ileana let out a frustrated sigh. "Everyone assumes that my family and I are dead. I cannot risk them being exposed. I don't even know where The Dark Sisters are nor how much stronger their dark magic is."

"We must find who betrayed you and make them talk."

The doors were forced open and smashed against the walls.

"Baltaan," Thaddeus said with the utmost confidence.

"Baltaan is alive?" Ileana asked Thaddeus, feeling relief and sadness at the same time.

"It was she who betrayed you. When the chaos began at the palace, I saw her encased in a protective bubble. She had forged it prior to the attack happening… She knew."

"Where is she now?" Queen Sharon asked him.

"I followed her to the City of Witches. The city had been cloaked. No one saw it coming until it was too late for anyone to give aid to the palace." He looked at Ileana. "There were no survivors," he informed her. "The Dark Sisters know that you were the last hope for peace among the kingdoms."

"You are not safe," Queen Sharon told Ileana. "And neither is that book."

Thaddeus' attention was drawn to her words. "So, that rumor is true."

"Not now, vampire," Queen Sharon ordered.

"Your family is part of the prophecy. They cannot be discovered to be alive," Thaddeus reminded her. "Ileana! Your family must separate."

Ileana pulled the book with the rose gold spine from her bag. The griffin-hide leather cover was of similar color to the spine and the pages were empty and sharp white. They made a crisp sound as Ileana flipped through the emptiness upon them.

Ileana held the book with her eyes closed. She stopped on a particular page.

"This book has as many pages as it would take to create the most difficult and detailed spell. Every spell is contained within it but only one can be called at a time. The particular spell begins on a page based on how many total pages are required to complete it."

"We should give you some privacy," Queen Sharon said.

"No," Ileana replied. "This will only take a minute." As she flipped the pages, she stopped with only a few pages left. She spoke the incantation and then closed the book. "A protective spell for the children." Thaddeus and Queen Sharon looked at one another. "Thaddeus," she began. "You will convince Quentin that the children must be separated and that he must distance himself from them. Sharon. You must rally your forces and those kingdoms who you can trust to prepare to fight. That includes Water. Have her convince the other Elements that they must fight with us."

They both nodded in agreement.

"And you?" Thaddeus asked.

"Me? I must learn this book and then hide it. I will have to teach what I learn to my people to be able to destroy The Dark Sisters with spells that haven't been produced in over a century… But first, I have to find Baltaan."

Chapter 10

Ileana entered the chambers that had been set up for her family. *He looks so peaceful,* she thought as she watched Quentin being attentive to their baby boys. The boys were asleep and holding tight to one another as usual for them. Their daughter was smiling as she crawled towards Ileana. Ileana picked her up and nuzzled her. *They are just babies.*

"What did you discuss with Queen Sharon?" Quentin asked.

Still dressed in the unflattering brown cape, Ileana walked over and handed their daughter to Quentin.

"Don't worry. It's all taken care of." She spoke as she kissed his forehead. "By the way, Thaddeus is here."

"Where are you going?" Quentin asked as he found his arms holding tight to the squirming girl. Ileana said nothing and walked out. He turned to put the baby girl into the crib with her brothers. He attempted to control his emotions. "Ileana?" he whispered with force.

Their daughter started to cry and drew his attention. He motioned back to Ileana but she was gone.

The door was closed and locked from the outside. Quentin went to the window and threw it open. He saw no one. He was cautiously relieved to note the lingering aroma of orange and vanilla in the night air and the sound of silence as the baby had stopped crying. The distraction was momentary. Where are you going? Quentin refocused but was apprehensive to yell out his wife's name.

Ileana did not tell him about the plan to separate the family. As she walked through the streets of Mortua, her simple brown cape exposed nothing of a queen's glamour. It served its purpose to conceal her identity as she moved past people and carts traveling in both directions on the road.

She heard a "caw" from a raven in the distance. Her heart relaxed. Yes, she thought. Allies. The raven's call was repeated but this time closer. "Hello, my friend," Ileana said to the air as her eyes turned purple and she was seeing the streets from above. She had taken on the raven's vision. She spotted the familiar woman walking towards her.

"Seems like the end of the line," she heard from the voice behind her. "My... queen," Baltaan added with venom in her words.

"The end of this path is definitely not the end of my line, Baltaan," she replied without turning around. Her eyes returned to her own perspective. "How did you find me?"

"That foolish vampire led me right to you," Baltaan told her. "Pathetic."

"You've made a very poor choice."

"I had no choice," Baltaan answered with whispered hate.

"Be careful, Baltaan. You're showing your anger." Ileana walked over to where Baltaan stood with a strong pose. "Anger will attract them." She came to stand directly in front of her. "And we are in Mortua. You have no allies here."

"I want them to come. I want them to find you."

"You think that they will destroy me and then just go away. That you will become the leader of the Witches? Your quest for power has led you down a very dark and hateful path."

Baltaan attempted to maintain her hard stare.

The caw of the raven is closer.

"When they destroyed our sister, Natasha… you wept. As did I. And what of Esmeralda and Ariel. Are the rumors of their deaths true? Did you assist in destroying them as well? You know what is coming."

"I have protected myself."

"Marrying that beast will not protect you."

"The Palace of Tebbs is a magical fortress."

"Not against them."

"Against them?" Baltaan laughed. She pulled open her top and exposed the deformity as a badge of honor. "No. They arranged it for me. They respect me and my power. Once this is done and you are destroyed, I will have my throne and my peace."

"Oh, Baltaan. Don't be delusional. They have manipulated you. You have nothing to protect you other than us working together to fight back, to destroy The Dark Sisters."

Baltaan turned to walk away. Ileana grabbed her at the wrist. Baltaan took offense and drew the emerald blade from its holder on her side. Ileana fought to hold back her reaction.

"Yes, Ileana. The Sword of Sansit."

The Sword of Sansit was the weapon of the Immortal warrior, Sansit. It was lost in battle and had not been seen for eons.

The raven landed on a statue behind Baltaan.

"How is it that you have come to have it?" Ileana questioned as she backed away.

"A wedding gift," Baltaan told her.

"Baltaan. You didn't."

"Yes. I already did," Baltaan told Ileana with an air of superiority. "Don't worry. The formal ceremony will be a full-on extravaganza, but unfortunately, you won't be able to attend. I pushed for the Bonding Ceremony and got what I wanted." She stared at the green blade.

"That is not for you to use, Baltaan."

"Why not? It was gifted to me by my husband, the King of Tebbs."

"It was not his to give."

"Nor yours to take," Baltaan replied as she continued to admire the light that reflected off the emerald sword with a smirk.

"But it is mine to protect. Ours actually. But if you are planning on using it, I'll have to take it from you."

"Good luck," Baltaan threatened and moved herself and the blade to mimic using it.

"Baltaan. Please don't."

"I'll be quick about it," she said, ignoring Ileana's request. "I'm doing you a favor. The Dark Sisters would have no pity on you."

"Nor I on them," Ileana said.

The raven was quick to flight and came at Baltaan from behind.

Ileana used the distraction and conjured a burst of purple light which she pushed forth from her hands.

Baltaan instinctually dove out of the way. Ileana was quick again to push forth another burst of magic which knocked down the trees along the road and created a wall between them. She hurried to the river's edge, spoke an incantation that produced an invisible raft from the water and pushed off. The raven flew past her to scout ahead.

Baltaan cast a green burst of light. It hit the trees, and they exploded. She walked cautiously towards the river. "Yes. Use your magic. Draw them." Ileana was gone.

Chapter 11

Ileana woke with a strong inhalation and was immediately en garde. She was quick to feel for the book. She focused on the spells that she had learned from the book prior to falling asleep. It took time before she felt the cold and the wetness. She was deep in the underbrush of the marsh surrounded by the razor-sharp poisonous thorns of the vines.

The raven announced herself and Ileana's mind snapped back to the present.

She smelled for aromas… no one was around. She sat on the raft, Ileana removed the book from under her cape and held her hand atop it. She closed her eyes and calmed her breathing. With a golden glow, the book's content began to flow freely until encasing her. The spells bonded with her aura and entered her consciousness.

Night had fallen as Ileana stood atop the invisible raft. Her hood and dark cape camouflaged her. The only resemblance to herself was the robin's egg colored stone bracelet that she felt moved back and forth on her wrist with each stroke of the invisible oar. The feeling of the bracelet allowed her a meditative sense of peace as she paddled the rivercraft forward. No water was disturbed. No sound was made. Bioluminescent fish swam opposite her with the flow of the river's current. Ileana steered away from the brightness of the fish.

The flow of the river was hypnotic as Ileana listened carefully. There was no sound other than the movement of the water. Ileana's focus went inward and her thoughts returned to her memories.

She stopped paddling. The raft moved backwards with the flow of the river's current. She closed her eyes and focused on the book, still under her cape. We are all connected through magic, she enchanted with her thoughts. With that the book released its golden energy. She began to further channel the knowledge within it. She exhaled through her mouth and allowed the exhalation to extend for as long as the breath was able. Her ability to access higher magic was getting stronger.

The sound of the water was deep and echoing. It rippled from the riverbanks towards her. The ripples grew closer to each other as they approached her. They became higher and more aggressive. Ileana felt the energy of magic. The raven swooped down and cawed three times before soaring again. The wind blew and her hood was pushed off her head, she was now fully exposed.

Was I again betrayed?

The water pushed frantically closer to where she stood.

"Aid me, Water," she requested.

The water rose and fell, she felt resistance in the water from itself. Yes, she thought as she knew that the Ruler of the Seas had come to help her.

The water gave in and launched aggressively from each side of the river growing into waves that turned to fire midair. She had no choice but to use magic. Ileana moved with quick and precise patterns. She was using the spellwork that she recalled from the book. The waves of fire came to connect above her, looking to devour the fallen queen. She pushed her arms up overhead and released the spell. The fire turned blue. Water rose in the same pattern and doused the fire. Only steam remained.

The sound of a step on the dry reeds grabbed hold of her full attention. Her eyes turned purple as she moved into her mind's eye and spied the scene from the eyes of a raven that circled high above. "Three," she said to herself. "Two on the left and one on the right."

The raven circled in the sky. Ileana moved in a swooping fashion that shook the invisible, hovering raft. She was still looking through the raven's eyes.

"Uhh…" she held back as the air was pushed from her lungs.

The bird dropped from the sky and landed at her feet. A hard dry reed was through its heart and blood spread from the corpse.

"No!"

Ileana looked up with concern and turned her head repeatedly to look at each side of the riverbank. There was movement. Running. The crunching of the dry reeds was harder and faster than before. It was growing closer, and she knew that she had been discovered.

The bird did not make a splash. She realized that the silence gave her away.

Ileana closed her eyes and spoke the incantation. What she had gathered from the Book of Spells was serving her well. The raft levitated higher above the river. Then, she summoned the invisibility spell and finally, a protective spell that would hide her presence from any anticipated Witchcraft that would expose her.

She saw the first of The Dark Sisters appear on the left bank of the river. The evil Witch yelled an incantation. She willed fire to engulf her head in flames to use as a weapon. She threw her arms forward blindly. The flames that had surrounded her head traveled down her arms and came out of her hands. As her magical fire aggressively pushed itself across the river, it did not meet with Ileana in the river, as the Witch expected. It hit the dry reeds on the right bank which immediately became an inferno.

The sister on the right bank was conjuring her own spell to expose Ileana when she was engulfed in those enchanted flames and screamed out in pain.

Ileana remained on her path, above The Dark Sisters. The other two Dark Sisters flew across to the right bank and came to the aid of their suffering sibling, although too late to have prevented the magical flames from doing their worst. The scourged Witch was alive, but her skin and hair had been burned off.

Ileana floated through the night sky, protected by her spell and the distraction of the burned Witch. Her spell bound her to the river's path, but she remained unseen. Her right hand was to her chest. She continued to feel the dry reed that had murdered the raven as if it had penetrated her own heart. She wept.

Ileana knelt down on the invisible raft and with her left hand, picked up the raven's limp body. She lifted it and held the lifeless animal to her heart. She closed her eyes and spoke the words of the spell. She felt the heat ignite from within. It traveled through her body and to her hands. The magical warmth surrounded the bird. The raven's body turned to light and then broke into sparks that floated away with slow weightless movement through the air.

She looked back and saw that the reeds on the riverbank continued to burn in the distance. She knew that she had gotten away but continued to worry about The Dark Sisters' powers and reach.

Her only peace came because Baltaan had mentioned nothing of her family. She was successful in protecting them when she cast the illusion spell over her triplets. Ileana reminded herself that she was not alone in this fight. Her allies had presented themselves and she knew that they were preparing for battle.

And what of the book? She needed to protect The Book of Spells and continue to gain its knowledge in order to reclaim control of her throne and bring balance back to the land.

She closed her eyes and reconnected with it.

Chapter 12

Ileana's journey continued through the system of rivers that made their way through the land. The raft continued to float above the water leaving it undisturbed.

She approached the towering cliffs of Mount Condamner. The raft had come to a remote dock hidden within a cave near the shoreline. Above was the city of Dremora. This, like many other caves, had paths that led up to the city. Ileana paused. She took in a deep breath and the aromas of anyone nearby.

"Cadet," she said.

"Word came quickly, your majesty," Cadet, the Leprechaun, told her from her respectful bow. "It is rumored that you were destroyed. I have been worried so for your safety."

She turned and led the Queen of Witches by her hand.

"This way," Cadet insisted and guided Ileana behind a waterfall in the cave.

They walked cautiously through a dark tunnel and entered a cavern illuminated in blue light by small glowing creatures scattering in all directions along the walls and ceiling of the cold grotto.

Ileana's face snarled as she took in the foul scent of the cave.

"An entrance to another realm," Cadet told her. "We've been waiting for you."

"I can only imagine." the queen replied. She looked at Cadet with disappointment. Cadet looked down with embarrassment.

"He was very convincing," Cadet confessed.

"Imagine no longer," Lucifer, the demon ruler of the Sixth Circle of Hell, announced.

Ileana shook her head at the demon.

"I understand that you need to hide something," Lucifer said to her.

"Not just something," she told him. "But before I continue, know that it is prophesied that if this goes wrong, it will go wrong for all of us. Everything. Everyone. Every moment will be destroyed. Nothing will have ever existed, and you will have no one to bow to you or praise you or admire your beauty." She ended with a gentle rub on his cheek and a squeeze of his muscular arm. The strong stroke of his demonic ego was necessary. "Even you will never have existed."

Cadet was silent in admiration of the Witch's self-control in the presence of the demon that she was unable to resist.

Ileana pulled a book from under her cape.

Lucifer was quick to become excited. "Is that…"

"The fabled Book of Spells," she said, finishing his thought. "It is the last high text and indeed holds every spell from every ancient book that was found in the Library of Witches. Every… single… spell can be found within its pages." Ileana opened it and showed him the blank pages. "But even you cannot read it. Only a Witch. And if it falls into the hands of the wrong Witch-"

"Or Witches," he added.

Ileana paused at his awareness of The Dark Sisters. "It will mean the end for us all. Why would I trust you?" she asked.

"The Dark Sisters have launched their attack with the aid of the King of Tebbs. Once they conquer the Kingdom of Witches, their plan is to take everything else between the two kingdoms." Lucifer told her. "That bit of information should prove my allegiance to your cause."

Ileana said nothing.

Lucifer sighed, annoyed that he needed to continue to prove himself. "The blade that Baltaan possesses is a weapon with the power to destroy them, you know. Now, do you trust me?"

Ileana ruffled her brow.

Lucifer walked over to her. "Who gave you this?" he asked of her robin's egg colored bracelet. "It's a tracer." The demon took the bracelet and destroyed it. Ileana could not hide her realization.

"Now you should trust that I can keep it for you," he assured her.

"To hide it," she reminded him.

"I can do that," he told her.

"Temporarily," she added and handed it to him.

Lucifer looked at the book greedily.

Ileana had no choice. "You need to give me something… Something I can use."

Lucifer offered nothing.

"Hmmm," Ileana let out with a cocky smirk. Cadet stayed close to her. Ileana walked towards Lucifer. She leaned in close enough to press her cheek against his. She moved her hand lower, slowly hovering over his body until she swiped a yellow orb that was at his feet. "This seems like something you would not want to part from. I'll hold onto this for you," she said. "Until I come to get my book back. And thanks for the tips."

Lucifer looked at her with full demonic anger but did nothing. "I will not be able to come back to your dimension without that," he informed her.

"Then, I guess, the ball is in my court," she said carelessly tossing the orb up in the air. "Be sure to keep my book safe."

Ileana led Cadet out of the cave.

"What is that?" Cadet asked her.

"His portal key, his way of transporting to our dimension," Ileana told her.

Chapter 13

Ileana rushed out of a different opening in the cave and found herself on an active street along a canal in the city of Dremora. The brightness of the sunlight caused her to feel lightheaded. She had been traveling by night. She quickly recovered from a loss of balance and pulled the hood to hide her identity.

"Your majesty," Cadet rushed as Ileana emerged. "Are you alright?"

"Yes. Fine." She looked around with concern. "Do not call me that," she demanded of the Leprechaun.

"He will return to Hell and not be able to come back. The book is safe," Cadet told her as if it were part of her plan. She pointed to the yellow orb.

Ileana paused in thought. "Unorthodox approach. But, yes. I believe you are correct."

Cadet looked around to be sure that they were not being followed.

"Queen Ileana —"

"No!" Ileana demanded as she turned and stared hard into Cadet's eyes. "No names. The Dark Sisters have a greater ability to search your energy and hurt those who you love if you speak their names. Too dangerous. We will no longer be using names. Not mine. Not my husband. Not my children."

"Yes, my lady —"

"Not just the ones I love," Ileana said to her. "Everyone. The word must be spread to no longer use names," she demanded again with her hands in tight grips around the Leprechaun's arms. "Erase everything about me. They will destroy your mind to get to me. You must get away from me and forget that you even know me. Do you understand?"

"But —"

"Do you understand?!"

"Yes…Yes. I do."

"Go," Ileana demanded of Cadet. "Go now. And do not turn back."

Cadet walked away from the fallen Queen of Witches and, as instructed, did not look back.

Ileana shaded herself and walked along the open streets down to the river. Hiding in plain sight, she thought to herself as she rolled the orb in her hand. Ileana held the orb to her mouth and whispered the spell that gave access to the Book of Spells. She turned and walked across the bridge and then down the stairs to the path along the lower river.

Ileana's mind wandered. She had made mistakes in the past and had sacrificed her people. She now understood that by agreeing to limit magic, she opened the door for the rise of warped magic. But she was well on her way to make up for her failures.

She knew the content of the Book of Spells enough to confront The Dark Sisters and bring proper magic back to her people. The book was now hidden and with Lucifer's orb, she was able to make it impossible for The Dark Sisters to access it. Ileana smiled at her last thought.

"I'm ready for you."

Chapter 14

Night fell. Boats were docked at the back of the houses along the river. Some of the merchants were busy unloading the goods that they had not sold earlier in the day. Other boats sat empty and were either tied to the docks or anchored.

A storm was coming. The air had turned cold, and the stars were beginning to show themselves through the fast-moving clouds. Ileana looked up as she lowered her hood. She walked confidently along the riverside houses. The path ended at the back of the final house and a wall protecting the property from unwanted company. She felt an uneasy presence behind her.

Baltaan launched herself from the shadows. Ileana maneuvered her hands and arms and shot a ball of energy at Baltaan who kept running towards her. Baltaan hit the magical ball of light back towards Ileana with the Sword of Sansit. Ileana ducked as the ball of light hit the wall behind her and smashed it. Ileana was quick to run through the fallen wall and to keep running.

"Yes, Ileana," Baltaan yelled with laughter. "Use your magic. Draw them to you." She yelled, chasing her through the orchard of orange trees.

Ileana moved the clouds to cover the moonlight and starlight. Baltaan stopped. She could not see Ileana in the dark. She listened and heard the water rushing on the nearby river. She inhaled and smelled the aroma of the oranges on the trees. It was the same as Ileana's scent but without the vanilla. Vanilla was faint, but Baltaan could not find its source. She closed her eyes and looked within to find Ileana.

The sound of water became clearer and even louder. The scent of the oranges remained fragrant. Baltaan began to feel humidity and quickly opened her eyes.

"No!"

She was immediately caught up in a large wave that pulled her into the river as she struggled for air. The water pulled her under and was fighting her for the Sword of Sansit. Baltaan held tight to the golden handle of the emerald dagger. Ileana too was surrounded by water and pulled under towards where Baltaan fought.

Water fought for the sword and Ileana joined in the struggle. Forces pummeled the Witches and pushed them to the bottom of the river. They hit the mud and rocks. Baltaan focused on holding tight to the blade. She could not lose it. Baltaan kicked off Ileana's attack knocking the orb to the bottom of the riverbed.

Ileana came at her as she was producing a spell and reached for the blade. Baltaan sliced downward and cut Ileana through the hands. The spell exploded and pushed the Witches away from each other. Ileana's blood spread throughout the water and made it even harder to see. Baltaan swam hard until she reached the surface. She was gasping for air and swam as quickly to the bank as possible. Baltaan pulled herself out of the water and struggled for air. She turned to look and see the lingering white light of Ileana's failed spell diminish under the water until it was fully extinguished.

Baltaan had dropped the Sword of Sansit to her side as she continued to recover. She was not yet aware that the blade had been broken. She began to cry through her gasping. "She's gone," she said with manic laughter. "Ileana, the Queen of Witches, is dead."

PRINCESS

The three of legend

Chapter 1

Marching armies protected the elaborate coaches that were filled with royals and representatives from neighboring lands. Each came across one of the seven bridges that connected the city state of Mortua to other parts of the mainland. The nobles who had to cross borders into other kingdoms prior to entering into Mortua worried for their personal safety. They chose to travel by motorized airships with jetpacked guards flying alongside, weapons drawn and on high alert. The breeze blew in their favor to assist their speed. Those from the farthest lands arrived by sea. Their vessels were guarded by propellered divers and single carrier submarines armed with explosive harpoons. They sailed past the Mermaids' burial ground at the protected entrance of the harbor and beyond the cliff that led up to the Monastery of the Order of the Brothers of Naa.

One by one, the officials entered the stately grounds of the palace and acknowledged the sibling rulers, Queen Sharon and her brothers Kings Charles and Jax, and the queen's daughter, Princess Brae. They all arrived at the palace of Mortua with their flags and their distrust proudly displayed. It had been agreed that Mortua would host the proceedings of the Council of Kingdoms which was created to allow for open discussion among more than a dozen nations with the utmost goal of maintaining peace.

Over fifteen years ago, the political landscape had become one of violence and tension among the kingdoms. The Dark Sisters, using a warped, unnatural magic, had taken over the Kingdom of Witches and joined forces with the Kingdom of Tebbs through the marriage of his royal highness to the Witch, Baltaan. The king felt that an alliance with The Dark Sisters would go unchallenged by the other nations and became aggressive in his pursuit of conquering the neighboring lands. However, Tebbs had found itself unsupported by the Kingdom of Witches, which led to many failed invasions.

Mortua had become a fortress unto itself. Geographically, it did not share borders with either of the offending kingdoms. Mortua was a peaceful nation. Her military was strong and unsurpassed in size and skills. The city-state had, on multiple occasions, given aid to the Kingdoms of Caarfu and Dremora in holding off invasions from the Kingdom of Tebbs. Yet, King Dubair of Tebbs did not relent. The uncertainty of what the intentions of The Dark Sisters were seemed only to delay a larger scale war. This gathering of the Council of

Kingdoms was occurring to prevent such a thing. "These negotiations are bullshit," King Charles of Mortua said to his sister, Queen Sharon. Through his facial expression, King Jax showed his agreement.

"Over my dead body!" the representative from Bacaa yelled and looked back at his king.

"That could be arranged," replied the King of Tebbs.

The doors opened and a fearful hush came over the gathering hall. The representative from Bacaa sat slowly so as to not be seen. The Dark Sisters entered the great hall. He cautiously looked over from his seat with a feeling of concern as he saw The Dark Sisters collectively smirk. They walked to their seats at the table but looked at no one. They said nothing. The three Witches sat sullen in their seats next to the King of Tebbs. One of the three kept her face fully covered. The King of Tebbs relished in the power of the attention the Witches were now drawing. Yet, they showed no interest in being a part of this gathering, other than to bask in their intimidation of the other monarchs.

The King of Tebbs argued for the turnover of rule to him to the northwest and to The Dark Sisters in the southeast. They would then decide how the lands would be divided. The representatives from Caarfu and Dremora, and the head of the Monastery of the Brothers of the Order of Naa, were quick to stand and argue against the demand. However, Monsignor Quahin quieted his yells as the others continued to scream out and draw the attention of the room. He used the distraction of the other arguments to call over a page who answered to The Dark Sisters.

Princess Brae raised an eyebrow as she spied the exchange and the note that the monk handed to the young man. She imagined reading the treasonous contents of that note and how Mortua would take the monastery and destroy the monks who sided with the opposing forces. This act of defense would stop any further consorting and continue to allow Mortua unopposed access to the sea. Her mother, who also noticed the exchange, watched the princess' reaction.

The King of Tebbs turned to The Dark Sisters for support. He did not receive any. He became uneasy with his words. The Witches gave the continued appearance of disinterest towards any further discussion. They stood in unison as the room again fell silent and moved to the doors and out of the negotiations. The page returned the note unopened to Monsignor Quahin. He made the attempt to hide the exchange. The princess shook her head. The King of Tebbs was left alone with squinted eyes staring back at him as he had now lost his bargaining power. The tone of the room flipped, and whispers began among the other rulers to possibly take his kingdom and his rule.

Queen Sharon stood tall and proud. It was now she who said nothing but commanded the attention of the gathering hall. A hush fell over the room. "We have passively defended our borders in the hope that the kingdoms would cease the violence on their own. However, the time has come to end the tension that exists among us. No further attacks will be tolerated. Any attack on any of the kingdoms present here will be met with the full retaliation of the forces of Mortua, as if the attack had been launched against the crown itself." Bacaa, Tamsu, Dremora, Caarfu, and even the monks applauded her valor and agreed to stand beside her against Tebbs. The king had been unforgiving in his pursuit of power but was wise enough to know when to step back. Queen Sharon was victorious in her efforts.

She turned her attention to her daughter, Brae, who sat near her at these trials and gave her a discreet wink.

"You have very big shoes to fill," King Jax joked to his niece.

"Sharon can rule the world," King Charles added.

"Without us," Jax said humbly to the teenage girl who smiled and looked at her mother who had just ended the war that had not yet started.

Amazing, Princess Brae thought in response to her mother's diplomacy and her ability to take control.

Chapter 2

The rulers all exited the gathering. The King of Tebbs and the rulers of Mortua were the last ones present in the hall. As King Dubair exited, he handed a scroll to King Jax.

"My marriage to the Witch, Baltaan, has shadowed my judgment and allowed me to… regretfully… agree to conspire with the current rulers of the Kingdom of Witches-" King Jax read.

"This is bullshit!" King Charles interrupted.

"Charles, please," Queen Sharon intervened with a sense of calm. "Dubair is," she began to search for the right words, "ridiculous," she agreed. "But he is kin-"

"Distant kin," Charles reminded her. "And so what. We just forgive him for his transgressions? His words mean nothing other than to now cry for our protection. I say again… This is bullshit!"

"Distant kin. Yes," she acknowledged after a collected pause. "But this serves as a peace offering."

"We should destroy him," King Charles told her and paced with full anger.

The princess took those words to heart. She played a mental version of an invasion of the Kingdom of Tebbs and her own success in capturing the king. She visualized him surrendering to her with his arms up over his head.

Queen Sharon looked to her other sibling, King Jax. "And what do you think?"

"I think that Charles is right," he told her. "We should destroy him."

The princess heard louder cheers in her head as she presented the fallen king to the people.

King Jax turned his attention to King Charles. "But we won't. Remember? 'Any attack on any Kingdom...'," he said with air quotes.

The vision dissolved from the princess' mind. Her mouth had opened in offense to his words.

King Charles threw his hands up. Queen Sharon did her best to hide her smile. She and Jax regularly agreed on most matters.

King Jax argued that attacking Tebbs would only put the other kingdoms on high alert against Mortua. The veil of trust was thin.

"And I can see that you are planning out an attack in your head," Queen Sharon voiced with concern. The princess looked back with worry that she had just been caught. "Seeing yourself win is not how military strategy works, my child. You need to study. You need to know your opponent and figure out their strengths and weaknesses as well as your own. You have to act and react at the same time."

The princess looked down as if she were being scolded.

Her mother came to sit beside her. "Brae, it is more than just fighting. Going to war is a last resort. The best option is avoiding war, avoiding the losses… lives, ways of living, and cost." She paused as her tone had softened enough for the princess to look up at her. "Your time will come when you will rule Mortua and command the armies. But there is a lot to learn before that and that time is not yet here. You saw how the political climate is currently. It is dangerous and foreboding. I would rather that you enter into this arena when it is safer so that you can start with a fresh understanding."

The princess nodded. "I understand, mother. I just want to be able to be as good a ruler as the three of you…when the time comes," she added to the laughter of them all.

"Good," King Jax replied. "I wasn't looking to be dethroned for quite a while."

They all laughed as Queen Sharon kissed her daughter on the forehead and held her tight.

Chapter 3

"You're going to lead the armies?" Tinker asked her with excitement. "I have so many ideas-"

"In time, Tink," the princess interrupted. "My mother lectured me that my imagination is not going to help. Mainly, I need to stop seeing myself as victorious and need to figure out how to become victorious."

"Huh?" Tinker replied with a confused expression.

The princess sighed out of frustration for having to explain herself. "I've been going about this all wrong."

"In your mind," Tinker added.

"Yes, in my mind," she agreed, adding to her frustration. "Apparently, I need to start thinking of avoiding a war... even more than winning a war."

Tinker was a boy, several years older than the princess, who had been brought to the palace when he was a child. As a favor to a respected friend, he had been taken into the guardianship of the crown and had lived with the rulers. The boy had been rescued from an abusive situation and needed a safe and private environment. A few years later, at the arrival of the princess, he had been immediate in his attention to her. Tinker had always been a shy boy, but he had found joy in his playing with the princess. He had taught her how to see situations from a less expected point of view and she was always eager to learn. His innate kindness taught her to think of others and their situations from their perspectives. Her imagination was as limitless as his. They were commonly in whispered conversation and together all the time. They considered each other to be brother and sister and held an unconditional love for one another.

"I think that you need to think for yourself," Tinker argued.

"I dare you to tell that to my mother," the princess challenged.

"Nope," Tinker was quick to reply and then retreated into thought as they walked.

"In time, I will. But Tink, Mortua has the most powerful military. It has never been defeated. And most of the time, just knowing that any branch of Mortua's forces is going to be involved, stops the battle before it begins."

"But things have changed. And they will continue to change. The Dark Sisters-"

"Oooh, did you see them in the Council of Kingdoms? They did not seem interested in what the King of Tebbs was arguing for. He handed my uncle a scroll which basically apologized for all the invasions. I don't think that they are siding with him any longer."

"All the more concerning," Tinker said. "What are they up to? I mean, if world domination is boring to them and they continue to seek power, then what kind of power are they looking at?"

Princess Brae pulled Tinker into an empty chamber.

"What are you saying?"

"They have something bigger planned." Tinker gave her a look that made it seem that his statement was obvious.

"But what could be bigger than world domination?" she asked.

Tinker took one of the books in his hands and opened it. "Control between dimensions… Or in more than one dimension." Tinker had educated the princess on portals that existed between dimensions. He had told her about the types of inhabitants that lived in some of these other dimensions and the powers that they possessed.

"Angels, demons, spirits, Immortals-"

"Yup," Tinker said, still very matter of fact. "All types of things in all types of places. All living in different dimensions with different powers."

"Too much, Tink. My head hurts. For now, I just have to learn the basics."

"I'm hungry," he told her to no surprise. Tinker was always hungry.

"Oh no!" the princess yelled. "We're late. Hurry! We are supposed to be at the reception. It's being thrown to calm tensions before the other rulers leave Mortua."

"You are in so much trouble," Tinker told her.

"Me?" she argued back as they ran to change. "What about you?"

"I'm the poor orphan who the rulers took in to protect," he reminded her.

"Good luck with that. Change quickly!"

Chapter 4

"Ah," Queen Sharon sighed as the princess and Tinker rushed into the ballroom. "Where have you been?" she questioned with a smile on her face and an annoyed tone in her voice. She straightened the princess' crown with a sense of longing. The single emerald spike that sat atop it reflected light as if repelling it.

"That ability to smile through your anger is impressive, your majesty," Tinker told her.

"Thank you, Tink. But it does not get you out of trouble." The queen looked between them. "I will deal with the two of you later. Go and mingle."

The princess walked off and was whispering to Tinker. She turned to realize that he was not there. Tinker suffered from severe social anxiety. He looked to spend as much time as he could alone reading, theorizing, making gadgets, and being in and preferably, under water.

"Thanks, Tink," she said to the air.

"Talking to yourself, weirdo?"

"Estab," the princess said with a socially responsible curtsey.

He snickered as if mocking her.

"I am the Princess of Mortua, Estab. You will respect me," she demanded.

"No. I will not," he countered. "You are only a girl." He moved in closer as a group of boys surrounded them. "And you will never be the ruler. You see, you are… a bastard."

The other boys laughed.

"My mother is the Queen of Mortua," the princess reminded Estab with anger squinting in her eyes.

"And your father?" he questioned with his pompous tone.

The princess felt her blood begin to boil at Estab's disrespect for her mother. A breeze blew from behind her and caught her hair and gown.

Calm, she reminded herself. Avoid the war. She needed to keep her head about her and maintain her regal composure. No.

The princess then extended her hand and Estab took it. She immediately responded by pulling him forward and punching him straight in the face. He dropped to the floor. Queen Sharon saw the exchange and went aghast.

"Expect the unexpected," the princess said as she walked away as if nothing had happened. After the initial shock, the circle of his friends that attempted to hide the exchange from public view did the same. Estab was left squirming on the floor with blood gushing from his nose.

"Not bad," Tinker told her as he caught up with her.

"Oh, now you're going to be helpful," she said with a scoff at him.

"My advice seemed to help you to win that battle," Tinker reminded her.

Princess Brae stopped. "Guess you're right," she admitted. "I'm going to have to learn the basics… and incorporate your unexpected, rogue techniques."

Tinker blushed with joy that he was right. He gazed at the boys that the princess had just humiliated. "That one is brooding over you," he said about the boy who was continuing to stare at the princess.

"Azurus Perculfilus?" she questioned with disgust. "Gross."

"Don't gloat, boy," Queen Sharon charged and looked with wide angry eyes at the princess.

"Mother-"

"No," the queen told her. "So you tell me that you want to be involved with military strategy and this is what you do? Unbelievable." The queen paced as she thought.

"So much for avoiding a war," Tinker whispered to the princess.

Queen Sharon stopped and looked at them. "You know what? You are right. It is time to start your military training," she said to her. "You need to start thinking about the big picture. Avoiding a fight is as important as winning one, and you need to learn when to use that skill."

"What?" she begged. "But when avoiding it is not an option, I will need to defend myself. I need to be able to attack, and in a way that is unexpected."

Queen Sharon attempted to hold her tongue. She maintained her regal appearance and minimized her pacing.

"You think too small. You have to learn the art of war. Your training will start tomorrow."

The princess and Tinker looked at one another, unsure if this was a punishment or a reward.

Chapter 5

A month had passed. The princess was completely engaged in her military training. As per her norm, she was early for the classes. Each day began with the new recruits reporting to their particular commander in the designated part of the school. The princess had remained within the palace grounds and had limited social engagements. Time with Tinker was the only socializing that she did outside of her squad. Both cases were more academic than social.

She was already deep in books that described great battles and how one group was able to overtake the opposition. Her focus was still on winning wars, not avoiding them. As she read, her imagination allowed her to see herself being victorious in each of the conflicts. She came across the recounting of the night of the fall of Ileana, the Queen of Witches. "They were able to cloak the palace and the City of Witches with a spell," she said with worry about how The Dark Sisters defeated the former matriarch of the Kingdom of Witches. A chill came upon her. "That was definitely unexpected."

As the sun rose higher that morning, the other squad members arrived. They caught sight of her eagerness and several of them mocked her.

"Trying way too hard," one boy said and drew laughter from Magurie Sanpe and an insecure giggle from Arurus Perculfilus.

"Leave her alone," two other girls demanded. "She works harder than the rest of us," they argued but did not receive a respectable response. "And we function as a single unit," they reminded him.

As their commanding officer entered, they were all quick to stand in formation. The twelve new recruits in Squad C maintained their four by three positioning until ordered to head out to the field. They fell into line in perfect time and marched out onto the grass. Their commander ordered that they stay in position until she returned. No one moved.

The sun was getting hotter as they waited for the staff sergeant to come back from the whispered conversation that she was having with another instructor. The two instructors saluted each other, and the leader of Squad A walked off with a brisk pace.

"We will be having a scrimmage today," the commander told her recruits. "We will be going up against Squad A in hand-to-hand combat." She walked amongst the group. No one moved. They each maintained a cold and distant stare and held their hands behind their backs with their chests up and strong.

The princess was running strategies through her mind. I guess I won't be avoiding a conflict today, she told herself. She began to hear the commander's words as if they were distant. Her mental attacks and defenses took the forefront of her concentration. She felt a kick from the girl to her left. The other recruit motioned with her eyes and pointed with her head.

The commander had called the princess who did not respond. The commander was facing away from the recruits as Squad A entered the field. The princess understood what the other girl was communicating and walked up to stand next to the commander. The commander did not turn.

"You will not be participating in this exercise," the commander explained. The princess could not hold back her disappointment and reacted with a gasp. "I know that you would fend well, but I am not taking the chance of you getting injured."

"But-"

"My order is final," she told her and walked forward to meet Squad A and its commander. After a prompt salute and greeting, she whistled for Squad C to approach. They moved in perfect unison and came to a halt behind their commander. They spread into a semicircle, which met with the semicircle formed by Squad A.

A member of Squad A hit into a member of Squad C.

"Ooops," he said with arrogance.

"Ooops, my ass," the Squad C member replied and launched at him.

A fight started and all the other squad members began pairing off as if they were all going to brawl.

The commanders blew their whistles to force a cease and pulled the recruits apart.

"This will be a true scrimmage," the commander of Squad C yelled. "We will not tolerate any nonsense."

The commander of Squad A nodded in agreement, but when he turned to his recruits, he winked.

"The rules are simple," the commander yelled. "You will each be assigned a random number and when that number is called, you will enter the circle. You will use the tactics that you have been taught here to engage in fair hand-to-hand combat. When you hear the whistle, you will stop. The victor will remain in the center of the circle and will call the number of the next opponent. The challenger will not be known until he or she comes forth." From the center of the circle, the commander looked around and stopped her gaze on the princess.

As the instructions were being given by the commander of Squad C, the other commander had been arranging the recruits and whispering in their ears their assigned number.

"Three," the princess heard. She took this as an opportunity to participate. My commander must have forgotten to say anything to the Squad A commander.

"We will begin with number three from Squad A and number ten from Squad C." The princess tensed at hearing the number, but it was for the recruit from Squad A.

Both recruits entered the circle and stepped as they sized each other up. Their cautious movements showed that they were planning, using the theories that they had been taught. The princess saw herself actively sparring and winning against both recruits with each move that they made. The sparring recruits moved into lunging and spinning as they acted and reacted to each other as they attempted to incorporate their training.

The whistle blew and Squad A was called as the winner.

The sparing continued and both Squad A and Squad C were demonstrating a good performance. The recruits were taking a mental count as to which class was winning. This had not been the intent of the commanders, but the recruits were teenagers and competing was in their nature.

"Four," the recruit yelled out.

Azurus Perculfilus stepped into the circle, attacked from behind, and knocked his opponent clear out of the circle. He was called the winner. "Seven," Azurus yelled out.

Estab, the princess thought to herself with disgust as he removed his helmet and stood behind Azurus in the center of the circle. Azurus saw his shadow and pulled his hands into fists. Estab snarled and rushed towards him. Azurus sidestepped and avoided his attack.

And clothesline him, the princess thought and saw herself doing just that in her mind. She saw Estab flip over and land face down in the dirt. Battle won.

But in the circle, Estab was quick to recover and expressed that he did not like that misstep. Azurus smiled involuntarily with pride. Estab attacked again, but this time, he did hit the mark. Azurus was knocked to the ground with a hard crack on his helmet.

"He's breathing," the commander of Squad A informed them all.

"You," the commander of Squad C ordered two recruits who had already gone into the circle. "Come with me. You will carry him to the medical hall." They did as instructed as the rest stayed in the circle. "Well?" she asked of Estab. "Continue."

Estab looked around the circle. He looked at the princess and squinted. He continued turning and stopped with his left side to her. "Three." He smiled as he said it. "I saw you flinch when the number was called out earlier."

The princess entered the circle and pulled her wooden sword. She waited. She pictured the attack in her mind. She would begin with a standard lunge and then a turn to attack from the side. Estab would try to push forward. She saw herself knock him in the back of the neck, which would push him to his knees and when he would turn, her blade would be in his face. She was ready, and she attacked in the same way as she had just practiced in her mind.

Estab threw his wooden blade at her, which drew a collective gasp from the others. The princess was knocked off guard and double stepped.

Estab ran towards the princess and tackled her. He straddled her arms under his knees and drew a wooden dagger, which he held to her neck.

The whistle blew repeatedly. "That is not a tactic that you have been taught here," the commander from Squad A yelled as he pulled him from atop the princess.

"Expect the unexpected," he said to her with an angry smile and then spit on the ground. Estab pulled himself from his commander and stormed off.

All members from both squads were now pairing off and fighting. The commander kept blowing the whistle but with no success. Two girls from Squad C came to her. "Are you okay?" they asked.

"Yes," she said, although embarrassed. They all joined in the fighting as well.

Chapter 6

For the next six weeks, the feeling between squads at the academy was tense. Squads B and D had heard what happened and had taken sides with either Squad A or C. The princess continued to rise early. Tinker had manipulated battle dummies made of straw and metal into having moving parts, including swords and daggers that actually injured if struck by them. She sparred with them daily. The princess balanced herself on thin wooden poles that were suspended in the air and moved with every step and sway. She yelled out as she launched forward and pulled back. Sweat dripped from her nose as the cold air and fog fought her comfort.

"You have good technique," the stranger said with a surprised tone. "Not bad for a princess."

The princess snarled and shielded her blade. "I am more than a princess."

The handsome stranger in a purple overcoat raised an eyebrow.

The princess looked around. "How did you get in here?" she asked but had no concern about the stranger being present. She figured if nothing else, he could be practice.

"My name is Thaddeus. I am a friend of the queen and kings," he told her. "I've been watching," Thaddeus said. "You still think too small. You think about winning the fight, the battle. You need to think bigger if you are to command Mortua's defenses."

"What do you know about that?" the princess asked.

"Nothing more than that you are the Princess of Mortua and when you are the ruler of this kingdom, you will also command the armed forces."

The princess said nothing more.

"You have to win the war with the least casualties," he told her. "Remember, in the end you will still need the respect and support of your people. Most commanders are not rulers, but you will be both. And since being defeated by that boy, you are only focused on the loss. You are still only able to see what is in your mind and not what lies in front of you."

The princess rolled her eyes and walked over to pull her daggers from one of the practice dummies. "Meaning?" she asked with an angered tone.

"Meaning you are only on the attack. You have to respect that if you look to solely be on the offensive, then you are not accounting for the skill of your opposition. You are not respecting the art of war. You are only seeing how you expect your opponent to react. And therefore, you will leave those under your command and your reign unprotected."

The princess thought about what he was saying.

"You seem to know a lot about military strategy," she said to him.

"I've seen a battle or two in my day," he confessed.

"My mother would have me avoid war," she told him and awaited a reaction.

He thought about it. "An excellent strategy…But not always an option."

Thaddeus now had her attention. "You are being groomed to one day lead all of Mortua. You need to balance your planning as you do your footwork. Remember, it is not only you who has to win. It is the coordinated efforts of the leaders and the combined efforts of individuals working together to create a single unit, a formidable military."

"Chess," she said her thought aloud.

"Exactly," he agreed.

"I can do that," she told him with a sly grin.

"Your majesty," Thaddeus began. "It is imperative that you know how to fight, both in battle and in life."

"Dramatic," she replied.

"You are a target. People come for you simply because of your position in life."

"Of this, I am well aware."

"However," he moved closer to her and elevated his sword. "These are dark times, and the darkness will stop at nothing to destroy the light." Thaddeus dodged forth with his sword.

The princess was swift to move and turn to counter. "But without light, there is no darkness… It is mutual assured destruction."

Thaddeus cracked a smile as he faced away from her.

"Not bad," he told her.

"My sword work or my philosophy?"

"Both, actually," he said with a lighter tone.

Chapter 7

"Tink! Wake up," the princess yelled as she entered his chambers.

Tinker was already awake and working on one of his gadgets. He looked at her from behind a pair of goggles that made his eyes look huge.

"It's time that I master the game of chess," she announced.

Tinker snickered. "Okay."

"Chess, Tink! It's the utmost in military strategy. It's offense and defense at the same time…watching the whole board, not just the individual battle but the whole war, at once."

Tinker sat quiet.

"Speak!" she yelled.

Tinker covered his workstation. "Estab embarrasses you after you embarrass him and now you are just going to go back and forth."

She paused. "No. I just need to be better at planning out a complete strategy." She paused again as she searched for the right words. "Yes," she admitted, "I would love to take down Estab again. But that is only because it is the only way to gain his respect. I worked it out earlier this morning."

Tinker shook his head. "Uh huh."

The princess stood in front of him.

"You ran in here to wake me up with this thought?"

"Yes," she told him.

"No, you didn't," Tinker countered.

"Fine," she said. "I worked it out while I was training."

"Keep going," he demanded.

"With Thaddeus."

"Who's Thaddeus?" Tinker asked her with concern in his voice and searched through a book.

"A friend of my mother's."

"A stranger? That scares me."

"Everything scares you," she reminded him.

"True." Tinker reached into a cabinet and took out a chess set made of crystals. "Ready?"

"Yes."

The princess spent the next few weeks continuing her military training with the recruits in Squad C, but also sparring with Thaddeus.

Tinker spent those few weeks teaching the princess everything that he knew about chess and strategy. He taught her that you can create an advantage and throw your opponent off guard by not reacting. He even referenced her mother's speech from the Council of Kingdoms. Tinker went into his personal texts and then the palace library to show her even more examples. They studied together until the day the princess announced...

"Checkmate."

Tinker was appalled and thrilled at the same time. He nodded after taking a second to confirm that what she had called out was in fact true. She had beaten him. No one else had ever beaten him. He held no ego when it came to the princess. He was proud to have taught her and to have her win. "Let's take that back to Thaddeus."

Chapter 8

"Tink!" the princess demanded as she beat her hand on the locked door of his chambers.

"What are you doing in there?"

"What do you think I'm doing in here?" Tinker thought quickly. "Don't answer that. What?"

"I received this letter from one of my Squad members. They are all going to fight… Tonight!... In the empty fisherman's market on the water."

"And?"

"And I need you to get me out of the palace. I need to be there!"

"No way!"

"Oh yes you are," she threatened. "Otherwise, I'm going to have to tell my mother that you have something explosive under that tarp," she said and pointed to what was covered on his table.

"How do you know it's explosive?" Tinker whispered with a strong concern in his voice.

"I didn't until just now," she told him. "Checkmate."

Tinker let out a sound of frustration. He led her to the far wall of his chambers and pushed a particular stone in the wall. She looked at him with total surprise.

"I'm sure that your room has this too," he told her.

She followed him through the hidden passage that ran between the walls and out into the public gardens. Once the concealed door closed behind them, there would be no reentering.

"We'll think of something," Tinker said. "Come on."

Under hooded cloaks, they made their way through the city. No one recognized them.

"There!" the princess told him and pointed to the sign that read, Casa de Pescado. "In there."

They entered the dark empty warehouse.

"No one's here," Tinker said.

Immediately after saying that, the recruits from all four squads came in from different entrances.

"The Princess of Mortua," Estab mocked.

"Keep your voice down," Tinker demanded.

"You don't get to tell me what to do, peasant," he retorted and evoked laughter from his squad.

"Are we doing this again, Estab?" the princess asked with a twitch of readiness in her fists. The princess was immediately thinking about how the exchange would play out. The members of Squad C came around her and squared off against Squad A who all stood with Estab. Squads B and D looked around but now unsure of what alliance they might choose.

Estab was looking for another fight. Both he and the princess had successfully used the element of surprise in previous fights. But now it would be anticipated and not a viable option.

I must think bigger than this battle, she thought.

Estab made a motion to intimidate her.

She was lost in her own thoughts and did not react. To win the war, she reminded herself. She looked around and saw how the squads were each working to intimidate each other. Her mind switched gears as she realized that most of them did not want to fight. They were just going along with what they were told to do. But this was Mortua. And these were the citizens and future leaders of Mortua. Fighting against one another would only set up for a future of disharmony.

This is war? she thought and felt a sense of nausea. No! She realized that there were options.

One… Fight Estab and his gaggle of entitled pretty boys and beat them until they no longer felt the desire to bully anyone again.

No.

Two… Convince the other squads to join with Squad C by promising them something.

No.

Three…

Three… Yes! Three. Be like my mother at the Council of Kingdoms.

"Tink! Give me a boost," she said and climbed atop a booth. She whistled loud and grabbed the attention of all the squad members. She looked at Estab and motioned to tell him that he was the cause of the problems. She stopped herself. She realized that calling him out in front of the others would only continue this back and forth battling.

"I am Brae Salingalees, the Princess of Mortua. But you already know that." She now looked at Estab. "Some of you want to minimize my position and my power because I am just… as you have previously stated… a girl." She stopped as she stared at him. Several of the girls from each of the squads moved forward and held their heads up to her. "But you see, despite my title, because I am a girl, I've had to work harder, move faster, think bigger. And I am not alone." Two of the girls gave each other a high five hand shake. "And it does not matter that I am a girl. What matters is that we… collectively… are the future of Mortua." A few of the boys and girls gave small nods. "We are the leaders of tomorrow. Who here really wants to fight tonight?" The air was silent. "Neither do I," she told them. More kids joined in with stronger clapping. "And we... working together... are what is needed to defeat anyone and anything that tries to take our life and our home from us!" All the squad members were now applauding. Estab looked around and shook his head. He too was taken by what the Princess was saying. "The future of Mortua is in our hands. And our training, not our squabbling, is what will keep her great and keep our people safe and happy. So I say this. No more pointless fighting and bickering. We can disagree and we can work out our disagreements. We can scrimmage and battle when we are called to do so. But looking to hurt and destroy each other will only weaken Mortua and will only cause us distrust in one another."

Tinker gave her a thumb's up and a smile.

"First round is on me," she said. "The Taverne Ayer will serve us... right Estab?" she said with a wink and a joking tone.

He laughed and bowed to her, knowing that it was true.

The princess turned her back to the recruits. She spread her arms and leaned back. She knew that they would catch her. That simple exercise in trust brought all four squads together. And the drinking that followed created the first of many times that would bond the recruits in treasured memories.

Chapter 9

“I have to admit, that was impressive,” Thaddeus told her as she and Tinker attempted to sneak their way back into the palace.

“You were there?” they asked.

“In the shadows,” he confessed. “You read your opponent, swayed his allies, and disarmed the situation. That speech reminded me of your mother.”

“Offense and defense,” Tinker said.

“Yes. It seems you have won that war and gained allies. That boy will not bother you again,” Thaddeus agreed. “Continue to work on your diplomacy. That speech was powerful enough for you to gain the favor of the people. You will need to work together in order to be a successful leader,” he advised.

The princess looked at Tinker and smiled. She squeezed his hand and led him to stand beside her in front of Thaddeus.

“If anyone knows anything about working together, it is us.”

"But you wouldn't understand," Tinker told him. "You see, we are the biggest outcasts ever. We've always had to work together."

"I wouldn't understand?" Thaddeus questioned with an uncommon annoyance. "I will let you in on a little secret. I am a vampire, an Immortal," Thaddeus confessed. They scoffed in disbelief. "If anyone understands how you feel right now, it's me!" Thaddeus turned and looked at an area of the night sky that was void of stars. "I know what it feels like to be alone… to be an outcast." He turned back to them. "I don't want to feel like that anymore."

Tinker motioned to speak but was lost for words. He squeezed the princess' hand, and she squeezed his back.

"This world is changing," he told them. "You need to be able to protect yourselves… and each other. Like you've always done." He attempted to hide his proud smile as they stood quietly in front of him. "Get back inside the palace. Train," he told them and pointed to the high walls that surrounded the palace. "Always know your way out… or in this case, in."

"Are you leaving?" the princess asked him.

"Yes," he told them. "I received some information that will aid in my quest. It is time for me to leave Mortua."

"Thank you, Thaddeus," the princess said and hugged him. "It has been an honor."

"Your majesty," he said with a bow. "And you," he said to Tinker. "Do not fear me. You carry a scent in your essence that has drawn me to you. Our paths will cross again, and when they do, we will find that we have much more in common." He looked at the main gates to the palace. "Go," he ordered them. "I will distract the guards."

And with that, the vampire, Thaddeus, was gone.

AZ
Sword and shield

Chapter 1

"Hi, AZ," the flirtatious girl said as she passed him on the street. AZ ignored her and walked on with complete disinterest. However, in his mind, he thought of Brae, the Princess of Mortua, and stood a bit taller. Everyone in Mortua knew the beautiful princess and longed for her attention but was too afraid to seek it.

Throughout his seventeen years, AZ had always been part of a well- to-do family. His parents moved to Mortua when he was less than a year old. They told stories of how their older son, Saric, who died before AZ was born, was one of those special people with the rare ability to track priceless Cez stones. These stones, also known as Fallen Stars, were able to produce an unlimited amount of energy. Possessing Cez stones and temporarily loaning them to governments and private businesses was how AZ's parents amassed their fortune.

AZ never felt inspired to compete with the stories of his dead brother's legacy. His relationship with his parents was emotionally distant, mainly because of their constant need to make attempts at elevating their social status among Mortua's elite. AZ was never given a limit to his choices of how he spent money.

AZ, like many seventeen-year-olds, passed his days and nights with his circle of friends. This group of boys were all part of Mortua's high society. They constantly reminded him that because his family did not descend from Mortuan roots, he would always be seen as an 'outsider'. He spent money recklessly in attempts to secure his status within this circle.

The leader of this group was another tall, handsome teen named Estab Roncols. Estab was entitled and spoiled, as he descended from one of the founding families of the citystate of Mortua. Having heard the stories of AZ's brother, Estab made it a regular point to remind AZ that his family would be nothing if it were not for Saric. AZ took these taunts as fraternal hazing and went along with it in order to be included. However, he longed for the day that he would stand up to Estab and no longer be the butt of the jokes.

Chapter 2

AZ arrived at school late but did not care that he would be in trouble. He was a decent student but never put in the time to make anything more of his studies. School was nothing more than a formality. AZ, like many other children of Mortua's elite, had, by birthright, already secured a future in the family business. And similar to other days when he found himself late, he found that he was not alone. Several other students entered the first period classroom at the same time. Some of them had slips from the headmistress' office excusing their tardiness. AZ considered buying a slip off one of them but then saw that the teacher was new and would not know any of the students.

"Azurus Perculfilus?" the teacher called as he sat in the back of the class. The teacher had become distracted by the other students bringing their forms to her. "Azurus?"

He did not reply to her calling him. He would be marked absent and would be free to head out of school for the day.

What's the point of being here anyway?

"Out sick, I guess," the teacher said and finished calling attendance. Several other boys ignored her when their names were called. The teacher did not realize. With chalk in hand, she turned and went to the board. She began writing, A life without purpose. "Is not worth living," she said aloud. "This theme comes up in classic and current literature. Reassessing your daily lives and where you expect them to go will be the theme of the five-hundred word essay due to me by Friday."

Several students let out loud sighs. Others began to take notes on what the teacher was saying about the assignment.

AZ felt a ball of paper hit him in the cheek. He turned to see Estab smiling and mouthing that he and some others were going to cut the rest of the day at school. AZ was quick to give him a thumb's up mostly because he was already planning on doing the same and looked around to three other boys who were also smiling.

The teacher continued with her lesson. With her attention drawn to scribbling on the board, the five boys quietly walked out of the classroom and through the empty hallway.

"The guards?" one boy questioned.

"Easy enough," Estab told him. "We'll pay them off." He turned to AZ. "Use some of your brother's money, AZ."

"It's my money," AZ argued but then pulled himself back. "I paid the past few times," AZ reminded Estab, timidly.

"Only commoners keep tabs, AZ," Estab said, quick with his comeback. "You want to go or not?"

I was going anyway.

The other boys laughed and encouraged AZ to pull out the money. He did.

"Remember this, boys," Estab said as they left the building. "Know where you come from and where those around you come from." The playful delivery of his dig at AZ's family did not go unnoticed by the others. However, AZ wanted to be accepted by this group and went along with what Estab was saying. He faked a smile. They walked aimlessly on the streets.

"Should we go to the harbor?" one boy suggested.

"And what?" Estab countered. "Throw stones at each other? That's a stupid idea."

The other boys laughed at Estab's comment.

"I know," another announced. "We can go to the Taverne Ayer and have a few drinks."

"Better," Estab said. "But they don't open until three o'clock."

He looked at AZ and the last boy for suggestions. AZ shrugged his shoulders and the other boy looked away. They knew that whatever they said, Estab would not agree to it. He, like always, already had a plan in his head.

"We are going to spend the night in Dellai," he told them with a smile.

"That's a long trip," AZ reminded them.

"That's why you're going to get us horses, dumbass," Estab said with a laugh from the others. AZ felt obligated to laugh at himself as well.

Chapter 3

Estab and one of the other boys waited in an alley as AZ and the other two came back with five horses.

"Took you long enough," Estab grunted. AZ said nothing. The other two boys offered apologies.

"Here, Estab," one of the boys said, handing him the reins of a white mare. "The stable manager said that this one is the fastest."

Estab slapped him on the shoulder and took the reins. "Mount up, boys. We have a long road ahead of us and the last one there buys dinner."

I bet I'll be buying it regardless of who is the last one there, AZ thought to himself.

The five boys rode through the streets of Mortua without any respect for pedestrians and other horses and riders. They crossed one of the bridges that led out of the city.

They had ridden for two hours when they entered an area that was outside of the borders of any kingdom. A tall, lanky rider came past them with strange-looking goggles over his eyes and a wrap covering his mouth and nose. He ignored Estab and the other three boys who all snarled and laughed at his appearance. However, he turned and stared at AZ, the last rider, and AZ stared back at him. There was no verbal exchange between them.

The road had become narrow and they had to continue to ride single file. To each side of the narrowing road was a lake of lava. The air was hot and heavy, with the unpleasant aroma of sulfur. The heat burned in their lungs and only shallow breaths could be taken. The boys all became quiet.

Beads of sweat began to form and run as their clothes became wet. They each covered their nose and mouth with the elbow of their jacket sleeves and squinted their eyes to protect them from the heat.

This is a bad idea, AZ thought. He turned his head to see the empty road behind him but knew that the horse did not have room on the road to turn.

Small black stones banked the sides of the road in steep angles that lead down into the lakes of lava. The stones were unstable for the footing of any creature larger than a rat.

"Maybe this is a bad idea," one of the boys said with a failed attempt to hide his nervousness.

Yes, AZ thought with hope that they would abandon this idea of Estab's.

"That guy made it," Estab reminded them. "And he looked like a wimp."

"A smart wimp," AZ said and motioned his hand for only himself to see to acknowledge the goggles and face covering.

Estab did not care for AZ's challenging remark. He turned to him with anger. AZ looked away and closed his eyes tight. He was mad at himself for what he knew would cost him, financially as well as with the verbal abuse.

AZ felt his body get hotter. He began to have difficulty breathing and looked at the others. No one else seemed to be having the same reaction to what felt like the heat. AZ became fearful as he looked over the banked edges of the road to the red and orange lava.

"Hey guys," he began saying as he fell forward. His horse was startled by the weight of his torso on its neck. It reacted by taking a double step that brought its hoof off the path and down on the angled bank. The horse neighed in fear and lifted onto its hind legs. AZ fell from his horse and was laying on the black road.

AZ's horse was now frantic, but the road was too narrow to turn around. It pushed the other horses forward. The other boys pulled on their reins to ride faster. They reached a widening in the road, beyond the lakes of lava, where they pulled to the side. AZ's horse kept running.

"What do we do?" one of the boys asked Estab.

"Hey, stupid?" Estab yelled to AZ who looked like he was attempting to get up. "He sucks," he said to the others. They all looked back to AZ and then to Estab. "Are you coming?" he yelled. AZ did not reply but was crawling on the road. "Fuck this," Estab grunted. The others sat quiet and nervous. "Don't look at me. This is his fault. If he can't handle a little heat, maybe he shouldn't have come with us to begin with."

"What about the runaway horse?" one of the boys asked.

"AZ paid for the horses, not us. So, that's on him," he told them and two of them nodded in agreement. "Let's just stick to our plan and go on to Dellai. He'll either meet us or go home. Problem solved."

The other boys went along with what Estab had said. They rode off towards Dellai without looking back.

AZ had crawled a bit but then rolled over, laying on the black road. He felt like he was dreaming as he saw a clear stone among the black ones. He reached for it, but then passed out.

Chapter 4

AZ awoke to movement, swaying forward and backwards. He opened his eyes and saw that he was back on a horse. His mouth was dry, and he desperately needed water. He was experiencing the worst headache he had ever had.

"Welcome back from the dead," he heard spoken by a masculine voice from over his shoulder.

"What?" AZ questioned as he tried to piece together what had happened. "My friends?"

"What friends?" the man asked. "You were alone on the road," the man told him. "A group of boys around your age rode past me as I approached the crossing from Dellai."

AZ was confused and then angered. The uncomfortable position of being seated in front of the man on the saddle added to his annoyance. He still felt weak and had no stability on the horse other than the man's arms on the reins that supported his trunk.

AZ squirmed and made an attempt to turn to face him. "Who are you?" he asked.

"My name is Th-" the man began and then stopped himself. "I go by Vampire. Names are not to be used for safety against dark magic."

"That's a ridiculous alias," AZ said. "There's no such thing as vampires."

Vampire motioned his face to question AZ's statement but said nothing more about it. AZ squirmed again and pushed against Vampire's arm. Vampire became annoyed with AZ's comment and squirming and removed an arm from supporting him. AZ fell from the horse.

"Damn it," he said as Vampire continued to ride along at a walkable pace. "Hey!"

Vampire ignored him. AZ ran up and stood in front of the horse. AZ saw him for the first time and noticed that he, like the rider who passed earlier, had his face covered. Vampire pulled on the reins and the horse stood still.

"Are you going to pull me back up?" AZ asked.

"No," Vampire replied.

"Do you know who I am?" AZ asked.

Vampire looked up in thought and replied, "No. But I do know that you're a mess. Your friends abandoned you and left you on the side of the road. You have a poor attitude and seem quite entitled. Who are you? Or better yet, what are you doing with your life?"

AZ made an attempt to offer a comeback.

"I've known others like you. You need to find purpose… Otherwise, you will end up dead on the side of the road." AZ was looking away at the road towards Dellai. "Good luck, kid." Vampire snapped the reins and the horse rode on.

AZ stood in place so annoyed that what Vampire said was right. He was aware that he had spent his entire life not doing anything that mattered.

Purpose? I can't even find a true friend. What kind of a future is there for me?

It would be a long walk back.

Chapter 5

It was near midnight when AZ walked past the guards at the gate of the Perculfilus estate. He entered the large villa and looked for signs of anyone waiting up for him. He entered the kitchen. No plate had been prepared and covered for him.

No one even thought to leave me dinner.

He went upstairs and opened the door to his parents' bedchambers. He was met with both his father and his mother snoring in a reciprocal pattern as if having a conversation in their sleep. AZ shut the door quietly and went to his room.

AZ stayed up the rest of the night looking out at the cracked moon. Its shape was distorted in its three-quarter stage. Thoughts about everyone in his life ran through his mind. None of them were good. AZ felt that he had no one. He had every thing but no one.

Hours later, AZ was still sitting in the same spot and looking out into the distance. The thin line of light on the horizon cracked to separate the sky from the land. He began to see movement outside as the servants were preparing the estate for the day. Rustlings began inside the villa as well. He heard a knock on his door but said nothing. Mrs. Perculfilus entered and went over to his empty bed. She pulled her hand to her mouth in a worried expression.

"Over here, mother," AZ said from the dark corner.

"Oh, my son," she said with relief. "Thank goodness. I became worried when you were not home."

"I noticed," he told her with sarcasm. "You and father were up all night," he added with the same contemptuous tone.

"We assumed that you spent the night at a friend's. Probably Estab." Mrs. Perculfilus walked over to him with her cheeks red with embarrassment. "But there was no note to confirm it, and it was too late to send a messenger." She walked closer towards him. "Oh, AZ," she said and took a knee at the window seat where he sat.

AZ stood and shook his head at her as he walked out.

Chapter 6

AZ walked aimlessly throughout the day. He was deep in thought about his life and how alone he felt. Being left on the side of the road to die proved that he had misjudged his friendships. The words of Vampire rang in his head.

I am a mess and I need to find a purpose. I need to get out of this city. But where would I go? And with what? To do what?

Three girls walked by the seawall on which he sat.

"I can't believe she is going to be in our cadet class," the one girl squealed.

"That will be amazing," the second girl added. "I don't think that she'll have guards around her all the time like in school. So, it will be easier for us to make friends with her. Think of the parties!"

"Hey," AZ yelled. "What are you talking about?"

"Hi, AZ," the first girl said flirtatiously.

"Princess Brae is going to be in our military training class," the second replied. "We start the day after tomorrow."

"How do I get in?" he asked.

"The classes are full," the first girl told him.

"Well," the third began. "Your parents could pay for you to get in. That's what Estab's did." The three girls laughed.

The sound of the name, Estab, caused AZ's face to tighten in anger. He was still quite upset with his supposed friend for what had happened. However, AZ took this as a sign. He would go to military training and get to know the princess. She would fall in love with him as she watched him defeat Estab in everything that happened in military training, whatever that was. He would finally be able to step out of Estab's shadow and shine on his own.

I guess, my parents will be paying too! he thought.

He was quick off the wall and walked with purpose all the way back to town. A carriage would take him home from there. AZ had no problem convincing his parents to pay for his way in. They were still embarrassed as he continued to guilt them about not looking for him the other night that they would do anything he asked.

Chapter 7

AZ showed up at the military training academy. He had an uncommon awareness about him. Everything seemed exciting. As he walked down the hallway to his assigned classroom, he found that it was beaming with energy. He could hear the buzzing of teen gossip and chatter from the hallway. However, when he entered the classroom the first person he saw was Estab. Estab looked surprised to see him and was quick to come over with a big grin and outstretched arms.

No, AZ thought and walked back into the hallway.

"AZ," Estab said loudly to draw enough attention to quiet any unwanted conversations regarding AZ walking away from him. Word had gotten around that AZ had broken away from the other boys and then went missing. The story that Estab and the others told was that they spent the whole day looking for him but could not find him.

AZ kept walking down the hall, away from Estab. This was a bad idea. He grunted as he pushed the door to exit the building.

Wait. What are you doing, AZ? he asked himself. You're not here to keep being part of Estab's crew. You're here to beat him… To no longer have to put up with his bullshit.

AZ sighed and tightened his fists in frustration. He went back in and found an empty seat near the back of the class. Estab took a desk behind him.

Damn it! AZ thought.

Several of the other students looked back and forth between AZ and Estab, waiting for something to happen. Nothing did.

A female commander entered. "Good morning, cadets," she said with authority. "I am Commander Nessel and I will be your Orientation Counselor." There was a knock on the door. Two members of the Royal Guard entered and stood at attention.

"Excuse me," the princess said with an apology as she entered. "Sorry for this," she added to the other cadets and motioned towards her escorts.

Did she just look at me? AZ questioned.

"No need to apologize, your highness," Commander Nessel told her and looked to the class of recruits who were standing in honor of her majesty. AZ was among them, but Estab was slow to stand in respect.

"Please, no," the princess began. "That will not be necessary here. Here, we are equals," she said and immediately wished she could take back her words. "What I mean to say is that we are all first-year cadets and need to work together to our best individual and collective abilities." Princess Brae looked back to the commander with humility and took the empty seat nearest where she stood. It was at the front of the class.

"Dismissed," the commander said to the Royal Guard who then tapped their heels and exited the classroom.

AZ wanted nothing more than to switch seats.

"She thinks that she's so great," Estab whispered to him. "My parents say that the royal family is more concerned with the threat of The Dark Sisters than taking care of the needs of Mortua. They're not even using names anymore. We're supposed to call her Princess."

AZ ignored him. His focus was on Princess Brae. Seated in a classroom like any other student, she was even more beautiful than ever before.

The day was filled with orientation, academic lectures, and introductions. There was a short break for lunch but it too was accompanied by a lecture. AZ was relieved by the idea of not having to put up with Estab's attempts at saving face in front of the others.

"At Oh-Six-Hundred tomorrow, your military training classes will officially begin. I suggest that you get a good night's sleep and be ready for a full day, tomorrow and for the next three years. For now, you are part of the military of Mortua. Those of you who will complete your training and graduate from this program will be at officer status in the branch of your choice. And for those of you who do not," she added and seemed to look directly at AZ, "we wish you the best as upstanding members of Mortuan society. Sleep well."

Estab was glaring at the back of AZ's head. AZ gave him no attention and left the classroom quickly to avoid having to interact with him.

She thinks I'm going to fail, AZ thought as he quickly left the building.

Chapter 8

It was five o'clock the next morning. AZ had refocused.

I'm going to be the best recruit that they have ever seen, he told himself. And the princess is going to know it. Fuck Estab!

He had been in the mirror for more than an hour with slight changes to his hair, posture, buttoning and unbuttoning his jacket, untucking his shirt to appear like a rebel. The princess was going to be there. He had to make an impression if he was to have a chance over the other boys in the training.

He made his way downstairs and to the dining table. "Mother? Father?" he questioned them regarding their being present at the table.

"We wanted you to know that we are happy that you have taken this interest in military training, AZ," his mother said.

"And that we are here to support you in it," his father added. "Wherever it leads you."

"Ummm… Thanks?" AZ said, immediately wishing that he had made his tone more grateful. He ate his breakfast and headed to the coach waiting outside.

"Go!" he said to the driver with his parents waving him off. AZ could not help but smile.

My parents seemed 'proud'.

It was a twenty-minute carriage ride from the Perculfilus estate outside the main city to the closest of seven bridges that crossed into Mortua. "Hey!" AZ yelled to the driver and pounded his hand on the door. The coachman stopped the carriage. "I'll walk from here," he told the driver.

"But-"

"I said that I will walk," he told him and motioned with his head for the man to return to the estate. AZ then changed his tone and apologized. "I'll make my own way home after classes let out," he told him, with an attempt at humility.

The driver nodded. "Good luck today," he told him. "We're all rooting for you," he added with a wave. AZ walked across the bridge with his posture turned upright and cocky, looking straight ahead and not at anyone else. AZ was on a mission to be the best recruit that the military training academy had ever had.

"AZ!" Estab yelled.

Damn it!

"AZ," he said again and ran over to throw his arm around his shoulder. "I can't believe the other losers didn't want to join us. We'll be surrounded by Mortua's finest girls. I mean, I'm not sure if any will go for an outsider like you, but still," Estab told him from behind a pair of sunglasses. "This is gonna be awesome!"

AZ was unsure what 'but still' meant. However, it did not matter. He and Estab would enter the classroom as if nothing had happened and everyone would swoon.

He saw a girl who looked like the princess enter a cafe and was immediately distracted. He pictured her blushing as he walked by and did nothing more than nod and wink. The thought lifted AZ's spirit.

AZ and Estab walked through the city. Estab was talking loudly and laughing just hard enough to garner peoples' attention. However, when they reached the military training school, the guards did not pay them any mind; Not until they attempted to enter the main gates. The guards were quick to draw their weapons. AZ and Estab were immediately taken aback. The guards told them that the cadets entered through the side entrance. Neither AZ nor Estab had ever entered through a side entrance. Estab attempted to bribe a guard and asked AZ for cash. "Side entrance," the guard repeated to Estab who still expected to enter through the main gates.

After entering the training grounds through the side entrance, they arrived at the classroom with forty-six other cadets. Several of them came running up to them. Both AZ and Estab were quick to hug and slap hands with them. They had arrived. Estab, loving the attention, got even louder. AZ began searching.

"She's not here yet," Beta Poclue told him. "The princess. I know that's who you are looking for."

AZ made it seem like she was wrong and walked away. He looked at the clock. It was three minutes before nine when they entered the classroom. Beta had been wrong. The princess was already in the classroom, deeply researching through a pile of books. She had no escorts. Her hair was pulled back and her uniform was in perfect order. AZ was quick to tuck in his shirt and stand upright. He watched with pain in his heart as Estab walked over to her.

"Go away," the princess told Estab who smiled as he went into a playful bow and did exactly that.

"She hates him," Beta told AZ. "She may be the only girl other than me who does not care about his looks... or his money. Or your money. Or looks. She is more interested in knowledge." AZ looked at Beta. "She's really nice," she added. "Too nice for you." Beta went and sat next to the princess as they exchanged a laugh.

Regardless of Beta's jab, AZ was full of excitement. The Princess of Mortua could see right through Estab's charms.

I have a chance.

Chapter 9

As the weeks passed, the recruits all realized that military training was more challenging than they had anticipated. Estab had never worked this hard without reward. The princess always seemed so focused. She worked harder than any of the recruits. They found that every day she was the first one to arrive in the classroom. AZ had refocused his plans from charming the princess with winks and nods to excelling in his academic and tactical training.

"Teamwork," the commander yelled, three months into training. "You will no longer be the class of first years. You will now split and train solely with your squad. Say goodbye to the other three squads because the only time you will interact on campus will be during scrimmages."

The cadets all pushed at each other playfully.

"The squads will be chosen at random. There will be twelve cadets per squad… to start. Not all of you will make it. Any loss of a member from any squad will be the result of not only that individual but also of that entire squad. Every branch of the military for the Kingdom of Mortua is of the highest quality. Mortua has never been defeated in battle. Let it not start with you."

The last order of business for the day was the splitting of the cadets into four squads, A through D. Every cadet was eager to hear their name called. Many gave respectful hugs to the one next to them to wish luck. AZ reluctantly accepted a handshake from Estab who was still putting his best foot forward to ease AZ's anger towards him.

Commander Nessel picked names at random out of a hat. Twelve cadets had already been placed into their respective squads.

"Azurus Perculfilus," she said aloud. "Squad C."

Estab attempted to congratulate him but AZ just walked away. The newly appointed members of Squad C embraced him with a strong welcome.

"Estab Roncols," the commander called. "Squad A."

The cadets of Squad A erupted in excitement as if they had just scored the top recruit.

The commander pulled a piece of paper from the hat. "Your majesty," she said with respect. "Squad... C."

Everyone gave a respectful round of applause. In his mind, AZ led an excited greeting, but in reality, he too just kept his distance. The princess was still humbled by the applause.

The rest of the names were called and everyone had been assigned to one of the four squads.

AZ and Estab looked at each other. Estab put his fist to his other hand. AZ looked at the princess and saw that she was staring at him. She winked and gave him a thumb's up. AZ could not contain his excitement.

"Yes!" he screamed. "Squad C!"

The other members of Squad C joined in with clapping and whistling and slapping hands in the air. The other squads challenged their excitement and did the same.

"Quiet down. Quiet down," the commander yelled over all the excitement. She blew her whistle three times and all of the recruits moved into formation and stood at attention. "You will train with your squads for the rest of this semester and then formal scrimmaging will commence. Winning or losing the scrimmages is not what is graded. Technique and application of the strategies taught at this academy is what will allow you to advance to second year status. Failing to abide by the techniques of this institution will call for your immediate dismissal from this academy."

All the recruits became more serious.

The commander continued, "By now you have become aware of the strengths and weaknesses of each other as individuals. However, teamwork and military strategies will be necessary in this first round

of official scrimmages."

Chapter 10

Two months had passed. Squad C had been training well together. Group challenges ranged from getting the entire squad over a wall to building a human pyramid to be able to reach a flag. The recruits went up against one another in mock combat drills using fake weapons and others in which they went hand-to-hand.

The princess was shown no preferential treatment. She would not allow it anyway. AZ respected her for that. She did befriend Beta and another girl with whom she would discuss the lectures. She was oftentimes escorted to the grounds by a tall lanky boy who always seemed to have a strange gadget in his possession.

A cousin, AZ told himself seeing that they never held hands or kissed. However, he was still jealous.

A few of the members had made it a point to challenge the princess. She rose to the challenge with each attempt that they made.

AZ began to see her no longer as the prize of his dreams but rather as a fellow contender for top of class.

The cadets were all buzzing in the early morning. It was rumored that today would be the official day of final grading for the semester. The test would be hand-to-hand combat. But the commander had not yet said anything. They collectively marched out into the open field and stood at attention. Their commander came back after talking to another commander a distance away from them. No one broke form as their superior returned. "We will be going up against Squad A," she told the recruits of Squad C.

Yes, AZ thought with excitement. He had done well with his training and knew that Estab was in Squad A.

"Your performance today in hand-to-hand combat will give you your grade for the semester and your rank for when you return for your second year. You will utilize the tactics that you have learned here in military training to scrimmage in fair combat."

AZ watched as Squad A came onto the field. All the recruits from both squads had helmets. It was a challenge to tell who was who, but he recognized Estab as soon as he came into view. His stature as well as the cockiness with which he continued to hold himself made it obvious. AZ wanted to be the one to take him down. Estab looked at him and smiled. He motioned that he knew it was him.

The recruits were instructed as to how the scrimmage would go. Each would be given a number and when the number was called by the other squad's victor, that recruit would enter the circle and scrimmage. The commanders called the first numbers. "We will begin with number three from Squad A and number ten from Squad C."

All the recruits clapped awkwardly and cheered on their squad members. As the scrimmage progressed, the support and encouragement grew. The commanders appeared satisfied with what they were seeing. Squad A had won the last challenge.

"Four," the winning recruit yelled out.

That's my number, AZ thought. He looked quickly to see the princess cheering him on and then the rest of Squad C. He turned his attention to Estab and saw that he was screaming, "Kill him!" He was immediately enraged but cautiously stepped into the circle. His challenger was facing away from him. He ducked low to get a running start as he was stealth in his approach and was quick to attack from behind. AZ jumped and grabbed the other recruit's trunk as he spun in the air and knocked his opponent clear out of the circle. AZ was called the winner. He felt like for the first time in his life, he was truly a victor.

This is where I belong.

Adrenaline flowed as AZ was cheered on by his squad. He saw the princess excited about what had just happened.

I will take down the rest of Squad A, he thought to himself as he too yelled out in excitement of his victory.

"Seven," AZ called out.

AZ focused on calming through his own breathing as he waited for the recruit to enter the circle. He saw no movement in front of him.

Estab, he thought as he then saw a shadow and pulled his hands into fists.

Estab pulled his helmet from his head and threw it at AZ. AZ ducked and the helmet missed hitting him. He turned to face Estab.

The squads cheered on their teammates but the commanders were arguing because of Estab's tactics not being what the recruits were told to do. They were supposed to only use tactics learned in their training so that the scoring could be consistent. However, Estab had gone rogue and had chosen to fight dirty. With his helmet removed, Estab snarled and rushed towards AZ.

No, AZ demanded and sidestepped to avoid the attack. He stuck out his foot and Estab tripped but was quick to recover.

Estab was now both embarrassed and infuriated. He expressed that he did not like that misstep by letting out a scream and pounding hard on his chest. AZ knew that he had both scored a point and annoyed Estab. He smiled involuntarily with pride.

Estab launched into another attack. AZ considered a possible counter. He got low as Estab charged at him. But Estab surprised him by throwing a fistful of dirt in his face. AZ turned away from him as the dirt came into his eyes and Estab pushed hard. AZ lost his balance and tripped on Estab's helmet that was in the ring. His vision went from seeing Estab's angry scowl through the dirt in his eyes to the blue sky to blackness.

Chapter 11

AZ awoke at home. His bedroom had been turned into a hospital room. He opened his eyes to a nurse sitting at the edge of his bed and a doctor reading through some papers.

"Doctor?" the nurse whispered so as not to startle AZ.

"Tell his parents," the doctor ordered.

AZ saw flowers and cards throughout his room. The doctor pulled his face to him with his hand on AZ's chin and shined a bright light into his eyes. AZ was temporarily blinded from the brightness and was only able to see red for a few seconds. He blinked repeatedly.

"What happened?" he demanded of the doctor who had said nothing to him.

"You were-"

"Oh, AZ," his mother let out with a sense of relief. "Thank goodness you are alive." AZ's father rushed in with her.

"He was always alive, Mrs.-"

Mrs. Perculfilus shushed the doctor with a displeased look on her face. She returned her attention to AZ with a smile that showed true relief. "It has been three days, my boy," she informed him. Mr. Perculfilus turned his attention to the doctor. "Can he stand?"

"Let us see," he told him and called for assistance. Mr. Perculfilus was standing to AZ's side.

AZ let out a sound of frustration from the pain. He threw his bed covers off himself and turned to sit up. He was immediately dizzy and almost fell back. He held up his hand to stop anyone trying to assist. He waited for the dizziness to cease. It did. AZ wanted no assistance from anyone. He stood and paused again. The dizziness came and went. He took his first step in three days.

Damn it! Military training was a bad idea. I just embarrassed myself in front of the whole squad and the princess. The thoughts of defeat and self-pity were practically visible in AZ's face.

"You were knocked out during the scrimmage," his father told him.

"You hit your head and have been in a coma for three days," his mother said. The doctor motioned to correct her again but she shot him a look that stopped him. She showed him his helmet and the crack in the back.

AZ said nothing. He thought only of losing to Estab. He thought of how he had not broken free from being in his shadow.

Am I destined to always lose to Estab, he thought. I will never be anything more than the loser who pays for his fun, the outsider. I need to get out of this city.

Chapter 12

It had been a week when AZ finally left his room. He took a horse from the stables and rode with no direction in mind, lost in his thoughts.

What is the point of trying to be something in life if when you fail, you end up in the same place you started?

He rode on with still no chosen path ahead of him.

But worse, now you're in the same place and with the shame of failure. I can't show my face in that training anymore.

He was wandering aimlessly.

Guys like Estab will always move through life however they choose… And anyone who challenges them will be destroyed.

AZ pulled back on the horse. The horse neighed.

But, it did feel good to be part of something, AZ sighed.

The putrid smell of sulfur pulled at his consciousness as he realized that he was back on the narrow road to Dellai. He looked back towards Mortua and then ahead to the black volcanic dirt road and the lakes of lava. The road was empty. It looked lonely and scary. The mountains in the distance, active with red and orange lava slowly traveling down to the lakes, looked like another hopeless challenge.

He dismounted the horse and stood next to it, holding tight to the reins. He turned and looked back at the road from which he had come and saw the familiar hills, trees, and green grasses. Even though it was home, it looked less inviting. AZ knew that the unknown laid ahead of him. He stared at the empty road and focused on the blackness, the emptiness. He looked back and forth several times as the thoughts emptied from his mind.

TINKER

Must come into existence

Chapter 1

With the cracked moon full in the night sky, the climber felt his way for any crevasse on the wall of the glacier. Wind and ice pelted at him as he kicked his spiked boots into the frozen surface. He was nearing the nest that sat upon a carved out cave midway up the glacier. The chirping of the chicks became audible over the howling of the wind. Almost there, he told himself.

His face was covered and his goggles were freezing over, making it difficult to see. The climber hit a button in the palm of his glove with his middle finger. It sent a charge through the cable that connected to the goggles and defrosted them. He was able to see again and looked to the ledge above him. He could almost touch it.

He attached another safety hook into the hard surface. With it came a muffled noise as the hook pushed through the ice. Even with the howling winds, he needed to be completely quiet. That slightest sound could risk him being discovered and then most likely eaten alive by the gryphon chicks. He required a small piece of gryphon hide to test a theory. The chick would not be injured; Not for more than a minute. It would heal itself without even a thought.

That's the last spike I can put in, the climber thought as he felt his way along the shallow ridges to continue his ascent. The gloves limited his ability to feel a safe surface. He felt his nose start to twitch.

He held himself suspended just below the gryphon's nest. He paused as he listened for changes in their chirping. The chicks were still calling out for their mother and food. She was not back, which was a good thing, but they were hungry. That was a bad thing. He swung his leg up and then pulled himself onto the surface. He rolled with his eyes closed and caught his breath. He stayed quiet as he opened his eyes.

One of the chicks was over him. "Chirp!"

"Oh shit," he said and rolled in time to miss the chick's peck.

He was crawling away and looking for a hiding spot. His nose was twitching again. He found a small area in which he could be safe. As he reached it, he felt a pull on the rope. He turned and saw one of the other chicks tugging at it. The baby gryphon's sharp beak cut through the rope.

"Oh shit!" he said again as he was relying on the rope for his escape. "Think Tinker! Think!" he argued with himself as his nose twitched harder. There were three chicks in all. Each was the size of a small horse.

A loud, deep shriek came from the sky. The chicks all turned and stood at the edge of the landing. They cried loudly in response to their mother's return. With their attention drawn away from Tinker, he pulled a stick from his belt.

No more than you need, he reminded himself as he focused and the twitching stopped. He knew that he had a tendency to overtake… No more than you need. He hit the button and the stick opened on the far end into a square wire. It illuminated as it heated. Tinker came up behind the closest chick and laid his device on its hind leg. The animal was so distracted by its mother, that it did not even feel the heat and the slicing of its skin.

The chick's hide healed immediately as Tinker removed the furry piece of skin. It looked like it had never been touched. Tinker rolled up his prize and put it in his backpack. Here goes nothing.

Chapter 2

"That was really dumb," the head palace chef yelled as Tinker recounted his tale while the staff prepared dinner for the royal family. "Good thing they did not follow you back to Mortua," he said, pointing at Tinker with the sharp tip of his knife. The chef examined the cuts and the bruised and swollen eye.

"What was I supposed to do?" Tinker asked him as he followed him from prep station to prep station and followed suit by tasting everything. "The mother gryphon was coming back and I had to get out of there. My rope had been cut. So, I had to improvise."

"I'll need a steak," the chef yelled. "The coldest you can find!" A kitchen worker was quick to oblige his demand and presented a fresh cut of cold meat to him. The chef picked it up and slapped it on Tinker's swollen eye.

"Ouch," Tinker yelled.

"Keep it there," the chef ordered with his knife again pointing at Tinker.

"I knew that the mother would rescue the chick," Tinker said as he continued to follow him around the busy kitchen. "So I kind of tackled one of the chicks off the ledge. And, it just turned out that the chick learned to fly."

"The princess was worried sick," the chef added with his knife pointed threateningly. The chef saw Tinker's nervousness and put the knife down. "Three weeks you were gone, Tinker. Three weeks! And not a word."

"She wasn't worried," Tinker argued.

"You didn't tell her that you were going away, never mind that you were going to track gryphons in the north!" He continued to yell as he stirred a pot quickly. "She was in here every day asking if I saw you. At least three times a day!" The chef looked off and smiled kindly. "She's a very nice young lady," he added. Instinctually, the chef picked up his knife and turned back to Tinker. He was back to pointing with it. "And then, a monk came looking for you. That was concerning."

"A monk? One?" Tinker asked.

"Yes. Just one." The chef looked around and then leaned in. He reexamined the cuts and bruises on Tinker's now concerned face. He shook himself upright again and went back to matters at hand. He was cooking and tasting and calling over the other chefs to make sure that the dinner was perfect. "That vampire is so particular," he said to himself. "He asked for you too."

"He's here?" Tinker yelled. "I mean, a vampire. That is fascinating," he added, changing his tone for an attempt at a matter-of-fact sentiment. "I hope he doesn't leave any gifts behind this time," he added, talking to himself.

"You can't fool me, boy." the chef said with laughter. "I know that he scares you. Everything scares you."

"Not everything," Tinker argued. "Just things that I don't yet understand."

"Yes. Like how gryphons fly! Stupid boy!" The chef changed his approach. "Why did you go and risk your life like that?" he asked but received no response. "We can have a place set for you at the table if you like."

"I don't think my appearance will be very appetizing to the rest of the dinner table."

"Well, you are welcome to serve tonight if you want to get an up close audience with the Immortal. Or better, the princess."

"Why is he here?" Tinker asked, ignoring the chef's comment. He was picking off the plates that were being prepared.

The chef motioned a staff member to prepare a plate for Tinker. "You will eat after you serve the royal family and their guest."

Tinker gulped but then continued to take food off a plate made for one of the royals. A member of the kitchen staff replaced what he took and then took the plate. He reached out for a final morsel. The chef smacked his hand with the side of the knife and then pointed it at him.

Chapter 3

The dining room staff entered with plates and the best wines from Quorca. "I am sorry, Vampire…" the queen continued her conversation. "But I do not know the one of which you ask," she said to her dinner guest. "The monastery is not exactly an open door, and the Order of Naa is an independent state. We do not have jurisdiction to go in unless invited."

Thaddeus, the vampire, looked to the queen's co-rulers, her brothers, King Charles and King Jax. They both shook their heads. He looked at the princess who mounted her elbows on the table in anticipation of more of this conversation.

"Hullo," Tinker said to the princess and kept eyeing the vampire as he served her. Other staff were serving the queen, kings, and the vampire. "He's back?"

"Tinker," the princess whispered with anger, ignoring his question. "I cannot believe that you went without me."

"Well-"

"Three weeks!" she added, interrupting him. "You were gone for three weeks!" She turned to him as the jarring scrape of her chair on the hard floor grabbed everyone's attention.

"What is going on over there?" Queen Sharon asked her daughter. "Why is Tinker serving as opposed to eating?" She looked, examining him. "And what happened to your face?"

"Sorry your majesty. I needed to speak to Princess Br-"

"It was decreed last week that, in the palace, we officially stop using birth names as a protection from dark magic." The queen interrupted him. "And you can talk to Princess… when you sit and eat." She motioned for another place setting and plate.

Tinker took his seat and thanked the servants for bringing his plate. The steak looked familiar. He kept looking up at the vampire from his plate, but was quick to look away to not get caught. He made unsuccessful attempts to stop his nose from twitching.

"A birth name is a calling card. Many have adapted to being referred to by their place in life. I will be known as Vampire," Vampire told him.

The princess said nothing but ate faster. She eyed Tinker who followed her lead and ate just as quickly. She took a napkin to the sides of her mouth and wiped. "May we please be excused?" she asked the queen.

Queen Sharon looked over at their plates which were clear. "I don't see why not," she said. "But go easy on him," she said to her daughter. "Practice diplomacy... and listening."

The princess nodded to her mother's request. She grabbed Tinker from his chair and pulled him out of the dining room.

Chapter 4

The princess led Tinker through the palace with haste as he continued to recount his adventure.

"So, there I was on the back of the gryphon chick plummeting down a cliff. I knew its mother was going to rescue her baby. The mother's claws were wide and looked sharp. But I needed to make sure that she didn't crush me. I pulled back on the chick's neck and its wings opened. It started to glide and then its legs began to run in the air. It was a bit awkward, but it was flying," Tinker told her with a sense of pride. "I taught it how to fly," he marveled, lost in his reverie.

"That's a bit much," the princess told him. "How did you escape the mother?" she asked.

"Truth?" he asked and looked a bit embarrassed. "The chick lost its rhythm for a second, and I fell off into a forest of pine trees."

"That explains your cuts," she said through a laugh.

"What's been happening here?" Tinker asked her, knowing that her lighter mood meant that he was forgiven.

"Since you went… missing… the Kingdom of Tebbs again attempted to invade Dremora. We aided in her defense and the combined efforts of six kingdoms were successful in stopping the attack. But The Dark Sisters were at his side for this attack."

Tinker motioned to speak, but the princess continued to inform him of all the news that he had missed.

"So it has become official, at least in the palace," she continued without taking a breath, "that birth names are no longer to be used. It is for the protection of all. Apparently, dark magic can access your mind by calling your name."

"Are you okay with this?" Tinker asked.

Princess paused as guards patrolled past them in the wide, dimly lit hallway. She shrugged to answer the question.

"And me? What am I to be called?" he asked with a touch of sadness.

"Tinker," she told him. "It's not your real name, so it should be safe." Princess attempted to be cheerful about it, but knew that Tinker's history was a sore subject for him. She continued with kindness. "Tink. If it makes you feel any better, I don't know who my father is. I don't think anyone but my mother knows who my father is."

"Good luck getting her to confess," he said. "Then Tinker I shall remain," he agreed with a false sense of strength. His nose twitched.

Princess paused again, but then questioned Tinker. "Do you know why a monk would come looking for you?"

Tinker's eyes tightened as he said, "No idea."

Chapter 5

Tinker and Princess continued walking until they reached his chambers. He motioned to enter, but the princess stepped in front of the door to block him. She gave him a look that told him that she was not moving until he confessed his concerns.

"Now, you tell me everything," Princess demanded.

"You never actually told me why you needed gryphon hide," she added and cocked her head to suggest that she was waiting for an answer. "I know that you are up to something, but I don't know what it is." Princess smiled at him, attempting to get him to confess.

"Since the vampire's last visit, I have been haunted by something," he told her.

"There is no reason to fear him."

"Not him," he said from a downward stare. "I think he left something behind." The princess looked at him with a confused stare. "A ghost. A spirit."

"Tink-"

"I know," he rushed. "But, this ghost is angry and he is looking for something."

"He?"

"I saw him… more than once he has rushed towards me screaming that I hold a scent that reminds him of his untimely demise. His words, not mine." Tinker was scared and the princess knew it. His nose was twitching and he was looking in all directions.

"Tink-" she attempted but he cut her off.

"I don't care if I sound crazy," he told her. "I usually sound crazy," he added, which the princess did not deny. "But I am also always right."

"Usually," she corrected him.

He ignored her. "I found a weapon to defend myself if the ghost does attempt to attack me, but I need the gryphon hide to wield it."

The princess waited for him to tell her more. He did not. Tinker began working on a project which she knew meant that he would say nothing more. She made an attempt to bring him back from his thoughts. She was cut off as Tinker presented the gryphon hide. It was about a square foot in size and had a slight glow to it.

"I have a lot to study," Tinker told her as they looked closely at the underside. It appeared to have veins of electrical activity that moved with a yellow glow.

"Yes," she agreed. "I believe you do."

Chapter 6

Tinker was up hours before the sun. He had been back and forth to the palace library at least a dozen times and grew increasingly frustrated with not being able to find out any information on how to engage the powers of gryphon hide. The day had passed quickly into night and he was back in his chambers looking through various texts.

"Am I the first to attempt this?" he questioned while pulling at his hair.

"No," he heard and covered his books and the animal skin. His nose began to twitch.

"You!" he gasped at the sight of Vampire. "Why are you here? When we last saw you, you were leaving on a quest to find someone. What happened?"

Vampire stood by the window and looked up at an area of the night sky that was void of stars. He looked back at Tinker who was eager for the rest of the story. "It did not pan out."

"Well, it seems that you left your spirit sidekick here to torture me," Tinker told him. "The lack of sleep has disrupted my ability to concentrate. I can't live like this."

"I do not know what you mean, Tinker."

"A ghost has haunted me regularly since you left. He says that I hold a scent that is attached to someone who caused his demise. His words, not mine." The vampire pursed his lips. "And that is why you needed gryphon hide. To rid yourself of a ghost?"

Tinker said nothing but stood up straight. He held the gryphon skin unrolled.

"How did you muster the courage to collect that?"

"I must know if what I read is true. So I climbed to a nest and took a sample from one of the chicks. It wasn't hurt, it repaired itself immediately," Tinker said with wonder in his memory of the experience.

"And your escape?"

"I had to improvise," Tinker told him without all the details. "My original plan got cut off, so to say."

Vampire made a sound that he was not interested in the full story. "In and of itself, gryphon hide has no known effect on ghosts."

"You said I wasn't the first to attempt this. Where can I find the results of those previous experiments?" he questioned and tried to maintain eye contact and not look towards a covered table. Vampire was quick to see his impulsive eye movements and walked over to the table and pulled the cover and exposed a pulley system.

Vampire's eyes and forehead moved to tell him that he wanted an explanation.

"Gryphon hide will help me lift something heavy." Tinker walked over and covered the pulley. "I needed the pulley to bring in that 'something heavy'." He held his nose from twitching.

"And that is?" Vampire demanded and pulled Tinker's hand from his nose.

Tinker could not control his excitement and impulsive eye movements.

"Damn it!" he said, knowing that he had again given himself away.

Vampire opened the door. There was a single object in the small room with a large window.

"Is that a troll sword?" Vampire asked. "Tinker, how did you get it from the troll? It's not like a troll is just going to give you his sword. Did you kill a troll?"

"No," Tinker demanded. "Of course not."

"Then how?"

"A story for another day. Let's just say that it takes a lot of alcohol to get a troll drunk." He offered nothing more and pushed the vampire out of the small room as he locked the door.

"Well, have you used the hide to lift it?" Vampire asked him and elicited Tinker's annoyed expression.

Tinker sighed. "Of course, but the sword did not move. That's why I'm looking to see why it did not work. Where can I find the literature on these experiments?"

"You're not going to like it," the vampire told him. "The results of those experiments are among other texts regarding mythical creatures in the Monastery of The Brotherhood of the Order of Naa."

Tinker's nose began to twitch.

"As expected," Vampire said. "Well then, I will leave you to it." The vampire took a deep inhale of the air around Tinker. He held it and exhaled. He smiled at Tinker and walked towards the door. "I'm sure I will be seeing you in the future, Tinker... If you survive your own curiosities." He nodded with a cocky smile and left, closing the door behind him.

"So strange," Tinker said to the air. He inhaled deeply trying to understand why the vampire had done it but smelled nothing.

Chapter 7

Tinker knew that he had exhausted the palace library and his own as he looked for anything to help him to learn how to use the gryphon hide.

He also knew that he did not want to go to the library at the Monastery of the Brotherhood of the Order of Naa. Although he did on occasion make attempts to sneak onto the monastery grounds and in particular, the library, memories of the torture that he endured there as a child always stopped him. He had been brought there as an orphan and was bullied by the other boys and most of the monks. He found protection in one of them, a monk named Phineas. Tinker followed him everywhere. For years Phineas would go to the library to learn about The Dark Sisters, and Tinker would get lost in the silence of the place and the expansive amount of knowledge for him to absorb. Even when Phineas attempted to ignore him, Tinker felt protected by him. It was Phineas who rescued him when Monsignor Quahin was about to punish Tinker with his spiked metal glove across Tinker's face. Tinker recalled an uproar and a brawl, and then, Phineas carrying him out of the monastery as a dark figure dropped from the ceiling to block the other monks from following them.

In the fifteen years that followed, Tinker had never made it back to the monastery. He had gotten no closer than sitting in a glass boat in the harbor and looking up the cliff. He imagined and even felt himself climbing up the far side of the cliff and then pulling along the strong grasses that grew on top and hung down over the edge. He shook off the thought and returned to the present.

Time to be brave, Tinker, he thought to himself. It was his personal mantra on the occasions that he did challenge himself to overcome his fears. And this was his greatest fear. Tinker thought of the knowledge he would gain, wisdom that was so rare even the Mortua Royal Library did not possess it. If Tinker was a glutton, it was more for knowledge than food… And Tinker was always hungry. He focused on the purpose of what he was doing as he felt the cold water of the harbor as Tinker again found himself in the glass boat in the middle of the night.

This time he had to get up there. He needed to figure out how to lift the troll sword, a weapon made of dragon bone which could destroy a spirit. He needed to know how to activate and use the gryphon hide to be able to lift the sword. But now, it was more so for his quest of knowledge than for the fear of a ghost.

He set up the docking area that was outside of the grounds of the monastery. The monks did not patrol the cliffs outside their borders. Tinker had drilled a hook into the stable rock below the water level to steady the boat. Time to go, he told himself and then looked at the water. He took his nose between his thumb and index finger. No twitch.

Tinker had always felt a sense of comfort with the water. He did not understand why, and it was one of three things that he never questioned. The others were his friendship with Princess and the protection that Phineas had given him.

Tinker put his gloves on. The yellow gloves would be concealed in the dark sleeves of his hooded coat. He knew that he would have to scale the cliff and avoid the monks who were patrolling the grounds. Climbing without the gloves would only leave a bloody trail from where his hands would have been sliced, and Tinker was going to need clean hands to search through the texts in the library of the monastery. Getting in would also be a challenge, but one step at a time. Tinker took his first grips on the jagged rocks.

Tinker was focused on his hand and foot placements. He got into enough of a rhythm so that when his mind wandered, he would be less likely to miss a stable hold. And as was a norm for Tinker, his mind did wander. He thought of the gryphons. He thought of their healing process that was instantaneous. He thought of potential uses for those healing powers. But then Tinker began to worry about how humanity might choose to farm and abuse gryphons for their hides. Tinker's thoughts shook him.

He was immediately called back to the present as a grip in the rock crumbled under his touch. He lost his footing as well and he was left dangling by one hand. Tinker focused. He was able to grip with his other hand and both feet. He steadied his breathing and focused on stopping the twitch of his nose.

The falling rock could draw attention from a patrol, so he waited. He heard nothing. It seemed clear for him to continue.

Focus, Tink, he told himself. He shook his head to clear his mind and then reached for his last gripping at the top of the cliff. To get inside the monastery grounds, Tinker would have to move along the wall of the cliff. He pulled on the grasses that were well rooted and hung over the cliff.

Once inside the border of the monastery, he peered over the edge and saw two monks patrolling the grounds by the bordering wall. The reflection of the moonlight off their swords was bright enough to act as a spotlight. He lowered his head and continued to move along the side of the cliff.

He thought himself far enough away from the patrol and pulled himself up. Tinker knew the full layout of the monastery, its grounds and all the buildings. He had to make it to the main building with the lighthouse which housed the library. There were no windows in the library and only one door to enter or exit the six-story gallery. He refused to believe that there were no secret passages in or out. He expected that this visit would not allow him time to investigate. He crept until he reached the main building of the monastery.

Tinker noticed that all the monks that were on patrol were running away from the main building. There seemed to be a commotion coming from the main gate at the wall. You have other things to worry about, Tink, he told himself as he made his way undetected to the main building.

Tinker was near the door when it crashed open and a dozen monks went running out. He had pushed himself against the wall and held his breath. His nose was twitching. He slowed his breathing until the twitching stopped.

With added caution and continued pounding in his chest, Tinker stepped towards the now open door. He let out a prolonged but silent exhale as he reached into the opening. No one. He looked ahead and saw the widened doorway that led into the library.

Tinker's mind snapped back to the night when he was taken from this place. He felt Phineas lift him and carry him out the main door. Tinker was walking towards the closed doors of the library. He fumbled around in his pocket and found the skeleton key that he kept with him at all times. He heard yelling from outside and ducked behind a pillar. As he looked up, he saw the glass ceiling that held the torch on the roof atop the spiral staircase. He looked back outside and saw no one crossing.

Tinker held caution with every step as he made his way to stand in front of the library door. He took the key and slowly inserted it into the lock. He heard low clicks as the key formed itself to the lock and allowed Tinker access into the library. He stepped through and turned as he slowly shut the door and locked it again, making sure to make no noise.

Chapter 8

Tinker turned and was staring at what he remembered to be the most beautiful sight, the library at the Monastery of The Brotherhood of the Order of Naa. The golden railing that wound around the ramped walkways were adorned to resemble the tail of a serpent. Yet, as he looked higher, he mired as he saw the railing climb beyond the end of the walkway and detach from the wall and attach to the center of the ceiling which was designed to resemble the back of a beast with hints of the expansive wings of a dragon on the tops of the walls.

Tinker turned in a circle in the center of the floor and looked at the binders of all the books being made of precious metals. The entire room was aglow. Tinker looked to his right and saw a particular book with a rose gold binder under glass. It seemed to sing to him with an echoing from under the glass. He reached for the glass cover, but heard a key being inserted into the lock of the door.

Tinker was quick to hide under one of the carts used to return the books to the shelves. Four monks entered and looked around the expansive space. "All clear," one of them said as four more entered in a protective formation around Monsignor Quahin.

Tinker gasped and held his hand over his mouth. He felt his nose twitch. His heart was racing and his eyes were wide. Fear. He watched through the openings between the books as the head of the Order of Naa was escorted through the library. He watched with his hand still covering his mouth as one of the monks pulled a silver book and a wall opened. They all went through and the wall closed. The book returned to its original position.

I knew it, Tinker thought. And I'm sure there are more. His excitement drew enough of his attention to get his mind off his fear and his nose stopped twitching. But if Quahin is here, who came to the palace looking for me?

Tinker looked around but knew that he did not have time to investigate. He was there with a purpose. Being right about the secret passages allowed his mind to forget the fear of seeing Quahin and to get back into its usual analytical processing. He was there to find out about how to use a gryphon hide to lift heavy objects. But where to start?

Tinker walked over to the official looking desk where the librarian would sit and the hundreds of drawers that housed the alphabetically cataloged cards for the entire library. The cards were categorized by key words in twenty-four languages. Tinker searched through the "G" cards to find gryphon and then the "H" drawer for hide, the "S" drawer for skin, and the "P" drawer for pelt. Only three books cross-referenced gryphon with one of the other categories. And they were on three different levels and in two different languages; but all in gold binders. Tinker was cautious as he stepped along the ramp that wound upwards. He did not want to miss any of the books.

His mind slipped into a memory of him as a boy following Phineas into the library that Phineas had snuck into. Tinker did this nightly and followed him through the ventilation system.

He snapped back to the present and stood in front of the first book. It was in Alloric, a language that Tinker was familiar but not fluent in. He thumbed through it and knew that it was not going to be giving him any useful information. He wiped it clean of fingerprints and replaced it.

Tinker walked along and kept his hands in his pockets. He wanted so badly to touch that railing but knew that he wanted to minimize his presence in the library. The second book was thicker and heavier. Tinker pulled it from its place with effort and almost dropped it. He was able to keep it from making a loud thud, but looked through it as it sat on the floor.

"Full moon," he read in a whisper. "It was a full moon when I took the hide." He continued reading in silence. He looked further back on the page for a better understanding. The neuroelectric current that stimulates a gryphon's skin allows for it to lift the full weight of the animal and assist the wings to attain flight… At the time of death, the current ceases to operate and the full weight of the animal limits any movement. An adult gryphon weighs between two to three tons. However, the removal of the hide of a living gryphon is only going to be able to function after being charged by the light of a full moon and will only last for one week. These experiments are considered a case study as they have only been performed once. The hide was obtained ethically just prior to the death of a gryphon that had been mortally wounded.

Tinker counted on his fingers as his mind ran through the calendar.

The next full moon is…"tomorrow night," he said with excitement.

He heard a sliding motion and saw the books begin to move a panel away.

Chapter 9

"**S**hit!" Tinker whispered as his eyes widened in panic. He fumbled with the weight of the book to get it back on the shelf.

He looked around and saw that there was no corner in which to hide. He turned his head back and heard the footsteps getting louder. Tinker looked down and saw a duct. He was quick to pull a compact tool from his belt and opened one of the attachments. He heard voices. He turned a dial and the head of the tool expanded and clamped onto the screw holding the cover in place. Multiple voices. All four screws were out. Tinker pulled the screen and slid into the duct. He pulled the cover back and held it from the inside. He kept his eyes tightly closed and wiggled his nose to keep the twitching from making him need to sneeze.

The footsteps and the voices moved past and away from him. He heard the door of the library open and close and then heard the sound of it being locked.

Tinker breathed a sigh of relief.

"But now to get out of here," he told himself.

Tinker figured that he was on the third floor of the building and would need to get back to ground level and then climb along the grasses until he was outside of the monastery's gates. He was crawling backwards until the duct met with a joint that he was able to maneuver and now pull himself forward.

Tinker was making his way down through the ducts and looked out the screens, both into the library and to the halls and rooms outside, to know it was safe to continue. The winding ramps of the library forced a single system of air flow.

He made it to the ground level and again looked out of the screens on both sides. He was laying at floor level and listening for any sounds that would make it seem like someone was present.

Monks were outside the library. He figured that if he unscrewed the screen inside the library, he would be stuck there. And he could not go out the other way because of the monks conversing there. He was stuck.

He searched his mind for options and accepted that the only thing to do was to take a nap. So, he did.

Chapter 10

Tinker awoke in the ventilation shaft. He peered through the grate but saw no monks present inside the library or in the hall outside. He realized that it was still night because the lights in the hallways were dimmed. No sunlight shined through. He was able to release the screws from inside the duct and then listened again before pushing the screen out. He waited and again heard nothing. It seemed safe to exit. Tinker pushed the screen and cringed his face with worry that someone might have heard. The twitching started but no one came. He pulled himself out into the long entrance hall of the building and then replaced the screen and the screws.

Tinker stood with a bit of pride but then wondered what might have been in that third book. Does it hold more information about the gryphon hide that could be useful? I am just looking to lift the troll sword, but what else can I do with it? Can it help me to fly?

Tinker was lost in his thoughts as he was walking towards the front door and accidentally hit into a coat of arms. It immediately fell to pieces and made hard loud crashing sounds as the pieces spread across the floor.

"Shit!" he said as he quickly ran towards the front door.

"Stop him!" he heard as monks came into the entrance hall from three openings.

Tinker was quick out the front door and ran across the field towards the edge of the cliff. More monks appeared as the night watch was now chasing him and blocking him from his path.

Tinker changed direction and ran towards the barn and stables. He knew that if he was able to make it there, he would be able to mount a horse and ride to the wall that bordered the monastery if not all the way to Mortua. He was completely out of breath when he entered the stables and knew that the monks were not far behind. The horses began neighing at his presence and moving about their stalls. Tinker looked back and saw the monks quickly approaching. He unlocked all the stables and made strong movements to get the horses to run out. He jumped on one and held tight to the mane.

Tinker rode the black stallion with the blanket still covering its body. The horse jumped out of the stables and pushed the monks out of the way. Tinker guided the horse towards the gates of the monastery, but the animal would not agree. Instead, the horse ran towards the cliff. Tinker found himself riding along the edge of the cliff to the wall.

"Smart move," he said to the horse as they came to a stop and he dismounted. "The monks will gather at the gate to stop us from running through." The horse neighed. He turned and ran off as several other horses were running nearby with monks attempting to round them up.

Tinker placed his yellow gloves on his hands and grabbed hold of the long grasses that grew over the edge of the cliff. He made his way along the side of the cliff by holding tight to the grasses and then down to the clear boat. He pushed off and then looked up to see the lanterns moving quickly in all directions.

"Keep looking," he said with a laugh. Tinker had escaped.

Chapter 11

It was sunrise when Tinker reached his chambers at the palace of Mortua.

He did not have the option of sleeping throughout the day. Questions would arise and he would have to make it seem as though everything was normal.

Tinker would find energy in his excitement about his newly acquired knowledge and activating the gryphon hide. Tinker thought of other possible challenges that could be overcome with the use of the gryphon hide. He did not waste his thoughts on wondering, What if it doesn't work? Tinker had the utmost confidence in what he read. But then he questioned letting this knowledge out. Maybe there's a reason why this knowledge has been kept secret. Tinker decided that his purpose for this hide was to rid himself of this ghost and that would be the last of it.

He kept his eyes on the time and on the sky. He could not wait until the full moon showed itself. He ate early and excused himself to his room. Princess was in military training. So, it did not appear odd that he did not want to be in the royal dining chambers with the queen and kings.

Tinker was sitting on the floor of his balcony as the moon appeared. He began to wonder if Monsignor Quahin had sent a monk to the palace to look for him. He had been in hiding and protected for the past fifteen years. Why now?

Then, he smiled as he thought of Phineas. He remembered hugging him so hard before he left him safe in the palace. He remembered that Phineas had come back several times to check on him, but even that was over a decade ago.

The brightness of the full moon caught Tinker's eye. He unrolled the gryphon hide and waited. At first, he thought that the underside should be exposed to the moonlight. "But no. I have to place it in the same way that it would be on the gryphon."

He took the hide from the floor and laid back, putting it on his bare chest. The sensation was immediate. He felt a charge that increased to a gentle and comfortable tingling. It was midnight and Tinker had spent the past few hours thinking of all the possibilities that he could use the hide for. He had committed to keeping whatever knowledge he learned on this night to himself in order to avoid the gryphons being hunted, farmed, and killed. He could not be responsible for that.

Tinker stood with the gryphon hide still on his chest. It stayed in place without any assistance. He went into the small room in his chamber. He wrapped his hands around the handle of the troll sword and gripped tight. It was with minimal effort that he was able to lift the sword. He held it up and slowly moved it as if defending himself. Tinker laughed at his success. He walked into his main chamber and then to the balcony. He held the sword up to the moonlight and it glowed pure white.

Tinker was so engaged in what was happening that he did not hear his chamber door open. But then, he heard a laugh. He turned quickly with the sword still in a defensive position.

"Up to your usual tricks. Huh, Tink?" Phineas said as he was leaning against the doorframe with his arms across his shoulders.

"You're not a ghost." Tinker said as he dropped the sword and ran to hug him tightly. Phineas did the same.

"It's time for us to go, Tink," Phineas said as he looked at the still glowing troll sword.

TWINS

For the beast to yield

Chapter 1

"So, a Scorpio, huh?" The young man leaned in. "I could fall in love with a Scorpio." He was flirting ferociously with the attendant who ran the information kiosk at the main port of the Isles of Mawt. What she did not see was his nervous, rhythmic foot tapping. He hid it well. Yet, there was an air of panic as the usually busy harbor had become overrun with ships in mass exodus from the islands.

"Child, how old are you?" She chuckled as she took a moment to forget what was happening around her.

"Age doesn't matter in love, and I am in love… especially with eyes so beautiful."

"Boy, you are crazy!" She chuckled again and rolled her eyes, but she couldn't hide her cheeks from blushing. She did however grab her final few trinkets from the booth and the keys as she was locking it up. "Anyways, the last ship leaving today is the HSS Lockeshwar." She pointed down to the farthest pier. "Those monks came to rescue the orphans after that plague killed off half of the adults on one of the other islands. But I'm not scared. If it didn't get me yet, it ain't gonna."

"You're the best!" he said. "I'll come back for you!" he yelled with a wink as he and his brother took off towards the ship.

"Did you hear that, Axel? Should we pass off as… orphans?" he asked with a cringe at the word. "Or crew members?" Aldrick asked his twin over the sound of metal clanking.

"We are orphans, as far as we know, so let's go that route," Axel remarked as he shuffled through the busy port. "Slow down, I can hardly move." He looked over his shoulder and then motioned to their pants stuffed with loot - jewels and coins.

"Those pirates can't be far behind us," Aldrick reminded his brother. "Move!"

"Not far at all!" A pirate appeared with a sarcastic laugh and grabbed Axel by the collar. "You ungrateful bastards! You'll pay for everything you stole and die a long and painful death for taking that ruby."

"Aldrick, run!"

Aldrick reached for Axel but felt hands attempting to grab his arms. He squirmed out of their calloused hold and took off down the gangway. He focused ahead and saw the last of the monks boarding the HSS Lockeshwar. He knew that the pirates were close on his tail.

He zigged into a cluster of fishermen unloading their catch of the day and zagged past others a few yards ahead.

"We gotta get on that ship, Axel," he whispered. When there was no response, his heart raced. Although he had been able to elude the pirates, he could not find his brother. This was one of only a few times they had been apart. His despair was noticeable.

"What are you doing?" asked the monk, aggravated with the wandering teen. "Get on the ship with the rest of them! We're about to push off before this weather turns." The monk shoved Aldrick up the ramp and onto the ship.

Aldrick wanted to believe that Axel was already on the ship, but knew the truth. He scanned the pier, the port, the crowd… nothing. Panic began to creep in. "Wait… my brother," he said to no one in particular, more of a prayer than a demand.

"Hush! What was the monsignor even thinking about taking in the older ones?" The monk was ordered on this mission against his will, and he made it clear every step of the way that he was not happy to be there. "Move! I'm going to get something to eat before I get seasick again!"

Aldrick was left alone on the top deck as the other children followed directions and went into the hull of the ship. The HSS Lockeshwar pushed off from the port with a blow of its horn. The cold rain started to come down, slowly. Aldrick was still hopeful that he would see his brother making his way towards the ship. They had gotten out of stickier situations before, but the pirates were a ruthless crowd. From behind him a shadow leapt from the ship onto the port. It sent shivers up Aldrick's spine.

"Come on, Axel. Where are you?" he whispered into the rain that disguised tears running down his face.

He looked around the deck of the ship but did not see Axel. He turned his focus back to the dock and saw the pirates standing in the rain. Axel was on his knees, bleeding from his nose and mouth. "Axel!?" Aldrick screamed. Fear had jumped into his heart. "Axel!"

The pirate captain pulled his sword and raised it.

Aldrick whistled and held a large crimson ruby over his head. Even in the rain and clouds, the gem caught light and shimmered in an unnatural way. "For my brother," he yelled to them.

The pirate captain ordered the others to take Axel and to follow the HSS Lockeshwar to retrieve the jewel.

The pirate captain threw Axel to the deck of his ship.

"He stowed away on that boat with the monks and kids," the captain told the other pirates. "Catch them!" he yelled to his crew. He then turned to Axel, "You bastards are going to make us capture a ship with monks and kids? Their blood will be on your hands, and the ruby will be in mine." The captain's ire was now more evident. "You could've had a swift death, but now you will both suffer a long and agonizing death-"

"Excuse me," the masculine voice yelled up from the pier. It came from a tall, slender man, dry under an umbrella, with long, gray-black hair, with classic features and an impressive ease in his style. "I must leave for the mainland immediately. I can pay ten thousand."

The captain's eyes widened at what the man offered. "We'll be making a stop first," the captain yelled down to him as the crew prepared to disembark. "Come aboard."

Chapter 2

The rain quickly grew more intense. The sea was raging and unforgiving as the HSS Lockeshwar crossed from the Isles of Mawt to the coast. The crew all began whispering and running up to the deck.

"What's happening?" the monk asked a crew member before he could dart out of the hull where the other monks and the orphans sat praying that the storm would pass.

The crew member looked around and then leaned in. "Pirate ship," he whispered.

"Pirates?" the monk screamed. He began nervously eating his 'snack', a handful of nuts, berries, chocolates and cheese.

"Shh," the crew member told him. "You'll worry the others. Stay here. We can handle this… as long as your God is with us."

Aldrick was standing behind the monk as the crew member went up to the deck. The monk turned and screamed.

"What are you doing?" he asked Aldrick.

"Sir," Aldrick began with teary eyes. "My brother was kidnapped by those pirates. They must be coming for all the children. You know, to train all of us to be pirates."

The monk shoved a chunk of cheese in his mouth.

"It probably also means that they'll either kill all you monks or make you walk the plank and drown or be eaten by sharks."

The monk's chewing was so fast that food was falling out. Then, it slowed. "Listen boy, the monks of the Order of Naa are trained for things like this."

"Monks?" Aldrick begged. "Trained killers?"

"Some," the monk admitted. "In the Order, we each choose a particular sin that we get to indulge in without repercussions. And most choose wrath and are trained to fight."

"You're a fighter? A killer?" Aldrick asked with disbelief.

"I took a different vow," the monk told him but said no more as he walked away.

One of the crew members pulled Aldrick into a huddled whisper. "These monks are not as pious as they let on. They relish this type of aggression. You seem like a quick thinker. My advice to you is as soon as we reach the mainland, get as far away from them as possible."

Aldrick had questions, but the crew member was called to the deck, and Aldrick had to make sure that above everything, Axel would be rescued.

"Get closer!" the pirate captain demanded. "I want that stone." He turned his gaze to Axel, who was bound in chains on his knees. "And I'm gonna kill you in front of your brother." He kicked him in the face and drew more blood, before walking away. The other pirates were readying the cannons and making sure that the ropes were untangled so that they could swing their way to capture the HSS Lockeshwar.

The man with the umbrella came near Axel. He was sniffing the air. He removed his glove and wiped blood from Axel's face. He licked his finger. "Hmmm. A good lineage," he said. Axel was too beaten to have any questions. "My name is Thaddeus, and I am a vampire," he told him. "We need to get you off this ship and back to your brother."

"Why?" was all that Axel could muster.

"Help you?" Thaddeus replied, finishing Axel's question. "Because in the future, you will have to repay me. And I will be coming to collect." Thaddeus held his umbrella over him and stayed dry in the now pelting rain. "Stay here," he said to Axel. "I mean, it's not like you have a choice," he joked in poor taste and knocked the chains with his foot.

"We'll have to be closer to swing over, captain," Thaddeus heard one of the pirates say. "But we'll definitely be able to cause some damage with the cannons from this range."

"Good," the captain said. "Kill them all if you must. Just make sure that I get that boy and that stone."

Axel looked to where Thaddeus had been standing and noticed that he was gone. He looked ahead and saw the HSS Lockeshwar getting uncomfortably close. He continued to fiddle with the lock on the chains. Panic set in as he felt a hand on his shoulder.

Shit, he thought.

"Relax, boy," Thaddeus told him. Axel kept his stare straight ahead. "You need to trust me. That is our only way out of this."

Our? Axel thought. When did you get involved? Who exactly are you?

Thaddeus pulled hard on the lock. It broke. "Do not move," he ordered and placed a key in his hand. "For your feet, but not until I say."

"We are going to jump," Thaddeus told him. "But first, we need to disable this ship from continuing its attack." He looked to the door that led down to the hull. "Do nothing until my word. I'll be right back," Thaddeus told him.

"This should do it," Thaddeus said and started to kick his foot with all his Immortal strength. The wood was sturdy, but after a dozen kicks, he had broken through. Sea water shot up into the hull. Thaddeus ripped the broken boards away to make a bigger hole that would not be able to be fixed while the pirates fought against the HSS Lockeshwar. He ran back up to the deck.

"Load the cannons. On my mark," the captain yelled.

"Captain!" One of the pirates came running in a panic.

"Get ready," Thaddeus told him.

The pirate captain blew a whistle. "To the hull," he ordered. "Make haste!"

The entire crew went into the lower hull of the ship.

"Now," Thaddeus told him. Axel unlocked his ankles, and they ran for the ropes.

"We're too far away," Axel yelled to Thaddeus but continued running. Thaddeus grabbed hold of a rope and swung out over the water. Axel did the same. As the ropes swung to their furthest potential, they both let go.

Axel closed his eyes before hitting what he expected to be water.

Instead, he felt a hard pull and then sensed like he was thrown forward. He landed alone with a hard thud and a roll on the deck of the HSS Lockeshwar. Aldrick was there to help him up. They embraced quickly as the crew and monks came around them with weapons drawn.

"No! No! This is my brother. The one that we were going to save." Aldrick hugged him again. The crew and the monks wondered how Axel made that leap. But more importantly, they realized they were safe from the pirates. Several of the monks seemed disappointed in the lost opportunity to go to battle.

They all watched as the pirate ship sank, almost majestically. There was a green aura around the whole scene. The pirates that managed to get to the smaller lifeboats were making hopeless attempts to navigate their way through the storm and the waves.

Chapter 3

The storm was moving so slowly that it seemed to have stopped atop them, as it continued its assault of rain, hail, and wind. The HSS Lockeshwar was making its way around the Kulkaati Peninsula to Mortua. The captain called a meeting of his crew and the head monk to let them know that the glow behind the pirate ship was in fact a sharp line of light that was moving… fast. Its path was erratic, but it was most definitely moving towards them. The news brought with it an ominous feeling which fell over the crew.

"A Ghost Ship?" the monk, Brother Jacob, questioned with a sense of frustration. "What's next?" he asked, as if blaming the captain for the current situation.

"I would not worry about what's next," the captain told him. "Focus on what is coming for us. A Ghost Ship is a vessel that was cursed by Water, the Ruler of the Seas."

Brother Jacob looked at the crew, who all stood with jaws agape and eyes widened. "What should we do?" he asked, now understanding that he should be concerned for the safety of everyone on board.

Brother Jacob was told to keep the children quiet and down in the hull. The crew too stayed off the deck of the ship. Nautical legend had taught crews to make their vessel appear uninhabited so that the spirits of a Ghost Ship would have no interest in coming aboard to steal their souls. The few crew members that stayed on deck were there to make sure that the ship did not capsize in the storm. Yet, they too stayed on their hands and knees and below the rail of the deck. They did not want to show any movement.

"Stay down," one of the sailors whispered to the pair of teenagers who were moving about the hull of the ship. "And stay quiet!" he demanded. Seafaring legends were at the forefront of their collective fear.

The Twins did not know what was happening. They looked at each other and shrugged their shoulders. What could be worse than pirates trying to kill you?

"Ghost Ship," one of the other sailors told them.

They again shrugged their shoulders.

"It's a cursed ship. One destined to float forever as a reminder never to cross Water, the Ruler of the Seas. Tales had it that the ship found its way into the Mermaids' sacred burial place, hoping to steal their jeweled remains." The sailor recounted the legend. "Water took full offense. She made sure that everyone on board was killed and left it to wander. It is said to seek out and devour the lives aboard any vessel that is caught in its path."

The teens looked at him with disbelief. Axel, the more superstitious of the two, felt and squeezed something just below the collar of his shirt. His brother took his hand away and attempted to change the subject.

"Hey?" Aldrick asked a sailor. "If I had to unload… something of value… and did not want any questions asked, where would I get the best payout?"

"This storm has us veering to Pemeta instead of Mortua. Vendors in Mortua would give you a fair price."

"And Pemeta?"

"Nah. Pemeta sucks. It's a shit town," he added. "Dellai. That's the place where you would have made out best. All the rich business folk. Those guys will overpay just to show off."

Too bad we are not headed to Dellai, Aldrick thought. "Thanks."

"Why are you asking about other places or selling anything? Anything you carry with you when you enter the monastery will belong to the brotherhood and you won't be let out until you have been brainwashed to be part of a mercenary army."

"They get to eat?" Axel asked. "And a bed?"

"Yes."

"Then it's better than anything we've ever known," Axel told him.

"Are we really going to trade in our freedom for a meal and a bed?" Aldrick followed.

"I guess not," Axel agreed. "We need to get off this ship," Axel whispered to his brother.

Aldrick nodded. "A distraction," he said. "Fire."

"Yeah," Axel agreed. "But a small fire, right? Just a distraction, not a destruction."

The Twins looked around. Everyone's head was down. Fear had taken control of the emotional state of the ship. They needed to keep moving. The teen boys made their way back towards Brother Jacob. He seemed to be a sloppy and uninspired monk.

"Shouldn't we douse that flame?" Aldrick asked regarding the candle that the monk kept lit out of fear.

"With the Ghost Ship and all," Axel added.

"What do you mean?" the paranoid monk begged. The ship caught a wave and was pushed with a hard thud against the outer wall. Brother Jacob squealed as he was knocked to his hands and knees. Aldrick kicked the candle, which rolled past the nervous monk and onto a blanket.

"Fire!" the Twins yelled.

The blanket caught fire. It would have been easily put out, had it not been for the fear and paranoia that were running high in the hull of the ship.

Chapter 4

The fire was enough of a distraction to allow the teens an unseen exit up the stairs and onto the now empty deck of the ship. The wind was pushing hard but the rain had stopped. As the boys forcefully pushed open the door, they were greeted by the most unexpected sight that was truly something to fear. A swirling curtain of light was just about to cut through the HSS Lockeshwar. It was nothing like what they had imagined. It appeared as a murky, transparent, greenish veil that floated through, and beyond anything with which it came in contact.

"What the fuck?" Aldrick asked rhetorically. He motioned to step towards the moving specter that was the Ghost Ship.

"There they are," announced one of the monks, angered by the boys for not obeying the rules. "These two will be spending a lot of time in the hole during training." Three other monks, all strong, muscular men held the same no nonsense anger on their faces.

"I know what you do with the orphans," Aldrick said. "You turn them into an army. You're not monks coming to save us. You're as bad as the pirates," he yelled.

"Nah," one of the monks said as he stepped forward. "We're worse."

Aldrick and Axel looked at one another. They turned to run and were met with a blinding green light that curtained them from the monks. They could not move at first, but after a few seconds, they were able to turn. They turned to see the monks' faces drain of blood in fear attempting to hold brave expressions but then retreat back to the hull of the ship. They stood in the middle of a translucent glowing ship that was crossing the HSS Lockeshwar. The ship was moving through the Lockeshwar and around them. It made both of them feel the need to draw their swords and to stand back-to-back. They were quick to survey the areas around them.

"Nothing," Axel whispered.

"Here either," Aldrick informed him. They were not on the Lockeshwar anymore. They walked towards the back of this new ship and looked out in the direction from which they had come. They saw through the deck of the HSS Lockeshwar and into the hull. They saw the frightened crew and passengers aboard.

Axel turned his head and saw, at the bow of the Lockeshwar, a few more children holding tight to each other. "It's like a knife cutting through the ship."

"A knife of light," Aldrick added.

"So how are we in a sliver of light…" Axel challenged.

"That houses a full ship?" Aldrick finished his brother's thought. "We're between worlds," Aldrick said as he realized what his brother was about to say.

"Yes."

"Does that mean that we're dead?" Aldrick asked.

"I don't think so," Axel told him and walked towards the passengers of the Lockeshwar.

Axel looked back at Aldrick with concern. Aldrick shared his worry but then turned and looked to see that the stern of the Ghost Ship was quickly approaching.

"Axel!" Aldrick screamed.

Axel saw that no one on the Lockeshwar noticed them; they were truly in a different dimension. Axel ran back and grabbed hold of his brother's arms to be sure that they would not be separated.

The light became blinding as the back wall of the Ghost Ship met up with them.

"I thought that the light would have just rushed past us," Aldrick said to Axel as they remained trapped in the light of the Ghost Ship.

"I was just hoping that it wouldn't burn us to a crisp," Axel replied.

The Twins realized that they were continuing on with the Ghost Ship which had broken contact with the HSS Lockeshwar. They were being moved along by the light.

"This was definitely not one of our better ideas," Axel said.

"Too late to worry about that now," Aldrick reminded him. "We're already here."

The Twins moved forward, away from the border of light that made up the back wall of the stern of the ship.

"So weird." He shrugged his shoulders. "Guess we should check this thing out."

The Twins rarely accepted fear and worry. Everything that they had gone through in their young lives, they did together. They were sure that the other would be there, that he would even sacrifice himself for his brother.

They stepped cautiously throughout the Ghost Ship. They walked on the floorboards made of pure light. They found no one. There were no evil spirits looking to steal their souls and torture them for eternity.

The Twins came back out onto the deck. They walked into the open space and saw the HSS Lockeshwar in the distance. The storm appeared to have calmed. The boys looked ahead and saw the thin line of light on the horizon.

"Aldrick?"

"I think that we should get off this ship in daylight."

Axel was looking around with concern. "But I do not see land anywhere. And there is nothing on this ship that will help us in the open seas."

Aldrick sighed in agreement with his brother. "We have some time," he said. "Let's see what happens between now and then." The Twins spent the next six hours looking out in all directions to see if they spotted land. They explored the entire ship. As daylight grew, the details of the ship became less visible. There was no one on board, nor lifeboats or buoys.

Axel said with building frustration, "Why call it a Ghost Ship if there are no ghosts?"

"Because the ship is a ghost," Aldrick reminded him.

"Yeah," Axel said, knowing that his brother was right. "But it would just make more sense to me if the ghosts of the sailors were still on board. I mean, that's what they tell people."

"I guess, they lie," Aldrick told him. "Come on. It has to be almost noon."

Chapter 5

The Twins stayed on deck and looked up at the sky. The sun was just about at its highest position.

"Axel?" Aldrick asked. "Do you feel…"

Aldrick and Axel fell from the sky into the water below. As the sun hit its peak, the green glow was completely gone from sight.

"What the hell just happened?" Axel asked as they came to the surface.

"The ship disappeared from underneath us!"

They felt pressure around them as the familiar glow began to emerge from the air.

"Swim away!" Aldrick ordered and began swimming as quickly as possible. Axel followed him.

Within one minute of them falling into the sea, the glow of the Ghost Ship began to have a very slight appearance. As they continued to tread water, the Twins watched as the glow became more vibrant and more distant.

"We couldn't see it because we were on the ship, but it must have been fading from sight as it got closer to noon," Aldrick said as the waves bobbed them up and down.

"And when it was completely invisible, we fell off it," Axel added to the theory. "That means that the original sailors must have fallen off as well…"

They looked at each other and said in unison, "And drowned."

"We're screwed," Axel said.

"Well," Aldrick began. "We're not just gonna tread water here and die. The crew member told me that Pemeta was the closest port."

"We traveled through the night and the morning on the Ghost Ship and the continent is west," Axel added. "We swim west."

They looked up at the sun and decided together which way was west. They began swimming at an easy pace. They changed their strokes to glide on their backs, to side swim, to traditional freestyle and breaststroke. The jewels and coins that they still held in their pockets added a significant amount of weight to them.

"No," Axel said. "Those pirates almost killed me. We are keeping this treasure and selling it to make a life for ourselves." He saw Aldrick's hands drop underwater. "Don't you dare, Aldrick!"

"Alright," he told him in a forced agreement.

The Twins had continued swimming with still no land in sight.

"Aldrick?" Axel questioned.

"Yeah, me too," Aldrick replied, knowing that his brother was going to say that he was getting tired. He figured that they had been swimming for at least two hours. Both of them were gliding on their backs. The weight of the treasure still in their pockets had become too much to bear.

"We have no choice," Axel said.

"Okay," Aldrick agreed, "but not all of it."

They each pulled jewels and coins out of their pockets and held them up out of the water.

"Goodbye beautiful life," Aldrick said as he released the riches from his hands.

"Goodbye house in the country," Axel added and did the same.

They again reached into their pockets and dropped more treasure. Aldrick was unaware that the large ruby had fallen out and sunk fast to the bottom of the sea.

"That should be enough," Axel said with disappointment.

There was silence, except for the water going across their ears. They looked at one another and forced smiles. The boys thought differently from most. They had been on their own since being abandoned by their parents and fending for themselves since they were five years old. They had been kidnapped by a slave trader who then sold them to the pirate captain. The boys knew pain.

Aldrick and Axel had only one thing worth living for: each other. They learned that they could get through this life together. They refused to see themselves as orphans; it felt too much like being victims.

"Our life sucks," Axel said.

Aldrick was quick to change his position and swim to his brother. "What? We have each other." Aldrick was fumbling under the water.

"What are you doing?" Axel asked him.

"Take off your pants," he told him as he was treading water again and tying knots in the foot holes. Aldrick pulled his pants over his head and caught the air which allowed them to inflate. He held the waist and rolled it to trap the air. He also made sure that he felt for whatever treasure was still in his pockets. "A float," he told his brother with a sense of joy.

"Yeah," Axel replied with a renewed sense of optimism. "Good idea." He too was now floating on his pants.

"But you are right, Axel," Aldrick told him. "Our life has not been as easy as the ones that we see other people living." He was looking off with a vacant gaze. "We have had to scrape for every crumb that has come our way. But I promise you… when we get back on dry land, things are going to change. We are going to be the ones who make the rules. We are going to be the ones who choose how we live. No more scraping by." This time, it was he who was holding the metal around his neck.

Axel had not said a word.

"Axel?" Aldrick asked, worried that his brother had drowned.

"Do you promise?" Axel asked him.

"Yes," Aldrick said. "Absolutely."

"Good," Axel said with a smile. "Then, turn around."

Aldrick turned and saw what Axel was smiling at. He saw land. "We made it." He kissed the metal.

"Not yet," Axel told him, "but we're almost there. Come on."

Chapter 6

The boys had made it to shore. They walked far enough from the break of the surf and dropped on the beach. They were panting hard from exhaustion and dehydration but looked to one another with smiles. They were alive and they were together.

They were unaware of the man who had approached them and dropped a jug of water between them. The Twins did not have the energy to fully react. Yet, they reached for their swords.

"Don't bother," the man told them. "I'll have sliced through you both before either of you could raise your blade." The boys relaxed their grips. "Drink," he ordered and dropped a second jug. "And then, we'll get food."

They sat up and began to chug the water.

"Slow," the man ordered but it was too late. The Twins were already coughing from the water backing up into their lungs. They continued to drink but at a slower pace, with breaks and full swallows.

"You boys look like you can use a hand," the man said. He was dressed in a patterned overcoat with tails. He had an oversized man with bulging eyes and a girl with a unicycle beside him. "It's pretty dumb of you to wash up here."

"Pretty formal attire for this time of day," Axel joked as he coughed on the words.

"We are heading to the courthouse. Regardless, you are dumb to be here," the man told them. "Pemeta is not a friendly place."

"We've never known a friendly place," Axel told him.

"My name is Celias Torreau, and I own a circus that is traveling through here. We are not staying." He offered no more. "I'm sure that you are hungry. Let's get you food."

The Twins helped each other up from the sand.

"And clothes," the girl with the unicycle added. "And showers."

Chapter 7

Celias did as he had promised. The boys were fed and showered and clothed in simple clothing, so as not to draw attention. The boys thanked them and offered some coins from what they had left in their pockets.

"Thanks kids," Celias told them as he refused the coins. "But, in the circus, everyone is welcome. We're family here and we look out for each other." The Twins looked at each one another, confused by the word family. "The religious zealots in this town have arrested some of my people for no reason whatsoever. That's why we're heading to the courthouse. We just have to get them out somehow and then we'll be on our way."

"Way where?" Aldrick asked.

"We're heading to Dellai," he said.

Aldrick sat up straighter and felt what was still in his pockets.

"Can we come with you?" Aldrick asked.

"You want to join the circus?" Celias asked.

"We want to get to Dellai," Aldrick told him. "And besides, you said that we are family," he added with a playful nudge.

"Yeah," Celias agreed with a giggle.

The Twins looked at one another with excitement.

"But first, we gotta go into town and get our people out."

Pemeta was a strange place. There was an air of oppression. The main streets were filled with people and traffic. Hoisted high above the congestion of the streets were individual cages with people screaming for mercy. They had been tried for minor crimes and put on public display.

Aldrick and Axel looked up at the cages that lined most of the block on the streets. They listened as those who were in them called down for water and food. No one else looked up; no one offered any assistance. Aldrick spotted a monkey climbing up one of the poles to the cage that held one of the circus performers. Several of the people were dressed like circus performers. The boys each reached for their own necks and felt for the pendants concealed beneath their shirts.

They continued to follow Celias through the crowd and crossed a wide concrete bridge that was adorned with life-sized statues. The statues were all religious in nature and showed angels triumphing over evil. Axel hit Aldrick on the shoulder as he recognized one of the statues. Celias and his colleagues were unaware that the boys had stopped. The Twins were lost in their gaze at the statue of the Archangel Michael.

"Axel," Aldrick whispered and gripped his pendant. He pulled it out of the collar of his shirt and was elated to see that the statue was in the same pose as the image on their pendants. "Is that-"

"Yes," Axel answered as Aldrick walked up and put his hand on the foot of the statue. Axel was a step behind his brother.

"Hands off!" yelled a parishioner. "You are desecrating that statue."

"No," Aldrick argued. "He protects us. We are praising him," he told him as Axel showed him his chain with the image of the archangel on the pendant.

The man blew a whistle three times and the other people on the bridge ran. The militia stormed in from both sides of the bridge.

"What's happening?" Aldrick argued. "We've done nothing wrong!"

"Three whistles," one of the men argued back. "Desecration. You will be tried for your insolence." The boys were both knocked out with a blow to the back of the head.

Chapter 8

"Axel," yelled the familiar voice. "Axel!"

Axel awoke to his brother's screams. He looked out and saw the street two stories down from where he found himself. He was in a cage, suspended high above the main street for all to see, mock, and judge.

"Axel," he heard again and lifted his head. Aldrick too had been locked in one of the suspended cages. He was rocking his cage back and forth so that he would be able to reach Axel's cage. What he would do after he reached and grabbed hold of it, he did not know. However, he did know that they would think of something together.

Axel pulled himself into a kneeling position and held the bars of the cage. He squeezed his arms out to be able to grab hold of Aldrick's cage when he swung it close enough. "Almost," he yelled to him.

A sparse late-night crowd had stopped on the street and watched in awe as the cage was making a greater arc. Aldrick pushed and pulled his body with all his might. He hit the cage behind him. The man in it grabbed hold of the bars. Aldrick turned and saw it was one of the circus performers.

"Do it for all of us," the man told him and pushed him off.

Aldrick's cage swung hard to a collective gasp from the crowd. He began laughing as he knew that the force with which he was moving would be enough to crash him into his brother's cage. Axel grabbed hold and Aldrick did the same.

"What now?" Axel asked.

"No idea," Aldrick replied. "Just keep swinging!"

The Twins were swinging their cages together and then realized at the same time that if they pushed off each other, they would crash into the next cages. They found that those who were locked in the other cages were now doing the same thing. They were all swinging their cages.

"The chains will break and when you hit the ground, the cage will burst open as well," Axel yelled out. One by one, the cages did just that. The aged links that held them above the street broke and the cages crashed down to the ground. Axel and Aldrick helped the performers to their feet. They had not eaten or had water for days. In all, eight cages crashed and opened before the militia was able to put a stop to it. This included the five circus performers and a local woman who ran away as quickly as possible. They all escaped into the darkness of the night.

Chapter 9

The circus caravan waited for the escaped performers outside of the city limits. The performers, along with the boys, arrived at the designated location written on the note that the monkey had delivered earlier that day. Once they were settled and fed, the performers recounted the tale of how the Twins led the escape.

"That was some act," the ringmaster of the circus said. "You should think of joining us," he added. "A bed and three square meals a day. You'll have to work for it, of course."

"It's a good place to hide for a while," Axel agreed.

"We've not had good experiences with joining groups in the past," Aldrick told him. "Slave traders, pirates, and those crazy monks?"

"Not for us," Axel added.

"It's not like that," the ringmaster told them. "We work together, but your life is your own. Every misfit here has made this their home, but we are free to leave whenever we choose."

"A circus," Aldrick said to Axel as they watched the kindness being shown.

"A family," Celias reminded them.

The Twins said nothing.

"Well, I can use some strong hands to keep this caravan moving quickly. You're not the only ones they'll be looking for. And I can work you into an aerial act. We have two weeks booked in Dellai."

The Twins looked at one another and smiled.

"Deal," they agreed and shook.

GHOST
Stones of eight

Chapter 1

The station felt familiar. There were trains and tracks and crowds hustling in different directions. The light that poured in from the windows had an unnatural greenish golden hue to it that made everything appear to have added tints and highlights.

He looked at his hands and his clothes. They too had the same greenish golden coloring with added shadows outlining his fingernails and wrinkles in his skin. A mirror, he thought, hoping to see his reflection. Yet, as he looked around he could not find a reflective surface.

A voice made several announcements over a loudspeaker, in what seemed to be different languages. However, the more announcements he heard, the more familiar the words became. Other patrons in the station walked by; many were human, but others were species that he had never seen before.

A dream, he told himself until one of the other patrons, a half bison - half man accidently bumped into him and pushed him back. The physical sensation was real; of that he was sure, but not of where he was or what was happening.

An overhead announcement echoed through the busy station. "All of those from Dimensions Three, Twenty-Seven, and Eighty-Nine who have been through the orientation process must proceed to Platform Five and be on board the train for immediate departure. Please have your ticket ready for stamping."

A crowd of characters rushed towards a train. He looked to see that he was standing at Platform Four and started to follow that crowd.

"You! You, there!" someone yelled out. He continued walking. "Hey! I'm talking to you." The voice got louder, as if right next to his ear. He turned to see an officer with a clipboard. "You cannot leave the platform yet."

"I- I-"

"Yes. You. You haven't been through orientation," the officer informed him.

"I- I don't even know where I am," he told the officer, who shook his head and let out a frustrated sigh.

"You died and now, you have to be oriented as to how to proceed into the next level towards Enlightenment." The officer looked at him with a sense of annoyance as added confusion took over and showed on the dead man's face. "You died," the officer said harshly. "Come with me," he added and turned to walk away.

As the officer moved through the crowd towards his office, he explained the process of what was to follow. The man remained in place, shocked by what he had heard. He looked at his hands again and then at all the other newly deceased, who were rushing by in all directions. The officer stopped when he realized that the man was not following him and whistled for him to catch up.

Instead, the man turned and ran in the opposite direction, past various lines of patrons; most of them were orderly and as their lines were long, he was able to duck between individuals that responded by moving closer together. He looked back to see that the officer pushed through them and continued his advance. He ran to a shadowed corridor and hid.

I lost him. The man stood in the dark opening which led to staircases that went up to the street level. What the hell is happening? He replayed the officer yelling callously, "You died!" but he heard it with a stronger emphasis. Died? he questioned.

He thought back to what had transpired. Quick visions ran through his mind. Paris. Night. The sound of a gun firing.

Chapter 2

The dead man walked along the dark echoing corridor and came out from his hiding spot. He quickly moved along with a group heading up the stairs.

I have to get out of this station.

He was at the street level and made his way towards the exit. A bright golden light was shining in through all the openings.

"Nope," he heard and was pulled back in by the officer. "You are presently in an undefined state and are not allowed to go anywhere until you are stamped."

"Then, stamp me," the man demanded.

"I would have had you come with me and did what you were supposed to do, like I asked. But instead, you decided to run and now you are tagged as a volatile spirit. You will need to be detained and counseled before you can move on."

"You said that I died." He drew the attention of some others nearby. They started to look quizzically at one another.

"Am I in Hell?" the man asked. "I am in Hell." He conceded to the thought.

"Not yet," the officer told him. "But everyone must go through Hell before entering Heaven and then into Enlightenment… Or repeat your karmic cycle to gain the understanding that will get you into Enlightenment."

"I'm sure that there is someone I can talk to about this," the man told the officer, easing off his failed approach at intimidation.

"Yes," the officer agreed. "Me!" He slapped a pair of cuffs on the man who reacted with total surprise. The officer turned dials and pressed keys on a tool that he pulled from his belt. "The first letter," he said and then turned the second dial. "The year that you died," he added while referring to a dirty piece of paper. "Number nineteen that year." He looked up with no empathy as he continued to explain. "From this point until your trial and arraignment, you will be referred to as D.91.19. That is your name until you are given either a new one or your previous name by the Holy Court."

"What?" D.91.19. begged. "I have a name," he yelled but could not think of what it was. "Where are you taking me?"

"I'm sure you've seen the inside of a cell once or twice before," the officer told him and pulled him along by the cuffs.

Chapter 3

D.91.19. found himself suspended in an olive-colored haze. The area beyond the haze felt void, with no sound, no light, and definitely no presence of life.

He finally heard a rumbling and then felt the pressure of the haze release. Before him stood a curvaceous woman of significant age. Her clothes were fitted as tightly as her skin.

"Well, hello." D.91.19. attempted to charm her with flirtation.

"Save it, kid," she told him. "My name is Mavi. I control everything between the dimensions, and I may be able to help you out of this mess."

"Oh! Thank you, Mavi! I knew that there had to be someone who would hear me out. I don't know where I am."

Mavi raised her hand to signal to D.91.19. that he should stop talking. Mavi smiled and sauntered over to a cushioned chair that stood beside a small table. A purple-colored cocktail in an etched coupe glass sat upon the table. Mavi relaxed herself into the chair and then reached ever so seductively for the glass. She took a sip and then licked her lips.

"Think of it as the in between," she told him. "Gokyuzu," she replied. "The cloud city that sits between dimensions. It is a transfer point for some and a holding station for others who await trial."

"Like Purgatory?"

"Some call it that," she said and took another sip. "It's a transfer depot really. Everyone and everything comes through, gets processed, and then moves on." She stood and walked around D.91.19. as she examined his stature. "But… then there are those like you. The angry ones. The rebels who cause problems and a ton of paperwork." Mavi was standing in front of him. "The ghosts."

D.91.19. listened intently, hoping that he would get some information that he could bargain with.

"Your case was brought to me because-"

"My case?"

"Spirits who go on the run become ghosts. Like you, they feel they were robbed of their lives; that the way they died was unfair. I reviewed your file, your life. It mostly sucked and it was mostly your fault." He held his gaze at the floor. "And from the things I read in there, the road to redemption will be a long one for you. But I can help you," she whispered leaning in. "After you help me." He looked up with determination. "It seems that you have the potential to bring to me something that I want… Someone actually." She waited. "Thaddeus," she said and watched his eyes for a reaction.

D.91.19. paused in thought. More of the visions flashed by. Night. Pont Louis Philippe. The sound of a gun firing. Thaddeus. Blood. He attempted to control his emotions but failed. "He murdered me," he told her.

"He freed you," she argued. "Your life wasn't so great. Now you have the opportunity for a fresh start. And it only takes one little thing… Bring me Thaddeus, the vampire," Mavi demanded.

Chapter 4

"What exactly is this new start you're promising? How do I get out of this station?" he asked Mavi as they walked along a pure white corridor with doors lining both sides.

"You were only supposed to transfer. But you refused to let go of your past and have now entered into a state of ghosthood." A hooded figure approached and held out a form for Mavi to sign. "Ghosts remain in such a state until they do two things. One: complete a task for someone else. And two: decide to move on. Only then will your case be heard in the Holy Court."

D.91.19. looked ahead in thought. He changed the subject. "Why are you here?" he asked.

"I choose to be here," she told him. He awaited more, but Mavi did not give any. "Why do you want me to bring you Thaddeus?" he asked, again attempting to get information. Mavi again said no more.

Mavi stopped in front of a door midway down the corridor.

"Time moves differently in different dimensions. You may not be familiar with anything." D.91.19. had a cautious expression on his face. "You're a resourceful lad," she said, stroking his cheek. "You'll figure it out."

"How do I find him?"

"Things will become familiar to you. You will start to remember." Mavi opened the door and D.91.19. saw the swirling portal. He maintained his concerned expression, cautiously stepped forward, and was pulled into the vortex.

Chapter 5

As he entered the portal, he found himself in a void. There was a clear delineated path that he walked and at the end was daylight. But different from the greenish hue of the light in Gokyuzu, this light had a familiar and natural golden quality. He looked to the cloudless sky and saw a moon lingering. It was cracked and resembled the head of a goat. I don't remember that. He stared out of the opening and saw a field along a wide river. Boats flowed in each direction. Huts and windmills sat scattered on flat structures that rose from the water. This was not the world that he left. He quickly turned back, feeling that there had been a mistake, but the portal had closed.

It was not until he looked across the landscape that he recognized the familiar structure on a distant island. Sacre Coeur, he thought, recognizing the cathedral on the hill of Montmartre. Paris. He looked around for signs of anything else that was familiar but found nothing. Time more than marched on. This is not the Paris that I remember.

D.91.19. could not believe that so much had changed. He could only remember the past two days at the station. Yet, everything in front of him told him that centuries had passed.

He stepped forward and found himself levitating just above the water. He truly was a spirit, unbound to physical constraints. It would have been helpful if someone explained these things to me, he thought. He decided to attempt to rise in the air and look down at the landscape. I'm a ghost. I'm sure that I can.

As he looked up and attempted to climb higher in the air, he found himself awkwardly stepping and tripping on the emptiness. He lost his concentration as his temper flared. He fell back towards the water. He hit it and went through, but the water was not disturbed. He stopped, pulled himself out and wiped his transparent form as if to dry himself out of instinct, but felt nothing. He heard laughing, "You're doing it wrong."

"Who's there?" he yelled, annoyed that someone was laughing at him. "Where are you?" He became more enraged as he continued to search for the person laughing at his expense. His ego would not accept this.

"I sense your energy, ghost," the voice continued.

"Don't call me that," he demanded.

"But that is what you are," he heard but could not see anyone nearby.

"Damn you! Reveal yourself," he screamed.

He continued to search to find who was talking to him. He found himself flying around and moving fast, without thinking about it. He was high above and looked down to see the wide river snaking its way through the landscape. Just under the water was the city that he remembered. A few towers shot out of the water and served as homes for the river dwellers. Huts had been set on the flat roofs of taller buildings, but the Paris that he remembered was now completely submerged in the river. This was Le Marais… my home.

"I'm sorry, ghost," he heard the voice say.

"Who are you?" he demanded as his thoughts came back to the voice that he heard.

"I am Kaas. I have the ability to communicate with beings like you."

"Are you alive?" he asked.

He heard laughter. "We are all alive, even those like you without bodies," Kaas replied. "It's just that we exist in different dimensions."

"Kaas?"

"Yes."

"What year is it?"

"The year is 4001."

"What happened to Paris?"

"Paris? That is what this place used to be called. But now, it is known as The Wastelands because marshes that border the river are too unstable to support building. Only the hilltop islands are able to maintain multiple structures, and they fall on a regular basis. The huts that you see on the ancient rooftops and the boats that move along the river… That is Paris, the sunken city."

D.91.19. was quiet, thinking about how centuries had passed him by in what felt like only a few days. He was lost in his thoughts about everything he had missed. My city is a ghost. He became infuriated and screamed. The wind blew hard and knocked the nearest hut into the river.

"I do not suggest you take that path," Kaas told him with a nervous quiver.

Ghost I will be, he accepted. He needed help. And Kaas knew the things that he needed to learn. But also, he did not know where Kaas was and could not force him to give him what he needed. "Okay," he agreed. "But I need you to show yourself to me."

A breeze blew from the north.

Montmartre.

Chapter 6

Ghost continued to follow in the direction from which the breeze came. The elevation of Montmartre had allowed it to be spared from the rising waters of the Seine River. The hilltop island was overrun with people and debris. Rats ran in the shadows searching for food, but oftentimes, they were trapped and became a meal.

Ghost reached what seemed like the source of the breeze. This is it, he thought as he hovered slightly above the street in front of a chartreuse door. As he waited for it to open, a frail young woman walked through him. She shivered but kept moving. At that moment, he remembered that he was a spirit, so he decided that he would go through the door. He closed his eyes as he pushed forward. It was a simple and effortless experience. Ghost felt an elated sense of power.

He went through the entranceway. The breeze, although diminished, was coming from the top floor. There was only one door. He floated through it with the same simplicity.

The apartment was an attic studio. Curtains had been hung to separate the space into makeshift rooms. A shadow moved from behind one of the curtains. Ghost moved towards it.

"You're here," Kaas said as he looked directly at Ghost.

"How can you see me? The people on the street did not see me," Ghost told him.

"They do not have my skill. It's how I make my money… Communicating with their loved ones who have passed on." Kaas walked around Ghost, examining his transparent form that others could not see. "You are fascinating," he said. "Did death hurt?"

"I do not recall," Ghost told him. "It felt only like a few days, but centuries have passed since I died."

"What is your number? The name that you were given," Kaas added.

"D.91.19."

"Those are clues to your identity. D is for your first name. 91, the year you died and 19, the nineteenth person to die that year," Kaas told him.

Ghost thought hard to remember his name as Kaas continued to examine him.

"Do you remember your name?"

"I am trying," he replied but hesitated to tell him more.

Kaas pushed to know what it was but Ghost could not remember it.

"I am looking for someone," he told Kaas. "A unique individual. If you can communicate with spirits, you might be able to connect with him."

Kaas showed excitement in his facial expression.

"He is a vampire," Ghost said and watched as the smile turned to concern.

"No," Kaas said. "I will not have anything to do with that demon. He is an Immortal that was sent to destroy us."

"Well, he destroyed my life all those centuries ago and it's not fair that he gets to live on unscathed!" Ghost felt his rage surfacing.

Kaas breathed in deeply. "I will not help you if you are angered."

"He killed me!" Ghost screamed.

"You need to control your energy," Kaas advised him. "The past does not matter. What does matter is what you choose to do from this point on."

Ghost found himself intrigued.

"Either way, I have been sent to find him," he told the medium. "Tell me where he is."

A glass vase began to rattle. The water inside it became unsettled and began to spill out.

Kaas thought for a minute. "I do not know where he is. I only know he came to me ten years ago demanding that I commune with the spirits to help find someone. The spirits would not cooperate and he left angry."

"And since then?" Ghost asked.

"I do not know," he replied. "I do not want to know."

"Well, I do," Ghost told him. "So, you will find him."

"No," he replied "Now please leave. I told you I wouldn't work with negative energy."

"I know you can and you will find him, Kaas," Ghost demanded. "I need him so that I can be free." The flames of the candles in the room flickered as a gust of wind swirled around them. The vase fell over and smashed on the floor.

"Your freedom doesn't depend on someone else!" Kaas pleaded.

"Do it!" Ghost ordered with an echoing scream. The glass in all the windows shattered and blew both in and out of the apartment. Pointed shards of glass moved through Ghost's transparent form but sliced into Kaas. His face, chest, and torso were cut and impaled by the sharp edges. Kaas fell back onto the sheets that served as partitions and then the floor, dead.

Ghost lingered in silence for a moment and then watched as Kaas' spirit separated from his physical form to rise above it.

"I'm sorry," he whispered.

Kaas' spirit looked down upon him. "I don't need your apology; I am free. I hope only the same for you one day." He rose to meet two bright lights that Ghost could only assume were angels and all three beings vanished.

Chapter 7

"I guess, it does not work like that," Ghost said as he tried to inhabit a soulless shell and use it to feel normal. Kaas' physical body had no use to him.

Ghost found himself floating along the streets of Montmartre, wondering what were the odds that he would find another person who could see him and knew of the vampire.

Ghost took note that fires were being used for cooking and candles for lighting the night. He smelled the oil in the streetlamps, a foul odor that did not seem to bother anyone else. "I can't concentrate with this stench," he voiced aloud.

Another voice laughed. "You must be new."

Directly in front of him, a spirit appeared. The spirit looked feminine and had hollow eyes. Her face and body were gaunt and sickly looking, and she glowed with a sad brownish light.

"I am Ditiris. I am one of you," she said as she introduced herself. "And you are one of me. We are spirits who have been robbed of what was owed to us and are forced to linger here between dimensions in this empty form. Don't worry. You'll get used to the smells."

"Ditiris," Ghost began. "How is it that you can speak your name?"

Ditiris cracked a smile. "The Peasant King," she told him. "He is the one who freed me to remember my name… And many others too."

"Freed you how?" he asked her. "You're still a ghost. Invisible. Voiceless."

Ditiris cracked a condescending smirk. "I guess you haven't noticed that your feet aren't touching the ground or that you have moved through solid doors. Being still a ghost has its advantages."

Ghost held his tight expression but wondered about what else he could find out.

"And besides, you don't have the struggles of the living… No hunger. No sickness. No pain."

That was not enough for Ghost. He shook his head.

Ditiris thought for a minute. She turned to him with her face cocked. "Being freed means learning your name and that will open all of your memories back to you."

Ghost considered what she said. "Okay. How can I get freed?"

"He will not free you out of kindness. You will need to strike a deal."

Ghost laughed. "This will be my third deal today," he told her. "First, with Mavi in the cloud city. Then, with a medium-"

Ditiris floated around him as if she was pacing. "What deal did you strike with Mavi?"

He again hesitated, but then replied. "She asked me to find someone."

"The vampire?" she asked, seeming as though she already knew the answer.

"You know him? Do you know where he is?"

Ditiris laughed hard. "This will help you to bargain with the Peasant King."

"Then, you will bring me to the Peasant King?"

Ditiris motioned her arm and hand to point directly at the cathedral. "His court awaits."

Chapter 8

Ghost approached the dilapidated cathedral. He could not help but to feel sorrow for what had befallen such a beautiful architectural masterpiece. He entered through open doors that were lit by torches on both sides. It had fallen into ruin throughout time and had become simply a structure in which this Peasant King now held court. Ghost entered with Ditiris who was following closely.

The Sacre Coeur had become a home for vagrants. This supposed court had destroyed any semblance of what had once stood on hallowed ground. Yet, on a golden throne in the middle of the copula sat the Peasant King, drunk and debaucherous as he threw wine from his goblet and slapped the naked bottoms of those on his lap.

The Peasant King's attention was still on the antics that surrounded him. "This place has become a sanctuary for the downtrodden." He turned his gaze to where Ghost was hovering.

Ghost was surprised to find that the Peasant King was able to see him. A medium, he thought. That is good to know. He held his place hovering above the broken tiles.

The Peasant King stood and walked towards him. The others watched him in awe. He came to stand directly in front of Ghost. Ghost said nothing. He looked at all the others who followed the Peasant King.

"They cannot see or hear you," Ditiris told Ghost. "Only he and I can." She levitated and pulled Ghost up with her. The Peasant King looked up. The others followed his gaze.

Ghost maintained a locked stare with the Peasant King.

The Peasant King had a questioning look on his face. "Why did you seek me out?"

"I did not," he said and looked at Ditiris. "I was told that you can free me and allow me to speak my name, to unlock my memories so that I can know who I am. I figured if I can remember my life, then maybe I'll have a clue as to where to find someone."

The Peasant King too looked at Ditiris, who dimmed her glow. He thought before he spoke. "What you were told is true," he began. "But only if I get something I want in return."

"I know what you want."

"And what is that?" the Peasant King asked.

"The vampire," he said.

The Peasant King's eyes widened and he laughed hysterically. "The vampire," he yelled and many of the others flinched and looked around in fear. "The vampire, Thaddeus, who rose to destroy humanity?"

"The one and only," Ghost told him. "Why he came and why he detoured from his path are not my concern." He lowered himself to come face to face with the Peasant King. "But he is already promised to Mavi. I am to bring him to Mavi to be able to move on. I am not interested in lingering in this spirit form."

"Promised?" the Peasant King questioned. "So what? Moving on means nothing. I… We… exist only here. Here and now! You cannot move on because your life was stolen. It was ripped from your control and you chose not to move on until your justice is served."

"Exactly!" Ghost admitted. "The vampire was the one who killed me. This, I remember. He ripped my life from me and left me to die. It was so tragic that I am now in this state… between dimensions. Without a name." He became frustrated and screamed out as he repeated, "Without a name!"

The heavy metal doors blew open and the wind pushed all of the Peasant King's followers to the ground. The candles went out. The Sacre Coeur was in complete darkness. The Peasant King said a spell and waved his hands. The candles illuminated.

Ghost was surprised to see this magic.

"I am a student of The Dark Sisters," the Peasant King told Ghost. "They will be the ones to rule this dimension and combine it with the bordering dimensions. Those in their service will be the most powerful in all the dimensions. We will be the new gods!"

The Peasant King's followers cheered and rejoiced in what he said.

"Can Mavi offer that?" he whispered to Ghost.

"I can bring you the vampire, if I am freed. Are you going to help me?" Ghost negotiated.

The Peasant King adjusted his posture and broke into a cocky smirk.

Chapter 9

The cathedral was illuminated in candlelight. The Peasant King's followers sat swaying in a circle on the floor. One of the followers walked around the circle of people chanting and banged slowly on the echoing drum. Another walked in the opposite direction with the aroma of incense emanating from a decanter. Two others drew symbols on the floor in white chalk.

Ghost was in the center of the circle. Ditiris, who remained outside it, nodded to him to show support. The Peasant King entered the circle as his followers remained seated and held onto one another. They continued to sway as he took a goblet and said a spell over it. Their movements became bigger, faster, and more intense. He drank its full contents and then spit it out into the air above the followers.

The liquid surrounded Ghost and the chalk lines on the floor began to glow. Ghost inhaled the aroma of the incense and felt dizzy.

The glowing lines blinded him and he felt as though he was pulled backwards.

As the brilliance of the light dimmed, Ghost found himself in a more familiar time and place. He was in Paris, 1891, and it was just as he had remembered. The full moon in the night was a solid sphere once again. He felt relief to be back in the Paris that he knew. Ghost was on a bridge over the River Seine.

Pont Louis Philippe. This is… was… the night I died. He began to hear his own voice and could feel his body move. Yet, he was not in control of his words or motions. He realized that he was witnessing the events of that evening. Ghost found himself in a physical altercation with another man. Phineas, he thought, remembering the man's name.

"You took everything from me," he said to Phineas. "Now, you will know what it's like to be on the other side of a jail cell."

The altercation became more aggressive and Ghost felt himself pull a pistol from his jacket pocket. He kept it concealed and closed his eyes in anticipation of the pain as he pulled the trigger and shot himself.

"He shot me!" he lied and pointed at Phineas, who was frozen in place looking for someone who may have witnessed the incident. But the crowd rushed away, frightened and confused. Ghost stumbled back to the edge of the bridge and tossed the gun over the side. He watched as someone else pushed his way through the crowd. "Thaddeus," he whispered.

Thaddeus ran to Phineas with concern. Ghost saw Phineas motion an explanation and then Thaddeus ran to the far side of the bridge, along the Left Bank. In the midst of the chaos, Ghost observed as his old self pulled a second pistol. He shot Phineas, who fell onto the wooden planks as blood soiled his white shirt.

The police had arrived and held off the crowd, but Thaddeus had returned and burst through. He looked at Ghost with anger, but ran to Phineas. Phineas was dead. Ghost felt anguish in his chest. He watched as Phineas' spirit was escorted away from the scene by two angels.

Thaddeus was full of rage. "You killed him!" he screamed.

"Self-defense," Ghost heard himself yelling out.

"All of this to get back at me." Thaddeus pulled Ghost down, holding tight to his collar. "You will regret what you did... Dax!" He sank his fangs deep into Ghost's neck. The screaming faded to silence and the lights faded to darkness.

Ghost felt a hard shake and found that he was back in the Peasant King's court.

"I know who the vampire is," he told the Peasant King. "He is why I am in this state of ghosthood."

Ditiris was by his side and added, "You can use that memory to trace his energy."

"Bring him to us and the Dark Sisters will reward you with godlike powers," the Peasant King demanded and the crowd around him roared in cheer.

"I will find the vampire," Ghost told him and vanished into thin air.

The Peasant King stood and pushed a follower to the side. He could no longer see or feel Ghost's presence.

Chapter 10

Six years had passed, and in that time, Ghost had traced and trailed the vampire. He was still deciding which benefited him the most; to deliver Thaddeus to Mavi or to the Peasant King.

Mavi promised Enlightenment. Ghost had seen his own part in the events that ended his life. He no longer held any resentment towards Thaddeus over his death. That is one step closer to Enlightenment, he thought. He could bring Thaddeus to Mavi and choose to move onto the next stage of his existence and find peace.

So, for these past six years, Ghost lingered in the shadows. He often wondered how Enlightenment would be and if he would just be one more soul in the crowd. That thought would bring a chill to him. That is when he would turn his thoughts to the Peasant King.

The Peasant King had promised him godlike powers; to be able to join the Dark Sisters and be one of a hand-selected few that would rule entire dimensions. Ghost no longer felt the need to punish

Thaddeus over his death. But if that was to be the vampire's destiny in order for him to achieve godlike status, Ghost would not think twice.

It was not until the night Ghost learned that the vampire was operating off a prophecy, that his perspective changed drastically. There was another Immortal coming to finish what the vampire, Thaddeus, had been sent to do. However, this time it would destroy all of time and space.

The idea of being a god meant nothing if everything was to be destroyed. So, he followed Thaddeus to get information regarding this prophecy. If the prophecy is true and Thaddeus does destroy this new Immortal, then I will deliver him to the Peasant King and become a god.

But for now, there was no hurry, because he was no longer another number in the system. D.91.19... Dax, the nineteenth person to die in 1891.

Ghost now knew his name. But Ghost, he chose to remain.

VAMPIRE

Will lock their fate

Chapter 1

Thaddeus, the vampire, is an Immortal. He was sent to destroy humanity centuries ago, but a chance encounter with a mortal named Phineas changed his course. Thaddeus saw in this mortal humanity and compassion; he learned about love and light. Being a creature of darkness, these qualities intrigued him. Thaddeus chose to claim free-will and spare humanity, as he found himself in love with Phineas. And as Phineas' life was coming to an end, the Immortal pulled a constellation from the sky. This served as a tracer for Thaddeus to find Phineas whenever and wherever he happened to reincarnate.

Thaddeus had marked Phineas in their first lifetime together and had found and loved him in each of Phineas' next seven lifetimes. Thaddeus learned to distract himself and to tolerate the years of Phineas' absence. He traveled and became a confidant to the leaders of kingdoms. He participated in what is now history; as both hero and villain. He was a force to be reckoned with, but he attempted to be, for the most part, invisible.

Thaddeus had returned to his isolated mountain retreat after another clue had led to another dead end. He knew that Phineas was alive again. He had caught Phineas' jasmine and crisp citrus scent twice before over the past decades but the time was not right to approach him then. Thaddeus let out a frustrated sigh as he planned his next move.

Thaddeus was watching the snowfall. This rare moment of calm and reflection was interrupted by light and sound coming from the next room. As he went in to investigate, he saw a fox cautiously come through a swirling portal. The fox was spying on him, but stopped. His movements became anxious.

Thaddeus looked at the other end of the portal and saw the royal family crest of Quorca. Quentin? he thought.

The fox looked up at him to confirm his suspicion but immediately ran and hid under a chair as the portal closed.

"Come here," Thaddeus said to the fox, coaxing him from his hiding spot. "I won't hurt you." The fox came out from under the chair and nuzzled up against Thaddeus' leg. He then began pawing at Thaddeus with a sense of urgency. The aroma of cinnamon emanating from the fox, again confirmed to the vampire that the animal had been sent by the sorcerer, Quentin.

He turned back to where the portal had been and looked at the mirror on the wall. "Seems that we're going to have to get back there through a different path." Thaddeus picked up the fox and placed him in a satchel. "I'll have to cover you to get through the Mirror Realm, my mortal friend." He looked down at the concerned fox. "But don't worry. I have used this trick before."

Thaddeus walked across the cabin and entered a windowless room. The walls were covered in tapestries that had woven in them the royal family crests of many kingdoms. Quorca, Mortua, Dremora, Tebbs, and the ensnared Kingdom of Witches, were among them. He hit a button on the side of the entrance and, one by one, the tapestries rolled up. Behind each hanging was a mirror. Each mirror was framed differently with a semblance to reflect the metal, stone, or wood of the region. The shapes varied but the mirrors were all full length.

Thaddeus walked around the room and stood before each mirror. What he saw in them was not his own reflection, but rather what lay on the other side. He saw the rooms in the varied palaces where the connecting mirrors hung: bedchambers, receiving rooms, hallways, and views out of windows. Being able to see through a mirror to its connection and to use the pathway between them was a skill for any Immortal. This was the Mirror Realm and Thaddeus took full advantage of it.

Thaddeus had used the Mirror Realm, the paths between mirrors in different places and times, to travel quickly. Throughout his existence, he had collected the ones that he found benefitted him and brought them here to his snowy mountain retreat. The tapestries hung over them to keep anyone on the other side who shared his talent from seeing where the mirror led. He would not have ever taken kindly to unwanted visitors.

Yet, some of the other mirrors were damaged or missing. He looked at the empty space that once held the path through the Mirror Realm to Ileana's palace in the Kingdom of Witches and tightened his face in sorrow. He looked to the cracked mirror that stood in a birch frame that used to allow him access to the Palace of Tebbs. Although shattered, the mirror to Dremora stood in place. And then he looked into the mirror with the direct path to Quorca.

"Make sure not to come out from under my cover," he said to the fox and kept him in the satchel. He stepped through the mirror as if it were not even there.

Chapter 2

Thaddeus was consumed by his thoughts as he traveled through the Mirror Realm. It had been decades since he had been to Quorca, the childhood home of Prince Quentin. Around forty years ago, Thaddeus taught the young prince how to master the art of sorcery.

Quentin later married Ileana, the Queen of Witches. They ruled the Kingdom of Witches for years and the land was prosperous, until The Dark Sisters pulled a star from the Heavens and destroyed the queen's palace. Common belief was that Ileana, her entire family, and her court died that night.

Thaddeus stepped out of the mirror and into the palace of Quorca. He was surprised to find the palace so quiet. He heard no voices and saw no shadows lingering behind corners. Everything had been well maintained, but the halls were empty. Odd, he thought. As he moved through the halls, Thaddeus heard noises and went to investigate. He turned a corner and found himself in the center of the castle. The great receiving room from which each of the wings of the palace connected was bustling with activity. He took the fox from the satchel and placed him on the floor. The fox scurried away in the opposite direction. He slowly went back, being sure that he had gone unnoticed by the palace staff in the receiving room.

"Psst," he heard from the empty hallway. Thaddeus looked back from where he had come but the fox was gone. He looked around and realized that all the doors were partially open. "Psst," he heard again, this time from behind a door. He entered the room with caution. He sniffed the same cinnamon aroma that the fox carried, but no one was behind the door.

He was in the former bedchambers of Prince Quentin. At the far end of the room, he saw the red fox bathing in the sunlight. The animal appeared playful and rolled around, as if being rubbed and petted. Thaddeus squinted and saw the outline of an invisible figure that camouflaged itself well in the light and against the sandstone walls.

"She taught me how to do this. It is an ancient enchantment that leaves no magic trace," the rough but familiar voice told him. "I miss her."

"You've aged," Thaddeus pointed out. "I can hear it in your voice."

"Some of us don't have the luxury of Immortality."

"Luxury?" he questioned. "Or curse?" Silence followed. "Quen-"

"Sorcerer," Quentin forced. "I go by Sorcerer." Quentin slowly took form as he appeared from the sunlight. It was the first time in over twenty years. "Only my brother knows that I'm here."

"How long have you been here?"

Sorcerer looked down, embarrassed. "The whole time."

Only a handful of trusted friends knew that Quentin's family had survived the attack. Ileana drew The Dark Sister away from them but died in battle. Sorcerer and their children were separated and went into hiding. He never tried to reunite with the children for their own protection.

"And the fox?"

"He was a gift from Ileana. He's been with me all along." The thought brought a smile to Sorcerer's face. "The staff thinks I'm a ghost and the fox is here to protect them."

Thaddeus thought for a minute. "Why have you called me here?"

Sorcerer sighed and began pacing. He stayed far enough from the window to avoid the possibility of anyone outside seeing him. "Two reasons. First, I have only recently come across something that I believe tells of my children being in danger."

"A prophecy," Thaddeus said plainly.

Sorcerer's eyes became anxious. "You do know it. Three of Legend. I believe The Dark Sisters might release a beast upon my children."

Thaddeus said nothing as he watched his friend emotionally unravel.

Sorcerer continued, "How will they protect themselves? They don't even know who they really are."

Thaddeus held his strong posture as he contemplated what Sorcerer had just told him. "I have known about the prophecy and the implication of your family. That is why I was at the palace… To warn Ileana." Sorcerer's eyes widened, and he continued to pace back and forth.

Thaddeus waited for Sorcerer's energy to calm. The fox came to lay at his feet as he continued. "At the time of the attack, I too thought the prophecy was related to the rise of The Dark Sisters and the newly born triplets. But Ileana managed to protect your family, even after her death. I assure you that your children are safe. I have seen to it myself." Thaddeus said, which got the hint of a smile from his friend.

"When did you last see them?" Sorcerer asked.

Thaddeus paused, knowing that his answer would only add to Sorcerer's concern.

"Thaddeus?"

"I have not used that name for years. I am known as Vampire," he confessed, trying to change the conversation.

"When?"

"No less than five years ago," he confessed.

Sorcerer sighed and collected his thoughts. "Before she was killed, Ileana enchanted the children with a protection spell. It changed their appearances and disguised any essence that would connect them to us." Sorcerer began pacing again. "However, four years ago, on their eighteenth birthday, these symbols appeared." He pulled up his sleeve and showed his forearm to Vampire. The markings looked like three coin-sized tattoos of the elements fire, earth, and air. "They gave me comfort because it meant they were still alive. I was not concerned until I came across that prophecy and now, I am worried that these markings will expose them."

"I will say, The Dark Sisters have not been heard from in several years." Vampire attempted to put his friend at ease. "If you had stepped out of this palace, out of your fear, you would have noticed it as well."

Sorcerer took a deep breath and then looked at the fox. He stroked his fur to calm himself. The fox stared back with a smile.

"Have you talked to your brother about this? I am sure he has insight on any potential threats," Vampire asked as Sorcerer looked deep into his eyes with a sense of conviction. "It is time, my friend." Vampire assured him.

"Let's go see my brother." Sorcerer began to recite the incantation and within seconds was invisible.

Chapter 3

An invisible Sorcerer led Vampire and the fox through the castle. They walked past members of the royal court, politicians, and staff who paid them no attention. "Masquet is the only one who knows that I am here," Sorcerer again told Vampire, referring to his brother, the King of Quorca.

Once they moved into the king's wing of the palace, guards came from every corridor and pointed spears and swords at them. "Move no further," one of the guards ordered.

"I think that it's time you come out, Sorcerer," Vampire joked as they both stood with their hands up.

From behind a row of guards stepped King Masquet of Quorca.

"This way," he told Sorcerer and Vampire.

They entered his chambers, and the king closed the door after ordering that no word was to be spoken about this meeting. Sorcerer started to take form as he explained to his brother what he and the vampire had been discussing.

"All we have are rumors and hearsay," King Masquet told them. "But The Dark Sisters abandoned their political ties with Tebbs. They are up to something. I wonder if this prophecy is what they are focused on. If this prophecy directly mentions your children, I agree that you need to make sure they are protected."

"That brings me to my second reason for summoning you, Vampire," Sorcerer told him. "We need to locate the Book of Spells. Ileana copied into that book all the spells of Witches. I'm sure that there would be a spell to conceal the markings and protect the children." He stood next to his brother and looked back at Vampire.

"Few know of the book's existence. Ileana had it with her when she died. Yet, nothing else was said of it," Vampire added. "I doubt that Baltaan found it. Otherwise, we would be living in a much darker world," Vampire mentioned referring to the Witch, Baltaan, a close confidant of Ileana's who ultimately betrayed and killed her in allegiance to The Dark Sisters.

The king turned to Vampire. "Ileana was killed in Dremora, and the last person to see her alive was the Leprechaun, Cadet Le Bougier."

"She must have the book," Sorcerer said. Vampire nodded in agreement and pulled his lips tight.

The king continued. "Cadet came here after Ileana's death but mentioned nothing of a book. She was on a quest to spread Ileana's command to not use names, as names are a tracer, just like magic. She keeps a somewhat low profile but my spies tell me that she is definitely in Dremora. You must be very careful. Dremora has become a shadow, a land of darkness and fear. It is a haven for the followers of The Dark Sisters, both magical and non-magical. Higher bastardized forms of magic are practiced there. So, you will have a better chance to use your magic and not be traced."

"Thank you, brother," Sorcerer said to the king.

The king pulled his brother in for a tight hug. "Be safe," he whispered into his ear. He pulled back at arm's length. "Quorca and her forces await your commands."

Sorcerer turned to Vampire, "Are you sure that you're up to this?"

"If this prophecy is active and The Dark Sisters are behind it, who better to have by your side than an Immortal?" Vampire responded nonchalantly as he walked to the door.

Chapter 4

Vampire and Sorcerer moved along less traveled roads from Quorca to Dremora. The journey took them through the outskirts of villages and towns where outsiders were looked at with concern. Early on in their travels, they agreed to enter these villages only for supplies and to sleep under the cover of the forests. Under the stars and the cracked moon, they set up camp along a river. Vampire distracted Sorcerer from his own concerns by challenging him to figure out the rest of the prophecy.

"This prophecy is not new to me," Vampire confessed, "but I too do not yet have all the answers." He looked at Sorcerer's eyes which seemed wide with concern as Vampire showed him a rolled piece of parchment.

Sorcerer nodded his head as he took it and read:

All will come to light
But the end is not clear.
Fire will rain down
As the beast will appear.

The three of legend
Sword and shield
Must come into existence
For the beast to yield.

Stones of eight
Will lock their fate.

He mumbled to himself as he read the words a second time, pausing at the end of each line. "All will come to light… But when? A fiery beast?" He looked at Vampire. "My children," he said, still concerned for their safety.

"The Three of Legend," Vampire told him. "That part we know."

"The sword and shield?" Sorcerer questioned, lost in the fog of his concern. "There are too many of those in the world today to figure it out. Never mind all the ones from history and legend."

"Exactly. In Dremora, you could invoke a vision. Maybe we can see the rest of the prophecy," Vampire suggested, only to be met with Sorcerer's focus solely on the parchment in his hand.

"The end is not clear," Sorcerer said just above a whisper. "I am taking that to mean that anything about this prophecy can be altered."

"Yes. I agree." Vampire looked around to make sure they were not being followed nor overheard. "All the more reason that we need to know what we are up against."

"Like you said, I need to use my sorcery and create a vision… To see it clearly. I am sure that you know places that would be safe for me to conjure a spell." He walked over to Vampire and grabbed him by his arms. "You are the only one I can trust with this."

The fox stuck his head out of the satchel that Sorcerer held him in. The distraction relaxed him. "I don't think that you are the beast that the prophecy is talking about," he joked to the furry animal. He looked back at Vampire. "But maybe you are."

"I've been called worse," Vampire said with renewed positivity and jest to change Sorcerer's focus.

The next morning, they followed the river to the waterfall at Mount Condamner and knew that they had reached Dremora.

"Most of the city sits atop it," Vampire told Sorcerer. "But it extends down to this level. Some of these caves serve as portals."

"Why did she come here?" Sorcerer asked about Ileana.

"We will find the Leprechaun and ask her," Vampire told him.

They dismounted from their horses, and Sorcerer let the fox out of his satchel. The fox was quick to scurry and investigate the surroundings.

"He will spy ahead for us," Sorcerer told Vampire.

"Come on."

Chapter 5

As Vampire and Sorcerer entered the central part of the city, they were forced to be quick to hide their concern as they found no daylight. Sorcerer looked up and thought that high buildings must have blocked the sun but saw that the open sky above the city was dark. They walked on with a feeling of caution. As King Masquet had told them, the former mountain capital had fallen into shadow over the past two decades.

Vampire secured a building in the darkest part of the city. For most of his existence, he had maintained an identity as a parfumier. This building was one of his shops back when Dremora was a desirable place to be.

"No one will bother us here," he told Sorcerer as they went into the building.

"I would think not," Sorcerer replied as they entered and saw the place in complete disarray.

"It's been vacant for over fifty years," Vampire told him.

"Not exactly," Sorcerer said as he illuminated the room with a wand and a number of rodents and lizards scurried away from the light. "Let me start with this," he added and spoke an incantation that created an expanding bubble around them. It spread out and lit the room. "The light is only on the inside. Anyone outside the barrier will only see darkness."

"No more magic than is necessary," Vampire reminded him.

"Right," he said.

The fox was surveying the room. Sorcerer opened a leather backpack and pulled out vials of premixed potions and ingredients for others. He grabbed two larger vials containing different salts. "Salt is cleansing and allows deeper insight." He used the salt to trace a circle. "Once this spell begins, you cannot cross the boundary."

Sorcerer held an uncomfortable silence. The thought of having not practiced magic in so long concerned him. He inhaled deeply to calm himself and to allow his focus. As he began to speak the words of the spell, the salt began to glow. He continued with his incantation, now with a stronger tone, and the glow extended upwards. He was surrounded by a curtain of light.

The fox was quick to go to Vampire's side. Vampire found it difficult to see through the intensity of the light. He and the fox were squinting and shielding their eyes when they began to see subtle changes in the color of the light. Then, figures started to take form out of those subtleties.

The changes in color became more distinct. Vampire saw eight horizontal lines form and those lines became swirls of red, orange, dark blue, pale blue, yellow, green, purple, and pure reflective white. They became rough solid shapes of various sizes as they glowed brighter and then moved into a formation familiar to Vampire.

"Cez stones," Vampire whispered. "The constellation," he realized.

A figure of a young man appeared outlined in pale blue light. The other colors created a scene around him. Vampire recognized the landmarks and structures.

"Mortua," he said. "There's a boy in Mortua who can find Cez stones."

The light transformed into three lines of gold, copper, and patina. They became swirls and then slowed their rotation. The three swirls of metallic light unraveled into lines of light and blended into each other.

"The Three of Legend," he said, continuing to speak his thoughts aloud.

The colorful lights all came together into a single horizontal black line but then separated into two, red and green. These lines began to coil upon themselves and the newly formed circles moved slowly around the curtain of light. The green light took the shape of a sword.

Vampire looked at it with curiosity. He followed it as it moved and watched as the blade broke. The two parts were taken in opposite directions. The green faded back to the white light. "The Sword of Sansit," he realized.

Then the red coil took form as a solid circle. It pulsed as it grew and appeared embellished.

"What is that?" he questioned. The entire curtain of light turned red and then changed back to the white glow.

Vampire stood close. He reached out his hand but quickly pulled it back as the curtain of light turned to fire and then went out.

Sorcerer laid crouched on the floor. "Sorcerer?" Vampire questioned, unsure if he could cross the barrier.

"No," he ordered through a weak voice.

"Not bad for a guy who hasn't practiced magic in over two decades."

"Not funny." Mustering all the energy that he could, he turned to face Vampire. He was mildly burnt. "What did you see?"

"The stones are Cez stones," Vampire thought of the prophecy. "There is a boy in Mortua who can find the stones."

"What else?" he begged in pain.

"I believe the sword is the Sword of Sansit, but it was broken in two. That is all that I was able to figure out from the images. The light turned to fire. What was that?"

"No idea," Sorcerer told him as he stood and exited the circle. He inhaled to keep himself from crying. "The Three of Legend," he said and fell back to the floor.

Vampire knelt to support him. "I did not see any danger concerning your children, just the symbols of their elements," Vampire told him. "I saw nothing of The Dark Sisters."

Vampire helped Sorcerer up, held him by his shoulder and said, "Let's go find Cadet and that book. We might find something to conjure a stronger vision."

Chapter 6

They walked out of the dilapidated building, "Step one wasn't so bad," Vampire said as he examined Sorcerer's burns.

"I think it best to torch the place to the ground to cover our tracks," Sorcerer argued.

"Probably right," Vampire told him.

Sorcerer picked up the fox and put him in the satchel. "Do you mind?" he asked Vampire, who took the bag and put it over his shoulder.

Sorcerer spoke the words of the spell as they walked with a confident pace and did not turn back to see the structure burn to the ground.

"Your brother's spies said that she keeps a somewhat low profile. But if I know Cadet, I know that she will be somewhere where she can trick others," Vampire said. "After all, she is a Leprechaun."

"A bar, I would think. Drunks. Poor decisions." Sorcerer looked around. "But which one?"

"There," Vampire said and pointed with his head. "The one with the mirror ball on the vertical flagpole. "She cannot help but crave attention as much as she craves her own trickery. Screwing people over is her drug, her adrenaline. That place will draw her like a moth to a flame."

They entered the bar. The roof was clear and the light of the mirror ball shined and moved inside. The place was crowded and as unkempt as the building from which they had just come.

Sorcerer tapped Vampire on the arm and pointed at the red-headed beauty flirting with the military commander.

"We will need to trap her," Vampire told him. "I'll take the left."

"Good," Sorcerer told him and just walked straight towards her with his anger growing. "Hey!" he yelled to Cadet, whose back was to him. The man she was with looked up with a surprised expression as Sorcerer wound up his fist. The Leprechaun, who stood between them, turned, but it was too late to duck out of the way. Sorcerer knocked her hard in the face and she fell back into the commander. He fell to the floor and hit his head on the solid surface.

Sorcerer and Vampire were standing over them as Cadet looked up.

"We need to speak to you," Vampire told her.

"Hello," Cadet replied sarcastically. She turned to Sorcerer. "You could have just bought me a drink." She looked back at the commander who was unconscious on the floor. She reached into his pockets and took all the money that he had. "Great thing about a dive bar," she told them. "No one cares," she added, pointing to the crowd that was uninterested in the exchange which had just taken place. "But we should go before he wakes up." She grabbed Vampire by the hand and led them out the back door.

"Why are you here?" she asked them as she sauntered into the empty alley, adjusting her face from the punch.

"You have something that belonged to my wife," Sorcerer said.

Cadet stopped. She stayed facing away from them and felt her eyes tearing up. She held back the tears and turned. "And what exactly is that?"

"The Book of Spells," Vampire told her.

Cadet laughed. "That's why you punched me? Joke's on you then. I don't have it."

"Then, you know where it is," Vampire said quickly.

Cadet walked ahead of them as she thought about what to say.

"Cadet," Sorcerer pleaded. "Ileana lost her life trying to hide that book... Trying to protect us. All of us!"

She said nothing.

"Don't you remember what Dremora used to be? Before it fell into darkness?" Sorcerer asked.

She stayed silent as she attempted to keep an upper hand. However, Cadet did remember what Dremora was like before The Dark Sisters, and she did remember Ileana, one of the few people whom she had ever trusted and respected. But mostly, she remembered that Ileana forced her to stay away, to protect her from the dangers that she herself was not able to avoid.

"I would have gone wherever she led," Cadet said as if in a reverie. "She saved my life."

"Then repay her," Sorcerer begged. "Give us the book."

Cadet was quick to pull her emotions back. "I already told you. I don't have it," she said flatly.

"Then who does?" Vampire questioned.

Cadet sighed. "Lucifer."

"The demon?" Sorcerer asked.

She looked at Vampire and rolled her eyes. "Ileana gave him the book to hide."

"Vampire," Sorcerer tried to argue back. "If the book is there-"

"I'm sure that it is," he rushed. "Lucifer has not been seen nor heard from for decades. He must have it."

Cadet chuckled.

"Yes?" Vampire asked, awaiting an explanation.

Cadet shook her head. "Lucifer hasn't been heard from because he can't get here. Ileana took his portal key in exchange for the Book of Spells."

"And the key?" Vampire questioned.

"Oh, I searched," Cadet assured them. "But I could not find it."

Vampire and Sorcerer looked at one another. "The book is in Hell," Vampire said. "I will have to do this part on my own. Where can I find a large number of mirrors?"

Cadet pointed to the roof. The mirror ball continued to turn.

"Never a quiet moment with you," Vampire reminded her.

She shrugged her shoulders and led them back into the bar. They avoided the now conscious commander as she brought them to the stairs that led to the roof.

"The glass is thick," she told them, "But it's still glass. Anybody looking up will see us."

They rushed quickly to the moving mirror ball that was aglow from spotlights reflecting off it and creating the moving light in the bar and onto the clouds.

Vampire said nothing as he moved quickly from mirror to mirror. He was searching for a way in, an opening to Hell.

"Sorcerer, time may be of the essence. I need you to go and find the boy," he told him and looked as Cadet became more interested. "I will get the book and meet you there."

"What boy?" Cadet questioned.

"Not of your concern. You have done your part," Vampire told her. "Cadet Le Bougier. I have never been able to truly trust you." He stood in front of her and rubbed his hands up and down her arms. "It is not your fault. After all, you are a Leprechaun." Cadet pulled her arms from him, angered by his comment. "However, know this. I will cause you pain beyond your comprehension if you do anything to interfere. I will destroy you and leave you for the wretches of Dremora to take back everything that you have stolen from them. Do you understand?"

Cadet knew that what he said was true. She said nothing as she backed away from him.

Vampire looked at Sorcerer. "I will find you," he told him and motioned towards the fox in the satchel. "I can cover him and take him through the Mirror Realm and into Hell. He can find you like he did before."

Sorcerer nodded in agreement.

"Remember, do not approach the boy."

"Be safe," Sorcerer told him.

Vampire nodded and cocked a slight smile. He turned, touched a particular mirror, and disappeared.

Chapter 7

Vampire found himself running along the designated path through the Mirror Realm. He held the satchel tight to himself, under his flowing coat.

The glowing path was steaming hot, but he did not have time nor interest in stopping to investigate. The Immortal knew very well that these fires could not destroy him.

He reached the other side. The vampire rushed through the mirror, only to find himself still sweating.

Hell.

Something crashed behind him and a golden light shined.

"Hello, brothers," he said without turning.

The golden light faded, leaving the archangel, Michael, and from the shadows came forth the demon, Lucifer. The angel and demon looked at each other with detest. Their distaste for one another was palpable. The Immortal was surprised at Lucifer's disheveled appearance and looked at the archangel, who showed that same response.

The vampire cracked a smile, knowing that Michael's presence created the opportunity to pit the brothers against one another, find the book, and even slip out without them noticing the book was gone.

"But Lucifer. Your appearance-" Vampire said.

Archangel Michael spread his golden wings and floated down to where his brother cowered. He knew that even in this state, Lucifer's pride was strong. He held back any pity in his voice. The light of his presence illuminated on Lucifer and an immediate change came over his appearance. His physical beauty was restored.

"It won't last, but this will give you temporary relief," Michael told him and handed him a bracelet. "You can call forth short bouts of beauty by rubbing it."

"That's what happens when you stay in Hell. Even the most beautiful become almost unrecognizable," Lucifer told him with a sincere quiver in his voice.

"Rumor has it that you're stuck here," Vampire said to Lucifer.

"I am not stuck!" Lucifer yelled. "Over two decades ago, on your timeline, I made a deal with Ileana. However, things did not go as planned, and I have chosen to maintain my presence here in Hell."

Archangel Michael burst into laughter. "Liar! You gave her your portal key and you are trapped here in Hell… Unable to leave. Such a fool!" He continued laughing at his brother's misfortune.

"That is why I am here," Vampire started. "Did she have a book with her? The Leprechaun, Cadet, mentioned you might be in possession of that book. And if you choose to stay here, then that book is of no use to you."

Lucifer said nothing more. He maintained his angered expression, more so because his current situation delighted Michael.

He turned his attention to Vampire. "You were sent to that dimension with a purpose, but you chose to ignore it. You are the reason why you need that book. Yet, you have the audacity to come here looking for favors. You caused this imbalance."

"I came seeking help to restore that balance," Vampire told them. "When The Dark Sisters attacked and dethroned Ileana, the world fell into darkness. That book contains the power for her descendants to rise and defeat The Dark Sisters. Take a look." Vampire said, handing Michael the parchment containing the prophecy.

Lucifer and Michael looked at one another through squinted and unconvinced eyes.

As Michael read the words, he lifted himself with his casually fluttering wings. "Do not lecture us, Vampire," he told him. "You're a fool. This prophecy has nothing to do with The Dark Sisters!" Michael exclaimed.

"It has to do with you." Lucifer chimed menacingly.

"I am not the beast of which it speaks. I chose not to destroy humanity. I chose love."

"You created the beast of which this prophecy speaks when you chose love," Michael argued. "You pulled those stars from the Heavens, to be able to find your love. That was the day. This is all your fault."

"The beast, the Jeweled Dragon from the Dracu constellation, is poised on destruction. And she will start by destroying Phineas and anything else you hold dear. It is meant as a punishment to you."

Vampire squinted his eyes in anger. He looked up and stared at Lucifer. "Careful. You're starting to flake." He motioned towards his cheek. "I would start rubbing that trinket if I were you."

Lucifer was immediately doing so.

Vampire walked towards Michael. "This prophecy mentions nothing of Phineas. But know that I will be there to protect him."

"You would sacrifice your wellbeing for a mortal?" Michael asked through laughter. "I don't believe you."

"That will be a first," Lucifer added. "You are too selfish."

Vampire said nothing as he thought, but then looked up with confidence. "This Immortal is poised on full destruction. Not just

Phineas but humanity and eternity… All of space and time." He had taken back control of the conversation.

Michael and Lucifer looked at one another, but held their words.

Vampire reminded them, "And that means, you too. You will have no purpose. There will be no souls to abuse and rehabilitate. You too will cease to exist. And I am certainly not the only one present whose ego would allow that. We have no choice other than to work together to keep this from happening."

The angel and demon looked at one another, knowing that what Vampire said was true.

Michael broke the silence. "We need that portal key. Without it, Lucifer is of no use to aiding in turning the tides and preventing your prophecy."

"Ileana was killed," the vampire reminded them. "I have no idea where to find the portal key."

"She was destroyed. Her essence never came through here," Lucifer replied. "But the key was not. I would have felt it if it was." With his beauty and confidence temporarily restored, he sauntered over to a throne-like boulder. "But as to your purpose in coming here, I do know where the Book of Spells lies. I will tell you where it is, if you make a promise to me. Promise me that you will get my portal key back to me."

"And we need your word that we will not be seen as having any part in this," Michael said. "Balance is a delicate thing, Vampire. You should know better than anyone."

"Fine," Vampire told them. "I agree. Now, where is that book?"

Lucifer stepped towards Vampire. "When The Dark Sisters attacked and dethroned Ileana, she came to me with the book. She asked me to hide it and expected that I would bring it here. I thought that I would be playful and leave it in that dimension," Lucifer confessed. "I figured that by hiding it in plain sight, no one would find it."

"Where?" Vampire questioned with growing impatience.

Lucifer looked at Michael who nodded for him to tell him. "It is in the library at the Monastery of the Order of the Brothers of Naa. I placed it on the shelves randomly. It is the only text with a rose gold binder."

"Those hateful monks cannot decipher it. It takes a Witch to pull forth the spells and images," the archangel added.

"Even I was unable to do so before hiding the book at the monastery," Lucifer told them.

"Then, I will need a Witch," Vampire added. "But first, I need that book."

Archangel Michael and Lucifer looked at one another and nodded. "Then go," Lucifer said. "But you will not be able to return through the mirror. Follow my brother. He will lead you out of here and back to your dimension." Lucifer stood close to the archangel. "I will wait here for news and the return of my portal key."

"Thank you," Vampire said to him. "Thank you both."

Archangel Michael wrapped his wings around the vampire and everything turned to pure warmth.

Chapter 8

Vampire opened his eyes and found that it was night. He looked up at the sky and saw the red tinge to the cracked moon.

The Blood Moon.

The fox was nestled at his side. Vampire patted the animal, who awoke with a stretch and a shake of his whole body. The fox turned back and forth several times before running off.

"Yes," Vampire said. "Find Sorcerer."

The Immortal looked in the opposite direction and saw the lights of the Monastery of the Order of the Brothers of Naa. He inhaled deeply and caught the faint aroma of jasmine and crisp citrus.

"The time is near," he told himself.

All will come to light
But the end is not clear
Fire will rain down
As the beast will appear

The three of legend
Sword and shield
Must come into existence
For the beast to yield

Stones of eight
Will lock their fate

ABOUT THE AUTHOR
James Voorhees

James Voorhees is the author of The Ambassador Chronicles, a character-driven series of shorts that introduces the main players of The Dragon Constellation, the first book of The Ambassador Chronicles trilogy.

Voorhees began writing through sleepless nights during the COVID-19 pandemic. He was working as a physical therapist in a Miami-based hospital and needed a quiet outlet. Little did he know that his random thoughts would come together to create an epic fantasy adventure, pitting love and darkness into desperate conflict.

Voorhees was raised in Secaucus, NJ. He has spent his lifetime immersed in music, fashion, travel, art, and with people who bring him joy and laughter as his greatest forms of inspiration. He currently resides in Miami Beach, FL.